The Chosen People

Charlotte Mary Yonge

Contents

THE CHOSEN PEOPLE

BY

Charlotte Mary Yonge

"God, who at sundry times and in diverse manners spake in time past unto the fathers by the prophets, hath in these last days spoken unto us by His Son, whom He hath appointed heir of all things."--Heb. i, 1,

"Yes; so it was ere Jesus came--
Alternate then His Altar flame
Blazed up and died away,
And Silence took her torn with Song,
And Solitude with the fair throng
That owned the festal day;
For in earth's daily circuit then
Only one border
Reflected to the Seraphs' ken,
Heaven's light and order.

But now to the revolving sphere
We point and Say, No desert here,
No waste so dark and lone
But to the hour of sacrifice
Comes daily in its turn, and lies
In light beneath the Throne.
Each point of time, from morn till eve.
From eve to morning,
The shrine doth from the Spouse receive
Praise and adorning."--Lyra Innocentium.

PREFACE.

In drawing up this little book, at the request of several friends, the Author has been chiefly guided by experience of what children require to be told, in order to come to an intelligent perception of the scope of the Scripture narrative treated historically. Since a general view can hardly be obtained without brevity, many events have been omitted in the earlier part, and those only touched upon which have a peculiar significance in tracing the gradual preparation for the work of Redemption; and though one great object has been the illustration of Prophecy, the course of types has been passed over, lest the plain narrative should be confused, since types are rather subjects of devotional contemplation than of history, and they should be perfectly comprehended as *facts*, before being treated as allegorical.

The next portion is little save an abridgement from Prideaux's Connexion, taken in connection with the conclusions drawn by modern discoveries, as detailed in Mr. G. Rawlinson's valuable edition of Herodotus. It is hoped that by thus filling up the interval between the New and Old Testaments, that children may thus be fairly able to understand what they read in the Gospels of the Roman dominion, the relation to Herod, the mutual hatred of the Pharisees and Sadducees, and the enmity to the Samaritans.

The concluding lessons are offered with great diffidence, and with many doubts whether the absence of detail may not prevent them from being easily remembered; but it has been felt important that the connection of the actual Church with that of the Apostles and Martyrs, should be made evident to the general mind, and the present condition of the Church accounted for. The choice of subjects has been very difficult; but it is hoped that those selected may be those most needful to be known as evidence that our present Church has every claim to the promise of Him Who will abide with her for ever.

If older and more critical persons than those for whom the little work is intended should cast an eye over it, the author hopes that they will bear in mind how the need of being both brief and clear is apt to render statements apparently bolder, and sometimes harsher, than where there is room for qualification or argument; and that they will not always accuse the work of unthinking boldness of assertion, where the softening is omitted for fear both of wearying and perplexing the young reader.

The chronology, for the sake of the convenience of teachers and scholars, is that of the margin of our Bibles.

The questions at the end are chiefly intended to direct the mind of the learner to the point of each lesson. It will be perceived that the answers must he prepared as well from the Bible as from the book; and in most cases the teacher will in use have to multiply, and perhaps to simplify them. One of their especial objects has been to show the ever brightening stream of prophecy, and afterwards, its accomplishment alike with regard to heathen nations, to the history of the Jews, of the Church, and, above all, to the Life of our Blessed Lord; and it is hoped that those who examine into them, cannot fail to be struck with the full and perfect accordance of the beginning with the end; and if they learn no other lesson, will have it impressed on them, how "the counsel of the Lord endureth for ever."

Two tables have been added for the convenience of the scholar, one giving the contemporary kings and prophets, the other the course of historical chapters, with, as far as possible, the prophetical, didactic, or poetical books, of the same date ranged in parallel lines. It is hoped that these may be found useful in arranging lessons for upper classes or pupil teachers.

May 20th, 1859.

LESSON I.
THE PROMISE.

"The creature was made subject unto vanity, not willingly, but by reason of Him who hath subjected the same in hope."--Rom. viii. 20.

When the earth first came from the hand of God, it was "very good," and man, the best of all the beings it contained, was subjected to a trial of obedience. The fallen angel gained the ear of the woman, and led her to disobey, and to persuade her husband to do the same; and that failure gave Satan power over the world, and over all Adam's children, bringing sin and death upon the earth, and upon all, whether man or brute, who dwelt therein.

Yet the merciful God would not give up all the creatures whom He had made, to eternal destruction without a ray of hope, and even while sentencing them to the punishment they had drawn on themselves, He held out the promise that the Seed of the woman should bruise the head of the serpent, the Devil; and they were taught by the sight of sacrifices of animals, that the death of the innocent might yet atone for the sin of the guilty; though these creatures were not of worth enough really to bear the punishment for man.

Abel's offering of the lamb proved his faith, and thus was more worthy than Cain's gift of the fruits of the earth. When Cain in his envy slew his brother, he and his children were cast off by God, and those of his younger brother, Seth, were accepted, until they joined themselves to the ungodly daughters of Cain; and such sin prevailed, that Enoch, the seventh from Adam, prophesied of judgment at hand, before he was taken up alive into Heaven. When eight hundred and nine hundred years were the usual term of men's lives, and the race was in full strength and freshness, there was time for mind and body to come to great force; and we find that the chief inventions of man belong to these sons of Cain--the dwelling in tents, workmanship in brass and iron, and the use of musical instruments. On the other hand, the more holy of the line of Seth handed on from one to the other the history of the blessed days of Eden, and of God's promise, and lived upon hope and faith.

Noah, whose father had been alive in the latter years of Adam's life, was chosen from among the descendants of Seth, to be saved out of the general ruin of the corrupt earth, and to carry on the promise. His faith was first tried by the command to build the ark, though for one hundred and twenty years all seemed secure, without any token of judgment; and the disobedient refused to listen to his preaching. When the time came, his own family of eight persons were alone found worthy to be spared from the destruction, together with all the animals with them preserved in the ark, two of each kind, and a sevenfold number of those milder and purer animals which part the hoof and chew the cud, and were already marked out as fit for sacrifice.

It was the year 2348 B.C. that Noah spent in floating upon the waste of waters while every living thing was perishing round him, and afterwards in seeing the floods return to their beds in oceans, lakes, and rivers, which they shall never again overpass.

The ark first came aground on the mountain of Ararat, in Armenia, a sacred spot to this day; and here God made His covenant with Noah, renewing His first blessing to Adam, permitting the use of animal food; promising that the course of nature should never be disturbed again till the end of all things, and making the glorious tints of the rainbow, which are produced by sunlight upon water, stand as the pledge of this assurance. Of man He required abstinence from eating the blood of animals, and from shedding the blood of man, putting, as it were, a mark of sacredness upon life-blood, so as to lead the mind on to the Blood hereafter to be shed.

Soon a choice was made among the sons of Noah. Ham mocked at his father's infirmity, while his two brothers veiled it; and Noah was therefore inspired to prophesy that Canaan, the son of the undutiful Ham, should be accursed, and a servant of servants; that Shem should especially belong to the Lord God, and that Japhet's posterity should be enlarged, and should dwell in the tents of Shem. Thus Shem was marked as the chosen, yet with hope that Japhet should share in his blessings.

It seems as if Ham had brought away some of the arts and habits of the giant sons of Cain, for in all worldly prosperity his sons had the advantage. In 2247 B. C. the sons of men banded themselves together to build the Tower of Babel on the plain of Shinar, just below the hills of Armenia, where the two great rivers Euphrates and Tigris make the flats rich and fertile. For their presumption, God confounded their speech, and the nations first were divided. Ham's children got all the best regions; Nimrod, the child of his son Cush, kept Babel, built the first city, and became the first king. Canaan's sons settled themselves in that goodliest of all lands which bore his name; and Mizraim's children obtained the rich and beautiful valley of the Nile, called Egypt. All these were keen clever people, builders of cities, cultivators of the land, weavers and embroiderers, earnest after comfort and riches, and utterly forgetting, or grievously corrupting, the worship of God. Others of the race seem to have wandered further south, where the heat of the sun blackened their skins; and their strong constitution, and dull meek temperament, marked them out to all future generations as a prey to be treated like animals of burden, so as to bear to the utmost the curse of Canaan.

Shem's sons, simpler than those of Ham, continued to live in tents and watch their cattle, scattered about in the same plains, called from the two great streams, Mesopotamia, or the land of rivers. Some travelled westwards, and settling in China and India, became a rich and wealthy people, but constantly losing more and more the recollection of the truth; and some went on in time from isle to isle to the western hemisphere--lands where no other foot should tread till the world should be grown old.

Japhet's children seemed at first the least favoured, for no place, save the cold dreary north, was found for most of them. Some few, the children of Javan, found a home in the fair isles of the Mediterranean, but the greater part were wild horsemen in Northern Asia and Europe. This was a dark and dismal training, but it braced them so that in future generations they proved to have far more force and spirit than was to be found among the dwellers in milder climates.

LESSON II.
THE PATRIARCHS.

"The God of glory appeared unto our father Abraham."--Acts, vii. 2.

Among the sons of Shem (called Hebrews after his descendant Heber, who dwelt in Mesopotamia) was Abram, the good and faithful man, whom God chose out to be the father of the people in whom He was going to set His Light. In the year 1921, He tried Abram's faith by calling on him to leave his home, and go into a land which he knew not, but which should belong to his children after him--Abram, who had no child at all.

Yet he obeyed and believed, and was led into the beautiful hilly land then held by the sons of Canaan, where he was a stranger, wandering with his flocks and herds and servants from one green pasture to another, without a loot of land to call his own. For showing his faith by thus doing as he was commanded, Abram was rewarded by the promise that in his Seed should all the families of the earth be blessed; his name was changed to Abraham, which means a father of a great multitude; and as a sign that he had entered into a covenant with God, he was commanded to circumcise his children.

One son, Ishmael, had by this time been born to him of the bondmaid Hagar; but the child of promise, Isaac, the son of his wife Sarah, was not given till he was a hundred years old. Ishmael was cast out for mocking at his half-brother, the heir of the promises; but in answer to his father's prayers, he too became the father of a great nation, namely the Arabs, who still live in the desert, with their tents, their flocks, herds, and fine horses, much as Ishmael himself must have lived. They are still circumcised, and honour Abraham as their father; and with them are joined the Midianites and other tribes descended from Abraham's last wife, Keturah.

Isaac alone was to inherit the promise, and it was renewed to him and to his father, when their faith had been proved by their submission to God's command, that Isaac should be offered as a burnt-offering upon Mount Moriah, a sign of the Great Sacrifice long afterwards, when God did indeed provide Himself a Lamb.

When Abraham bought the Cave of Machpelah for a, burial-place, it was in the full certainty that though he was now a stranger in the land, it would be his children's home; and it was there that he and the other patriarchs were buried after their long and faithful pilgrimage.

Isaac's wife, Rebekah, was fetched from Abraham's former home, in Mesopotamia, that he might not be corrupted by marrying a Canaanite. Between his two sons, Esau and Jacob, there was again a choice; for God had prophesied that the elder should serve the younger, and Esau did not value the birthright which would have made him heir to no lands that would enrich himself, and to a far-off honour that he did not understand. So despising the promises of God, he made his right over to his brother for a little food, when he was hungry, and though he repented with tears when it was too late, he could not win back what he had once thrown away.

His revengeful anger when he found how he had been supplanted, made Jacob flee to his mother's family in Mesopotamia, and there dwell for many years, ere returning to Canaan with his large household, there to live in the manner that had been ordained for the first heirs of the promise. Esau went away to Mount Seir, to the south of the Promised Land, and his descendants were called the Edomites, from his name, meaning the Red; and so, too, the sea which washed their shores, took the name of the Sea of Edom, or the Red Sea. They were also named Kenites from his son Kenaz. Their country, afterwards called Idumea, was full of rocks and precipices, and in these the Edomites hollowed out caves for themselves, making them most beautiful, with pillars supporting the roof within, and finely-carved entrances, cut with borders, flowers, and scrolls, so lasting that the cities of Bosra and Petra are still a wonder to travellers, though they have been empty and deserted for centuries past. The Edomites did not at once lose the knowledge of the true God; indeed, as many believe, of them was born the prophet Job, whom Satan was permitted to try with every trouble he could conjure up, so that his friends believed that such sufferings could only be brought on him for some great sin; whereas he still maintained that the ways of God were hidden, and gave utterance to one of the clearest ancient prophecies of the Redeemer and the Resurrection. At length God answered him from the whirlwind, and proclaimed His greatness through His unsearchable works; and Job, for his patience in the time of adversity, was restored to far more than his former prosperity.

Jacob's name was changed to Israel, which meant a prince before God; and his whole family were taken into the covenant, though the three elder sons, for their crimes, forfeited the foremost places, which passed to Judah and Joseph; and Levi was afterwards chosen as the tribe set apart for the priesthood, the number twelve being made up by reckoning Ephraim and Manasseh, the sons of Joseph, as heads of tribes, like their uncles. Long ago, Abraham had been told that his seed should sojourn in Egypt; and when the envious sons of Israel sold their innocent brother Joseph, their sin was bringing about God's high purpose. Joseph was inspired to interpret Pharaoh's dreams, which foretold the famine; and when by-and-by his brothers came to buy the corn that he had laid up, he made himself known, forgave them with all his heart, and sent them to fetch his father to see him once more. Then the whole family of Israel, seventy in number, besides their wives, came and settled in the land of Goshen, about the year 1707, and were there known by the name of Hebrews, after Heber, the great-grand-son of Shem. There in Goshen, Jacob ended the days of his pilgrimage, desiring his sons to carry his corpse back to the Cave of Machpelah, there to be buried, and await their return when the time of promise should come. He gave his blessing to all his sons, and was inspired to mark out Joseph among them as the one whose children should have the choicest temporal inheritance; but of the fourth son, he said, "The sceptre shall not depart from Judah, nor a lawgiver from between his feet, until Shiloh come." Shiloh meant Him that should be sent, and Judah was thus marked out to be the princely tribe, which was to have the rule until the Seed should come.

LESSON III.
EGYPT.

"When Israel was a child, then I loved him, and called my son out of Egypt."--Hosea, xi. 1.

The country where the Israelites had taken up their abode, was the valley watered by the great river Nile. There is nothing but desert, wherever this river does not spread itself, for it never rains, and there would be dreadful drought, if every year, when the snow melts upon the mountains far south, where is the source of the stream, it did not become so much swelled as to spread far beyond its banks, and overflow all the flat space round it. Then as soon as the water subsides, the hot sun upon the mud that it has left brings up most beautiful grass, and fine crops of corn with seven or nine ears to one stalk; grand fruits of all kinds, melons, pumpkins, and cucumbers, flax for weaving linen, and everything that a people can desire. Indeed, the water of the river is so delicious, that it is said that those who have once tasted it are always longing to drink it again.

The sons of Mizraim, son of Ham, who first found out this fertile country, were a very clever race, and made the most of the riches of the place. They made dykes and ditches to guide the floodings into their fields and meadows; they cultivated the soil till it was one beautiful garden; they wove their flax into fine linen; and they made bricks of their soft clay, and hewed stone from the hills higher up the river, so that their buildings have been the wonder of all ages since. They had kings to rule them, and priests to guide their worship; but these priests had very wrong and corrupt notions themselves, and let the poor ignorant people believe even greater folly than they did themselves.

They thought that the great God lived among them in the shape of a bull with one spot on his back like an eagle, and one on his tongue like a beetle; and this creature they called Apis, and tended with the utmost care. When he died they all went into mourning, and lamented till a calf like him was found, and was brought home with the greatest honour; and for his sake all cattle were sacred, and no one allowed to kill them. Besides the good Power, they thought there was an evil one as strong as the good, and they worshipped him likewise, to beg him to do them no harm; so the dangerous crocodiles of the Nile were sacred, and it was forbidden to put them to death. They had a dog-god and a cat-goddess, and they honoured the beetle because they saw it rolling a ball of earth in which to lay its eggs, and fancied it an emblem of eternity; and thus all these creatures were consecrated, and when they died were rolled up in fine linen and spices, just as the Egyptians embalmed their own dead.

Mummies, as we call these embalmed Egyptian corpses, are often found now, laid up in beautiful tombs, cut out in the rock, and painted in colours still fresh with picture writing, called hieroglyphics, telling in tokens all the history of the person whose body they contained. The kings built tombs for themselves, like mountains, square at the bottom, but each course of stones built within the last till they taper to a point at the top. These are called pyramids, and have within them very small narrow passages, leading to a small chamber, just large enough to hold a king's coffin.

They had enormous idols hewn out of stone. The head of one, which you may see in the British Museum, is far taller than the tallest man, and yet the face is really handsome, and there are multitudes more, both of them and of their temples, still remaining on the banks of the Nile. The children of Israel, being chiefly shepherds, kept apart from the Egyptians at first; but as time went on they learnt some of their habits, and many of them had begun to worship their idols and forget the truth, when their time of affliction came. The King of Egypt, becoming afraid of having so numerous and rich a people settled in his dominions, tried to keep them down by hard bondage and heavy labour. He made them toil at his great buildings, and oppressed them in every possible manner; and when he found that they still throve and increased, he made the cruel decree, that every son who was born to them should be cast into the river.

But man can do nothing against the will of God, and this murderous ordinance proved the very means of causing one of these persecuted Hebrew infants to be brought up in the palace of Pharaoh, and instructed in all the wisdom of the Egyptians, the only people who at that time had any human learning. Even in his early life, Moses seems to have been aware that he was to be sent to put an end to the bondage of his people, for, choosing rather to suffer with them than to live in prosperity with their oppressors, he went out among them and tried to defend them, and to set them at peace with one another; but the time was not yet come, and they thrust him from them, so that he was forced to fly for shelter to the desert, among the Midianite descendants of Abraham. After he had spent forty years there as a shepherd, God appeared to him, and then first revealed Himself as JEHOVAH, the Name proclaiming His eternal self-existence, I AM THAT I AM, a Name so holy, that the translators of our Bible have abstained from repeating it where it occurs, but have put the Name, the LORD, in capital letters in its stead. Moses was then sent to Egypt to lead out the Israelites on their way back to the land so long promised to their fore-fathers; and when Pharaoh obstinately refused to let them go, the dreadful plagues and wonders that were sent on the country were such as to show that their gods were no gods; since their river, the glory of their land, became a loathsome stream of blood, creeping things came and went at the bidding of the Lord, and their adored cattle perished before their eyes. At last, on the night of the Passover, in each of the houses unmarked by the blood of the Lamb, there was a great cry over the death of the first-born son; and where the sign of faith was seen, there was a mysterious obedient festival held by families prepared for a strange new journey. Then the hard heart yielded to terror, and Israel went oat of Egypt as a nation. They had come in in 1707 as seventy men, they went out in 1491 as six hundred thousand, and their enemies, following after them, sank like lead in the mighty waters of that arm of the Red Sea, which had divided to let the chosen pass through.

LESSON IV.
THE WILDERNESS.

"Where Is He that brought them up out of the sea with the shepherd of His flock? Where is He that put His Holy Spirit within him?"--Isaiah, lxiii. 11.

When Moses had led the 600,000 men, with their wives, children, and cattle, beyond the reach of the Egyptians, they were in a small peninsula, between the arms of the Red Sea, with the wild desolate peaks of Mount Horeb towering in the midst, and all around grim stony crags, with hardly a spring of water; and though there were here and there slopes of grass, and bushes of hoary-leaved camel-thorn, and long-spined shittim or acacia, nothing bearing fruit for human beings. There were strange howlings and crackings in the mountains, the sun glared back from the arid stones and rocks, and the change seemed frightful after the green meadows and broad river of Egypt.

Frightened and faithless, the Israelites cried out reproachfully to Moses to ask how they should live in this desert place, forgetting that the Pillar of cloud and fire proved that they were under the care of Him who had brought them safely out of the hands of their enemies. In His mercy God bore with their murmurs, fed them with manna from Heaven, and water out of the flinty rock; and gave them the victory over the Edomite tribe of robber Amalekites at Rephidim, where Joshua fought, and Moses, upheld by Aaron and Hur, stretched forth his hands the whole day. Then, fifty days after their coming out of Egypt, He called them round the peak of Sinai to hear His own Voice proclaim the terms of the new Covenant.

The Covenant with Abraham had circumcision for the token, faith as the condition, and the blessing to all nations as the promise. This Covenant remained in full force, but in the course of the last four hundred years, sin had grown so much that the old standard, handed down from the patriarchs, had been forgotten, and men would not have known what was right, nor how far they fell from it, without a written Law. This Law, in ten rules, all meeting together in teaching Love to God and man, commanded in fact perfection, without which no man could be fit to stand in the sight of God. He spoke it with His own Mouth, from amid cloud, flame, thunder, and sounding trumpets, on Mount Sinai, while the Israelites watched around in awe and terror, unable to endure the dread of that Presence. The promise of this Covenant was, that if they would keep the Law, they should dwell prosperously in the Promised Land, and be a royal priesthood and peculiar treasure unto God, They answered with one voice, "All the words the Lord hath said will we do;" and Moses made a sacrifice, and sprinkled them with the blood, to consecrate them and confirm their oath. It was the blood of the Old Testament. Then he went up into the darkness of the cloud on the mountain top, there fasting, to talk with God, and to receive the two Tables of Stone written by the Finger of God. This was, as some believe, the first writing in the letters of the alphabet ever known in the world, and the Books of Moses were the earliest ever composed, and set down with the pen upon parchment.

Those Laws were too strict for man in his fallen state. Keep them he could not; breaking them, he became too much polluted to be fit for mercy. Even while living in sight of the cloud on the Mountain, where Moses was known to be talking with God, the Israelites lost faith, and set up a golden calf in memory of the Egyptian symbol of divinity, making it their leader instead of Moses. Such a transgression of their newly-made promise so utterly forfeited their whole right to the covenant, that Moses destroyed the precious tables, the token of the mutual engagement, and God threatened to sweep them off in a moment and to fulfil His oaths to their forefather in the children of Moses alone. Then Moses, having purified the camp by slaying the worst offenders, stood between the rest and the wrath of God, mediating for them until he obtained mercy for them, and a renewal of the Covenant. Twice he spent forty days in that awful Presence, where glorious visions were revealed to him; the Courts of Heaven itself, to be copied by him, by Divine guidance, in the Ark and Tabernacle, where his brother Aaron, and his seed after him, were to minister as Priests, setting forth to the eye how there was a Holy Place, whence men were separated by sin, and how it could only be entered by a High Priest, after a sacrifice of atonement. Every ordinance of this service was a shadow of good things to come, and was therefore strictly enjoined on Israel, as part of the conditions of the Covenant, guiding their faith onwards by this acted prophecy; and therewith God, as King of His people, put forth other commands, some relating to their daily habits, others to their government as a nation, all tending to keep them separate from other nations. For transgressions of such laws as these, or for infirmities of human nature, regarded as stains, cleansing sacrifices were permitted. For offences against the Ten Commandments, there was no means of purchasing remission; no animal's, nay, no man's life could equal such a cost; there was nothing for it but to try to dwell on the hope, held out to Adam and Abraham, and betokened by the sacrifices and the priesthood, of some fuller expiation yet to come; some means of not only obtaining pardon, but of being worthy of mercy.

The Israelites could not even be roused to look for the present temporal promise, and hankered after the fine soil and rich fruits of Egypt, rather than the beautiful land of hill and valley that lay before them; and when their spies reported it to be full of hill forts, held by Canaanites of giant stature, a cowardly cry of despair broke out, that they would return to Egypt. Only two of the whole host, besides Moses, were ready to trust to Him who had delivered them from Pharaoh, and had led them through the sea. Therefore those two alone of the grown-up men were allowed to set foot in the Promised Land. Till all the rest should have fallen in the wilderness, and a better race have been trained up, God would not help them to take possession. In their wilfulness they tried to advance, and were defeated, and thus were obliged to endure their forty years' desert wandering.

Even Moses had his patience worn out by their fretful faithlessness, and committed an act of disobedience, for which he was sentenced not to enter the land, but to die on the borders after one sight of the promise of his fathers. Under him, however, began the work of conquest; the rich pasture lands of Gilead and Basan were subdued, and the tribes of Reuben and Gad, and half the tribe of Manasseh, were permitted to take these as their inheritance, though beyond the proper boundary, the Jordan. The Moabites took alarm, though these, as descended from Abraham's nephew Lot, were to be left unharmed; and their king, Balak, sent, as it appears, even to Mesopotamia for Balaam, a true prophet, though a guilty man, in hopes that he would bring down the curse of God on them. Balaam, greedy of reward, forced, as it were, consent from God to go to Balak, though warned that his words would not be in his own power. As he stood on the hill top with Balak, vainly endeavouring to curse, a glorious stream of blessing flowed from his lips, revealing, not only the fate of all the tribes around, even for a thousand years, but proclaiming the Sceptre and Star that should rise out of Jacob to execute vengeance on his foes. But finding himself unable to curse Israel, the miserable prophet devised a surer means of harming them: he sent tempters among them to cause them to corrupt themselves, and so effectual was this invention, that the greater part of the tribe of Simeon were ensnared, and a great plague was sent in chastisement. It was checked by the zeal of the young priest, Phineas, under whose avenging hand so many of the guilty tribe fell, that their numbers never recovered the blow. Then after a prayer of atonement, a great battle was fought, and the wretched Balaam was among the slain.

The forty years were over, Moses's time was come, and he gave his last summing up of the Covenant, and sung his prophetic song. His authority was to pass to his servant, the faithful spy, bearing the prophetic name of Joshua; and he was led by God to the top of Mount Nebo, whence he might see in its length and breadth, the pleasant land, the free hills, the green valleys watered by streams, the wooded banks of Jordan, the pale blue expanse of the Mediterranean joining with the sky to the west; and to the north, the snowy hills of Hermon, which sent their rain and dew on all the goodly mountain land. It had been the hope of that old man's hundred and twenty years, and he looked forth on it with his eye not dim, nor his natural force abated; but God had better things for him in Heaven, and there upon the mountain top he died alone, and God buried him in the sepulchre whereof no man knoweth. None was like to him in the Old Covenant, who stood between God and the Israelites, but he left a promise that a Prophet should be raised up like unto himself.

LESSON V.
ISRAEL IN CANAAN.

"But He was so merciful, that He forgave their misdeeds and destroyed them not."--Psalm Lxxviii. 38.

In the year 1431, Joshua led the tribes through the divided waters of the Jordan, and received strength and skill to scatter the heathen before them, conquer the cities, and settle them in their inheritance.

The Land of Canaan was very unlike Egypt, with its flat soil, dry climate, and single river. It was a narrow strip, inclosed between the Mediterranean Sea and the river Jordan, which runs due south down a steep wooded cleft into the Dead Sea, the lowest water in the world, in a sort of pit of its own, with barren desolation all round it, so as to keep in memory the ruin of the cities of the plain. In the north, rise the high mountains of Libanus, a spur from which goes the whole length of the land, and forms two slopes, whence the rivers flow, either westward into the Great Sea, or eastward into the Jordan, Many of these hills are too dry and stony to be cultivated; but the slopes of some have fine grassy pastures, and the soil of the valleys is exceedingly rich, bearing figs, vines, olive trees, and corn in plenty, wherever it is properly tilled. With such hills, rivers, valleys, and pastures, it was truly a goodly land, and when God's blessing was on it, it was the fairest spot where man could live. When the Israelites entered it, every hill was crowned by a strongly-walled and fortified town, the abode of some little king of one of the seven Canaanite nations who were given into their hands to be utterly destroyed. Though they were commanded to make a complete end of all the people in each place they took, they were forbidden to seize more than they could till, lest the empty ruins should serve as a harbour for wild beasts; but they had their several lots marked out where they might spread when their numbers should need room. As Jacob had promised to Joseph, Ephraim and half Manaseh had the richest portion, nearly in the middle, and Shiloh, where the Tabernacle was set up, was in their territory; Judah and Benjamin were in a very wild rocky part to the southwards, between the two seas, with only Simeon beyond them; then came, north of Manasseh, the fine pasture lands of Issachar and Zebulon, and a small border for Asher between Libanus and the sea; while Reuben, Gad, and the rest of Manasseh, were to the east of the Jordan, where they had begged to settle themselves in the meadows of Bashan, and the balmy thickets of Gilead.

Many a fortified town was still held by the Canaanites, in especial Jebus, on Mount Moriah, between Judah and Benjamin; and close to Asher, the two great merchant cities of the Zidonians upon the sea-shore. These were called Tyre and Zidon, and their inhabitants were named Phoenicians, and were the chief sailors and traders of the Old World. From seeing a dog's mouth stained purple after eating a certain shell-fish on their coast, they had learnt how to dye woollen garments of a fine purple or scarlet, which was thought the only colour fit for kings, and these were sent out to all the countries round, in exchange for balm and spices from Gilead; corn and linen from Egypt; ivory, pearls, and rubies from India; gold from the beds of rivers in Chittim or Asia Minor; and silver from Spain, then called Tarshish. Thus they grew very rich and powerful, and were skilful in all they undertook. The art of writing, which they seem to have caught from the Hebrews, went from them to the Greeks, sons of Japhet, who lived more to the north, in what were called the Isles of the Gentiles.

The Canaanites had a still fouler worship than the other sons of Ham in Egypt. They had many gods, whom they called altogether Baalim, or lords; and goddesses, whom they called Ashtoreth; and they thought that each had some one city or people to defend; and that the Lord Jehovah of the Israelites was such another as these, instead of being the only God of Heaven and earth. Among these there was one great Baal to whom the Phoenicians were devoted, and an especial Ashtoreth, the moon, or Queen of Heaven, who was thought to have a lover named Tammuz, who died with the flowers in the autumn and revived in the spring, and the women took delight in wailing and bemoaning his death, and then dancing and offering cakes in honour of his revival. Besides these, there was the planet Saturn, or as they called him, Moloch or Remphan, of whom they had a huge brazen statue with the hands held a little apart, set up over a furnace; they put poor little children between these brazen hands, and left them to drop into the flames below as an offering to this dreadful god.

Well might such worship be called abomination, and the Israelites be forbidden to hold any dealings with those who followed it. As long as the generation lived who had been bred up in the wilderness, they obeyed, and felt themselves under the rule of God their King, Who made His Will known at Shiloh by the signs on the breastplate of the High Priest, while judges and elders governed in the cities. But afterwards they began to be tempted to make friends with their heathen neighbours, and thus learnt to believe in their false deities, and to hanker after the service of some god who made no such strict laws of goodness as those by which they were bound. As certainly as they fell away, so surely the punishment came, and God stirred up some of these dangerous friends to attack them. Sometimes it was a Canaanite tribe with iron chariots who mightily oppressed them; sometimes the robber shepherds, the Midianites, would burst in and carry off their cattle and their crops, until distress brought the Israelites back to a better mind, and they cried out to the Lord. Then He would raise up a mighty warrior, and give him the victory, so that he became ruler and judge over Israel; but no sooner was he dead, than they would fall back again into idolatry, and receive another chastisement, repent, and be again delivered. This went on for about 400 years, the Israelites growing constantly worse. In the latter part of this time, their chief enemies were the Philistines, in the borders of Simeon and Judah, near the sea. These were not Canaanites, but had once dwelt in Egypt, and then, after living for a time in Cyprus, had come and settled in Gaza and Ashkelon, and three other very strong cities on the coast, where they worshipped a fish-god, called Dagon. They had no king, but were ruled by lords of their five cities, and made terrible inroads upon all the country round; until at last the Israelites, in their self-will, fancied they could turn them to flight by causing the Ark to be carried out to battle by the two corrupt young priests, sons of Eli, whose doom had already been pronounced--that they should both die in one day. They were slain, when the Ark was taken by the enemies, and their aged father fell back and broke his neck in the shock of the tidings. The glory had departed; and though God proved His might by shattering Dagon's image before the Ark, and plaguing the Philistines wherever they carried it, till they were forced to send it home in a manner which again showed the Divine Hand, yet it never returned to Shiloh; God deserted the place where His Name had not been kept holy; the token of the Covenant seemed to be lost; the Philistines ruled over the broken and miserable Israelites, and there was only one promise to comfort them--that the Lord would raise up unto Himself a faithful Priest. Already there was growing up at Shiloh the young Levite, Samuel, dedicated by his mother, and bred up by Eli. He is counted as first of the prophets, that long stream of inspired men, who constantly preached righteousness, and to whom occasionally future events were made known. He was also last of the Judges, or heaven-sent deliverers. As soon as he grew up, he rallied the Israelites, restored the true worship, as far as could be with the Ark in concealment, and sent them out to battle. They defeated the Philistines, and under Samuel, again became a free nation.

LESSON VI.
THE KINGDOM OF ALL ISRAEL.

"As is the fat taken away from the peace-offering, so was David chosen out of the children of Israel ... In all his works he praised the Holy One Most High with words of glory .... The Lord took away his sins and exalted his horn for ever, He gave him a covenant of kings, and a throne of glory in Israel."--Ecclus. xlvii. II.

W hen Samuel grew old, the Israelites would not trust to God to choose a fresh guardian for them, but cried out for a king to keep them together and lead them to war like other nations. Their entreaty was granted, and in 1094 B. C. Saul the son of Kish, of the small but fierce tribe of Benjamin, was appointed by God, and anointed like a priest by Samuel, on the understanding that he was not to rule by his own will, like the princes around, but as God's chief officer, to enforce His laws and carry out His bidding.

This Saul would not do. When, instead of lurking in caves, with no weapons save their tools for husbandry, the Israelites, under his leading, gradually became free and warlike; and his son Jonathan and uncle Abner were able generals, he fancied he could go his own way, he took on him to offer sacrifice, as the heathen kings did; and when sent forth to destroy all belonging to the Amalekites, he spared the king and the choicest of the spoil. For this he was sentenced not to be the founder of a line of kings, and the doom filled him with wrath against the priesthood, while an evil spirit was permittted to trouble his soul, Samuel's last great act was to anoint the youngest son of Jesse the Bethlehemite, the great grandchild of the loving Moabitess, Ruth, the same whom God had marked beside his sheepfolds as the man after His own Heart, the future father of the sceptred line of Judah, and of the "Root and Offspring of David, the bright and morning Star."

Fair and young, full of inspired song, and of gallant courage, the youth David was favoured as the minstrel able to drive the evil spirit from Saul, the champion who had slain the giant of Gath. He was the king's son-in-law, the prince's bosom friend; but, as the hopes of Israel became set on him, Saul began to hate him as if he were a supplanter, though Jonathan submitted to the Will that deprived himself of a throne, and loved his friend as faithfully as ever. At last, by Jonathan's counsel, David fled from court, and Saul in his rage at thinking him aided by the priests, slew all who fell into his hands, thus cutting off his own last link with Heaven. A trusty band of brave men gathered round David, but he remained a loyal outlaw, and always abstained from any act against his sovereign, even though Saul twice lay at his mercy. Patiently he tarried the Lord's leisure, and the time came at last. The Philistines overran the country, and chased Saul even to the mountain fastnesses of Gilboa, where the miserable man, deserted by God, tried to learn his fate through evil spirits, and only met the certainty of his doom. In the next day's battle his true-hearted son met a soldier's death; but Saul, when wounded by the archers, tried in vain to put an end to his own life, and was, after a reign of forty years, at last slain by an Amalekite, who brought his crown to David, and was executed by him for having profanely slain the Lord's anointed.

For seven years David reigned only in his own tribe of Judah, while the brave Abner kept the rest of the kingdom for Saul's son, Ishbosheth, until, taking offence because Ishbosheth refused to give him one of Saul's widows to wife, he offered to come to terms with David, but in leaving the place of meeting, he was treacherously killed by David's overbearing nephew, Joab, in revenge for the death of a brother whom he had slain in single combat. Ishbosheth was soon after murdered by two of his own servants, and David becoming sole king, ruled prudently with all his power, and with anxious heed to the will of his true King. He was a great conqueror, and was the first to win for Israel her great city on Mount Moriah. It had once been called Salem, or peace, when the mysterious priest-king, Melchizedek, reigned there in Abraham's time, but since it had been held by the Jebusites, and called Jebus. When David took it, he named it Jerusalem, or the vision of peace, fortified it, built a palace there, and fetched thither with songs and solemn dances, the long-hidden Ark, so that it might be the place where God's Name was set, the centre of worship; and well was the spot fitted for the purpose. It was a hill girdled round by other hills, and so strong by nature, that when built round with towers and walls, an enemy could hardly have taken it. David longed to raise a solid home for the Ark, but this was not a work permitted to a man of war and bloodshed, and he could only collect materials, and restore the priests to their offices, giving them his own glorious Book of Psalms, full of praise, prayer, and entreaty, to be sung for ever before the Lord, by courses of Levites relieving one another, that so the voice of praise might never die out.

David likewise made the Philistines, Moabites, Ammonites, and Edomites pay him tribute, and became the most powerful king in the East, receiving the fulfilment of the promises to Abraham; but even he was far from guiltless. He was a man of strong passions, though of a tender heart, and erred greatly, both from hastiness and weakness, but never without repentance, and his Psalms of contrition have ever since been the treasure of the penitent. Chastisement visited his sins, and was meekly borne, but bereavement and rebellion, care, sorrow, and disappointment, severely tried the Sweet Psalmist of Israel, shepherd, prophet, soldier, and king, ere in 1016, in his seventieth year, he went to his rest, after having been king for forty years, he was assured that his seed should endure for ever.

All promises of temporal splendour were accomplished in his peaceful son, Solomon, who asked to be the wisest, and therefore was likewise made the richest, most prosperous, and most peaceful of kings. No enemy rose against him, but all the nations sought his friendship; and Zidon for once had her merchandise hallowed by its being offered to build and adorn the Temple, Solomon's great work. The spot chosen for it was that of Isaac's sacrifice, where was the threshing-floor bought by David from Araunah, but to give farther room, he levelled the head of the mountain, throwing it into the valley; and thus forming an even space where, silently built of huge stone, quarried at a distance, arose the courts, for strangers, women, men, and priests, surrounded by cloisters, supporting galleries of rooms for the lodging of the priests and Levites, many hundreds in number. The main building was of white marble, and the Holy of Holies was overlaid even to the roof outside with plates of gold, flashing back the sunshine. Even this was but a poor token of the Shechinah, that glorious light which descended at Solomon's prayer of consecration, and filled the Sanctuary with the visible token of God's Presence on the Mercy Beat, to be seen by the High Priest once a year.

That consecration was the happiest moment of the history of Israel, What followed was mournful. Even David had been like the kings of other eastern nations in the multitude of his wives, and Solomon went far beyond him, bringing in heathen women, who won him into paying homage to their idols, and outraging God by building temples to Moloch and Ashtoreth; though as a prophet he had been inspired to speak in his Proverbs of Christ in His Church as the Holy Wisdom of God. A warning was sent that the power which had corrupted him should not continue in his family, and that the kingdom should be divided, but he only grew more tyrannical, and when the Ephraimite warrior, Jeroboam, was marked by the prophet Ahijah as the destined chief of the new kingdom, Solomon persecuted him, and drove him to take refuge with the great Shishak, King of Egypt, where he seems to have learnt the idolatries from which Israel had been so slowly weaned. Sick at heart, Solomon in his old age, wrote the saddest book in the Bible; and though his first writing, the Canticles, had been a joyful prophetic song of the love between the Lord and His Church, his last was a mournful lamentation over the vanity and emptiness of the world, and full of scorn of all that earth can give.

LESSON VII.
THE KINGDOM OP JUDAH.

"But if his children forsake My Law, and walk not in My judgments: if they break My statutes, and keep not My Commandments, I will visit their offences with the rod, and their sin with scourges."--Ps. lxxxix. 31, 32.

Rehoboam, the son of Solomon, brought about, by his own harshness and folly, the punishment that God had decreed. By the advice of his hasty young counsellors, he made so violent a reply to the petition brought to him by his subjects, that they took offence, and the ten northern tribes broke away from him, setting up as their king, Jeroboam, who had been already marked out by the prophet.

The lesson of meekness seems to have been the one chiefly appointed for Rehoboam, for when he assembled the fighting men of Judah and Benjamin to subdue the revolt, Shemaiah the prophet was sent to forbid him, and he submitted at once; and when again Jeroboam's friend Shishak invaded his kingdom, Shemaiah told him it was as a punishment sent him by God, against which he must not struggle; so he gathered all the riches left him by his father, paid the tribute that the Egyptians required; and for being thus patient and submissive, he was again blessed by God, and Judah prospered. No doubt Rehoboam's obedience saved him from sharing the fate of the other kings whom Shishak conquered and dragged back to Egypt, where he yoked them to his chariot, four abreast, and made them draw him about. Shishak was a great conqueror, and in nine years overran all Asia, as far as the river Ganges. All his victories were recorded in hieroglyphics, and the learned have made out the picture of a people with the features of Jews, bringing their gifts to his feet, no doubt the messengers of Rehoboam. He lost his sight in his old age, and is said to have killed himself.

In 955 Abijah came to the throne instead of Rehoboam, and was permitted to gain a great victory over Jeroboam, but he died at the end of three years, and was succeeded by his son Asa. The great temptation of the men of Judah seems to have been at this time the resorting to hill tops and groves of trees as places of worship, instead of going steadily to the Temple at Jerusalem; and the kings, though obedient in other respects, did not dare to put down this forbidden custom. Asa's mother, Maachah, a daughter of Absalom, even had an idol in a grove; but after the king had been strengthened to gain a great victory over the Ethiopians, he destroyed the idol, and put her down from being queen. His end was less good than his beginning; he made a league with the Syrians instead of trusting to God; and threw the prophet Hanani into prison for having rebuked him; and in his latter years he was cruel and oppressive. He died in 891.

His son Jehoshaphat was a very good and gentle prince, but his very gentleness seemed to have led him into error, for he became too friendly with the idolatrous House of Ahab in Samaria, and allowed his son Jehoram to take to wife the child of Ahab and Jezebel, Athaliah, who proved even more wicked than her mother. Jehoshaphat was in alliance with Ahab, and went out with him to his last battle at Ramoth-Gilead, where Ahab tried to put his friend into danger instead of himself by making him appear as the only king present, but entirely failed to deceive the hand appointed to bring death. Afterwards, when the Edomites, Ammonites, and Moabites came up against Judah, Jehoshaphat was commanded to have no fears, but to go out to meet them, with the Levites singing before him, "Praise the Lord, for His mercy endureth for ever!" So the battle should be his without fighting; for the three banded nations fought among themselves, and made such a slaughter of one another, that the Jews had nothing to do but to gather the spoil, which was in such heaps, that they spent three days in collecting it. And again, when Jehoshaphat went out with Jehoram, King of Israel, against the Moabites, with Jehoshaphat's tributary, the King of Edom, another miraculous deliverance was granted by the hand of Elisha, and the water which was sent to relieve the thirsty hosts of Israel and Judah, seemed to the Moabites as blood; so that, thinking the three armies had quarrelled and slain each other, they made an unguarded attack, and suffered a total rout.

Jehoshaphat was succeeded in 891 by his son Jehoram, who, though he had seen such signal proofs of God's power, chose rather to follow the will of his wicked wife Athaliah, than to obey the commands of God. To strengthen his dominion, he followed the example of the worst heathen tyrants, and killed his seven brethren; and he permitted and encouraged idolatry in the most open manner. He was first punished by the loss of the Edomites, who rose against him, and set up a free kingdom according to the prophecy of Isaac; next by an in-road of the Arabians and Philistines, who ravaged his very house, and killed all his children except the youngest, Ahaziah; and lastly, by a loathsome and deadly disease, which ended his life in the fortieth year of his age.

Ahaziah was only twenty-two, and was ruled by his mother Athaliah for the one year before, going to visit his uncle Jehoram, of Israel, he was slain with him in Jehu's massacre of the House of Ahab. Athaliah herself fulfilled the rest of the decree which she did not acknowledge. She was bent on reigning, and savagely murdered all her grandsons who fell into her hands; but as the House of David was never to fail, one tender branch, the infant Joash, was hidden from her fury by his aunt, the wife of the High Priest Jehoiada; and when the fitting time was come, the Levites were armed, and the people were shown their little king. They acknowledged him with shouts of joy, and Athaliah coming to see the cause of the outcry, was dragged out of the Temple and put to death. Jerusalem was cleansed from the worship of Baal, and all prospered as long as the good Jehoiada lived. After his death, however, Joash fell away grievously, and promoted idol worship; nay, he even slew the son of his preserver, Jehoiada, for bringing him a Divine rebuke, and for this iniquity his troops suffered a great defeat from the Syrians, and his servants slew him as he lay sick on his bed in 838. His son Amaziah began well, obeying the Lord by dismissing the Ephraimites whom he had hired to aid him against the Edomites, and he was therefore rewarded with a great victory; but so strangely blind was he, that he brought home the vain gods of Edom and worshipped them. He too was slain by rebels in the flower of his age, leaving his son Uzziah, also called Azariah, to succeed him at sixteen years old. Uzziah met with such success at first, that his heart was lifted up, and in his pride he endeavoured to intrude into the priest's office, and burn incense on the Altar; but even while striving with the High Priest, the leprosy broke out white on his brow, setting him apart, to live as an outcast from religious services for ever. His son Jotham became the governor of the kingdom during his lifetime, and afterwards reigned alone till the year 759, when he was succeeded by his son Ahaz, one of the worst and most idolatrous of the Kings of Judah. The Syrians made alliance with Israel, and terribly ravaged Judea, till Jerusalem stood alone in the midst of desolation; and Ahaz, instead of turning to the Lord, tried to strengthen himself by fresh heathen alliances, though the prophet Isaiah brought him certain messages that his foes should be destroyed, and promised him, for a sign, that great blessing of the House of David, that the Virgin's Son should be born, and should be God present with us.

LESSON VIII.
THE KINGDOM OF SAMARIA.

"As for Samaria, her king is cut off as the foam upon the water."--Hosea, x. 7.

Many promises had marked out Ephraim for greatness, and at first the new kingdom seemed quite to overshadow the little rocky Judah. But the founder of the dominion of the ten tribes sowed the seeds of decay, because, like Saul, he would not trust to the God who had given him his crown. He was afraid his subjects would return to the kings of the House of David, if he let them go to worship at Jerusalem, and therefore revived the old symbol of a calf, which he must have seen in Egypt in his exile, setting up two shrines at Bethel and at Dan, the two ends of his kingdom, bidding his people go thither to offer sacrifice. Thus he made Israel to sin; and while hoping to strengthen his power, was the cause of its ruin. Prophets warned him in vain, that his line should not remain on the throne; and in the reign of his son Nadab, the rebel Baasha arose and slew the whole family of this first king of the idolatrous realm, in the year 952. Baasha was not warned by the fate of Nadab, but followed the same courses; and his son Elah and all his house were destroyed in 928, when after the slaughter of two short-lived usurpers, the captain of the army, Omri, became king. Omri belonged to the city of Jezreel, in the inheritance of Issachar; but he built Samaria in the midst of Ephraim, between the two hills of blessing and of cursing, and this town becoming the capital, gave its name to the whole kingdom. In 918, Omri left his crown to his son Ahab, who allied himself with the rich Phoenicians, and took the Zidonian princess Jezebel for his wife; the most unfortunate marriage in the whole Israelitish history. Sinful as had been the calf-worship, it was still meant for adoration of the true God; but Jezebel brought her foul Phoenician faith with her, and tried to force on the Israelites the worship of Baal as a separate god, in the stead of the Lord Jehovah.

Ahab was weak, and yielded; and the greater number of the nation were so much corrupted by the breach of the Second Commandment, that they were not slow to break the First, although God had sent the most glorious of all His prophets to prove to them that "the Lord, He is the God." Three years of drought showed who commands the clouds, and then came Elijah's challenge to the four hundred prophets of Baal, to prove who was the God who could send fire from Heaven! All day did the four hundred cry wildly on their idol, while Elijah mocked them; at evening his offering was made, and drenched with water to increase the wonder of the miracle. He prayed, the fire fell at once from Heaven, and the people shouted "The Lord He is the God!" and gave their deceivers up to punishment; and when this partial purification was made, he prayed upon Mount Carmel, and the little cloud arose and grew into a mighty storm, bringing abundance of rain on the thirsty land.

Who could withstand such wonders? Yet they only hardened Jezebel into greater cruelty, and Elijah was forced to flee into the utmost desert, where he communed with God on Mount Sinai, even like Moses. Only once more did he appear again to Ahab, and that was to rebuke him for having permitted the murder of a poor subject whose property he had coveted, and to foretell the horrors in which his line should end.

Ahab was not wholly hardened, and often had gleams of good which brought favour upon him. A new enemy had risen up since the Canaanites had been destroyed, and the Philistines repressed, by David; namely, the Syrians, a powerful nation, whose capital was at Damascus, a city which is said to be a perfect paradise, so delicious is the climate, and so lovely the two rivers, one making the circuit of the walls, the other flowing through the middle of the town. These Syrians were appointed to bring punishment upon Samaria; but at first, two great victories were vouchsafed to Ahab, because Benhadad, King of Syria, fancied that the Israelites only won because their gods were gods of the hills. Afterwards, when Ahab went out to recover Ramoth Gilead, wilfully trusting to lying prophets, and silencing the true one, not all his disguise could avail to protect him; he was slain in the battle; and when his chariot was washed, the dogs licked his blood, as they had licked that of his victim Naboth.

Ahaziah, his son, soon died of a fall from the top of his palace, and the next brother Jehoram reigned, trying to make an agreement between the worship of God and of Baal. It was now that Elijah was taken away into Heaven by a whirlwind, leaving behind him Elisha to carry on his mission of prophecy and to execute the will of the Lord. It was Elisha who sent a messenger to anoint Jehu, the warrior who performed the vengeance of the Lord upon the House of Ahab. In the year 884 Jehoram was slain in his chariot; Jezebel, thrown out of window by her own slaves, perished miserably among the ravenous flocks of street dogs; and all the princes of the line were slaughtered by the rulers of Samaria; the worshippers of Baal were massacred, and the land purified from this idolatry. Still Jehu would not part with the calves of Dan and Bethel; and he was therefore warned that his family should likewise pass away after the fourth generation.

Elisha had already wept at the fore-knowledge of the miseries which Hazael of Syria should bring upon Israel; and Hazael, murdering his master Benhadad by stifling him with a wet cloth as he lay sick on his bed, became a dreadful enemy to Samaria. So much broken was the force of Jehoahaz, Jehu's son, that at one time he had only one thousand foot, fifty horse, and ten chariots; but after this, prosperity began to return to the Israelites. Joash, his son, was a mighty king, and would have been still greater, if he would have believed that obeying the simple words of the prophet Elisha on his death-bed would bring him victory. Yet so much greater was his force than that of Judah, that when Amaziah sent him a challenge, he replied by the insulting parable of the thistle and the cedar. Jeroboam II., his son, was likewise prosperous; but neither blessings nor warnings would induce these kings to forsake their golden calves. Amos, the herdsman-prophet of Tekoa, was warned to say nothing against the king's chapel at Bethel; and Hosea in vain declared that Ephraim was feeding on wind, and following after the east-wind, namely, putting his trust in mere empty air. So in the time of Zechariah, son to Jeroboam, came the doom of the House of Jehu, and in 773 the king was murdered by Shallum, who only reigned a month, being killed by his general, Menahem. Again, Menahem's son, Pekahiah, was killed by his captain Pekah, a great warrior, who made an attack upon Ahaz of Judah, and slew one hundred and twenty thousand Jews in one day. Many more with all their spoil were brought captives to Samaria; but there was some good yet left in Israel, and at the rebuke of the prophet Oded, the Ephraimites remembered that they were brethren, gave back to the prisoners all their spoil, fed them, clothed them, and mounted them on asses to carry them safely back to their own land. But Pekah, and his ally, Rezin of Damascus, were sore foes to Ahaz, and cruelly ravaged his domains; and though God encouraged him, by the words of Isaiah, to trust in Him alone, and see their destruction, Ahaz obstinately resolved to turn to a new power for protection.

LESSON IX.
NINEVEH.

"Where is the dwelling-place of the lions, and the feeding-place of the young lions?"--Nahum, ii. 11.

When the confusion of tongues took place at Babel, and men were dispersed, the sons of Ham's grandson, Cush, remained in Mesopotamia, which took the name of Assyria, from Assur, the officer of Nimrod, the first king. This Assur began building, on the banks of the Tigris, the great city of Nineveh, one of the mightiest in all the world, and the first to be ruined. It was enclosed by a huge wall, so wide that three chariots could drive side by side on the top, and built of bricks made of the clay of the country, dried in the sun and cemented with bitumen, guarded at the base by a plinth fifty feet in height, and with immense ditches round it, about sixty miles in circumference. Within were huge palaces, built of the same bricks, faced with alabaster, and the rooms decked with cedar, gilding, and ivory, and raised upon terraces whence broad flights of steps led down to courts guarded by giant stone figures of bulls and lions, with eagles' wings and human faces, as if some notion of the mysterious Cherubim around the Throne in Heaven had floated to these Assyrians. The slabs against the walls were carved with representations of battles, hunts, sacrifices, triumphs, and all the scenes in the kings' histories, nay, in the building of the city; and there were explanations in the wedge-shaped letters of the old Assyrian alphabet. The Ninevites had numerous idols, but their honour for the Lord had not quite faded away; and about the year 830, about the time of Amaziah in Judah, and Jeroboam II. in Israel, the prophet Jonah was sent to rebuke them for their many iniquities. In trying to avoid the command, by sailing to Tarshish in a Phoenician ship, he underwent that strange punishment which was a prophetic sign of our Lord's Burial and Resurrection; and thus warned, he went to Nineveh and startled the people by the cry, "Yet forty days, and Nineveh shall be destroyed!" At that cry, the whole place repented as one man; and from the king to the beggar all fasted and wept, till God had mercy on their repentance and ready faith, and turned away His wrath, in pity to the 120,000 innocent children who knew not yet to do good or evil.

The prophet Nahum afterwards prophesied against the bloody city, and foretold that her men should become like women, and that in the midst of her feasting and drunkenness an overflowing flood should make an end of her. But first God had a work for the Ninevites to do, namely, to punish His own chosen, who would not have Him for their God. Therefore, He strengthened the great King Tiglath Pileser, who already held in subjection the other great Assyrian city of Babylon, and the brave Median mountaineers, to come out against the Syrians and Israelites. Ahaz, King of Judah, hoping to be delivered from his distresses, sent messengers to Tiglath Pileser, to say, "I am thy servant and thy son," and to beg him to protect him from his two enemies, promising to pay him tribute. Tiglath Pileser did indeed take Damascus, and put the king to death, destroying the old Syrian kingdom for ever, and he carried away the calf of Dan, and severely chastised Samaria, where Pekah was shortly after murdered by his servant Hoshea; so that Isaiah's prophecy of the ruin of "these two tails of smoking firebrands," Pekah and Rezin, was fulfilled; but as Ahaz had tried to bring it about in his own way, he gained nothing. Though he went to pay his service to the conqueror at Damascus, Tiglath Pileser did not help him, but only distressed him; and instead of learning Who was his true Guardian, Ahaz only came home delighted with the Syrian temples, and profanely altered the arrangements in the Temple, which Moses and Solomon had ordained by God's command, as patterns of the greater and more perfect Tabernacle revealed to Moses in Heaven. He soon died, in the year 725, when only thirty-six years old, leaving his crown to Hezekiah, then only sixteen, the king whose heart was more whole with God than had been that of any king since his father David, and whose first thought was to purify the Temple, and to destroy all corrupt worship, breaking down idols, and destroying the high places and groves, which had stood ever since Solomon's time.

Hoshea, too, was the best King of Samaria that had yet reigned, for he encouraged his subjects to go to worship at Jerusalem, whither Hezekiah invited them to keep the Passover, and that feast had not been held so fully since Solomon's time. They came back full of zeal, and destroyed many of the idols; but the reformation came too late; the measure of Israel's sin was full. Hoshea offended Shalmaneser, who had succeeded Tiglath Pileser, by making friends with So, King of Egypt, and the Assyrian army came down upon Israel in the year 722, and killing Hoshea, carried off all the people as captives, settling them in the cities of the Medes, never more to dwell in their own land. Sargon seems to have dethroned Shalmaneser about this time, and to have completed the conquest of Israel, of which he boasted on the tablets of a great palace near Nineveh, which has been lately brought to light.

The remnant that was left, the small realm of Judah, took warning, and turned to God with all their heart, and therefore were protected; but they had much to suffer. Sargon's son, Sennacherib, was a proud and ambitious monarch, who used his Israelite captives in building up the walls of Nineveh, and making the most magnificent of all the palaces there, eight acres in size, and covered with inscriptions. He invaded Judea, took forty-six cities, and besieged Jerusalem, raising a mound to overtop the walls; but on receiving large gifts from Hezekiah, he returned to his own land. At Babylon a prince named Merodach Baladan had set himself up against Sennacherib, and sought the friendship of Hezekiah. When the good King of Judah recovered from his illness by a miracle, the sign of which was, that the sun seemed to retreat in his course, it probably won the attention of the Chaldeans, who were great star-gazers; and Merodach Baladan sent messengers to compliment the king, whose favour with Heaven had thus been shown to all the earth. For once Hezekiah erred, and was so much uplifted, as to display his treasure and his new-born son in ostentation. Isaiah rebuked him, telling him that his children should be slaves in the hands of the very nation who had heard his boast. He meekly submitted, thankful that there should be peace and truth in his days. Soon after, Babylon was reduced by Sennacherib, and Merodach Baladan driven into exile. In the latter years of his reign, Sennacherib undertook an expedition into Egypt, and on his way sent a blasphemous message by his servant, Rabshakeh, to summon Hezekiah to submit, and warning him and his people, that their God could no more protect them than the gods of the conquered nations had saved their worshippers. In answer to the prayer of Hezekiah, came, by the mouth of Isaiah, an assurance that the boaster who insulted the living God, was only an instrument in His Hands, unable to go one step against His will. Not one arrow should he shoot against the holy city, but he should hear a rumour, a blast should be sent on him, and he should fall by the sword in his own land.

Accordingly, on the report that Tirhakah, the great King of Ethiopia, was coming to the aid of the Egyptians, he hurried on to reinforce the army he had sent against him, intending to take Jerusalem on his way back. But on the night when the two armies were in sight of each other, ere the battle, the blast of death passed over the Assyrians; and in early morning the host lay dead, not by the sword, but by the breath of the Lord, and Sennacherib was left to return without the men in whom he had trusted! Even heathens recorded this deliverance, but they strangely altered the story. They said that it was the prayer of the Egyptian king that prevailed on his gods to send a multitude of mice into the enemy's camp, to gnaw all the bow-strings, so that they could not fight; and they showed a statue of the king with a mouse in his hand, which was, they said, a memorial of the wonder.

Sennacherib, in rage and fury, cruelly persecuted the Israelites at Nineveh for their connection with the Jews; and then it was that the pious Tobit buried the corpses that were cast in the street until he lost his sight, afterwards so wonderfully restored. Sennacherib was murdered in the year 720 by two of his sons, while worshipping his god Nisroch; and another son, Esarhaddon, became king.

Esarhaddon, who is known by many different names, soon after came out and marauded all over the adjacent country; and it is believed that it was about this time that Bethulia was so bravely defended, and the Ninevite general slain by the craft and courage of Judith. Esarhaddon took away all the remaining Israelites from their country, and filled it up with Phoenicians and Medes from cities which had been conquered. These, bringing their idols into the land of the Lord, were chastised with lions; and, begging to be taught to worship the God of the land, had priests sent them, who taught them some of the truth, though very imperfectly; and these new inhabitants were called Samaritans.

In the time of Hezekiah, many more of the Psalms than had been before collected, were written down and applied to the Temple Service. The latter part of the Proverbs of Solomon were first copied out, and the inspired words of the prophets began to be added to the Scriptures. Joel's date is unfixed, but Hosea, Amos, and Jonah, had recently been prophesying, and the glorious evangelical predictions of Isaiah and Micah were poured out throughout this reign, those of Isaiah ranging from the humiliation and Passion of the Redeemer, to the ingathering of the nations to His Kingdom, and Micah marking out the little Bethlehem as the birth-place of "Him whose goings are from everlasting."

Manasseh, the son of the good Hezekiah, began to reign in 699. He was in his first years savagely wicked, and very idolatrous. It is believed that he caused the great evangelical prophet, Isaiah, to be put to death by being sawn asunder, and he set an image in the Temple itself. He soon brought down his punishment on his head, for the Assyrian captains invaded Judea, and took him captive, dragging him in chains to Babylon. There he repented, and humbled himself with so contrite a heart, that God had mercy on him, and caused his enemies to restore him to his throne; but the free days of Judah were over, and they were thenceforth subjects, paying tribute to the King of Assyria, and Manasseh was only a tributary for the many remaining years of his reign, while he strove in vain to undo the evil he had done by bringing in idolatry.

Meantime the greatness of Nineveh came to an end. The Babylonians and Medes revolted against it, and it was ruined in the year 612. Sardanapalus succeeded his father at Nineveh, but was weak and luxurious. His brother, Saracus, was so like him, that what seems really to have been the end of Saracus, is generally told of Sardanapalus. He was so weary of all amusement and delight, that, by way of change, he would dress like his wives, and spin and embroider with them, and he even offered huge rewards to anyone who would invent a new pleasure. He said his epitaph should be, that he carried with him that which he had eaten, which, said wise men, was a fit motto only for a pig, not a man. At last his carelessness and violence provoked the Babylonians and Medes to rise against him, and they besieged his city; but he took no notice, and feasted on, putting his trust in an old prophecy, (perhaps Nahum's,) that nothing should harm Nineveh till the river became her enemy. At last he heard that the Tigris had overflowed, and broken down a part of the wall; and so giving himself up, he shut himself up in his palace, and setting fire to it, burnt himself with all his wives, slaves, and treasures, rather than be taken by the enemy. So ended Nineveh, in the year 612. No one ever lived there again; the river made part a swamp, and the rest was covered with sand brought by the desert winds. It was all ruin and desolation; but of late years many of its mighty remains have been brought to our country, as witnesses of the dealings of God with His people's foes.

LESSON X.
THE CAPTIVITY.

"Is this the city that men call the perfection of beauty, the joy of the whole earth?"--Larn. ii. 15.

Manasseh's son, Amon, undid all the reformation of his latter years, and brought back idolatry; and indeed, the whole Jewish people had become so corrupt, that even when Amon was murdered in 642, after only reigning two years, and better days came back with the good Josiah, it was with almost all of them only a change of the outside, and not of the heart. Josiah was but eight years old when he came to the throne, and at sixteen he began to rule, seeking the Lord earnestly with his whole heart, as David and Hezekiah alone had done before him. One of his first acts was to purify the Temple, and in so doing, the book of the Law of Moses was found, cast aside, and forgotten by all. Josiah bade the scribes read it aloud, and then for the first time he heard what blessings Judah had forfeited, what curses she had deserved, and how black was her disobedience in the sight of God. Well might he rend his clothes, weep aloud, and send to the prophetess Huldah, to ask whether the anger of the Lord could yet be turned aside. She made answer by the word of the God of Justice, that the doom must come on the guilty nation, but that in His mercy, He would spare Josiah the sight of the ruin, and that he should be gathered into his grave in peace; and at the same time Zephaniah likewise spoke of judgment, and Jeremiah, the priest of Anathoth, was foretelling that treacherous Judah should soon suffer like backsliding Israel. Yet even this hopeless future did not daunt Josiah's loving heart from doing his best. He collected his people, and renewed the Covenant, he rooted out every trace of idolatry, even more thoroughly than Hezekiah had done, overthrowing even Solomon's idol temples; and he went to Bethel, which he seems to have held under the King of Assyria, and defiled the old altar there by burning bones on it, as the disobedient prophet had foretold of him by name, when that altar was first set up. He likewise caused copies of the Law to be made, so that it might never be lost again; and the Jews have a story, that knowing the Temple was to be destroyed, he saved the Ark of the Covenant, Aaron's rod, and the pot of manna, from sacrilege, by hiding them away in the hollow of Mount Nebo, where they have never since been found; but this is quite uncertain.

Josiah lived between two mighty powers; the King of Babylon, who had newly taken Nineveh, and Pharaoh Necho, King of Egypt, a very bold and able man, who hired Phoenician ships to sail round Africa, and then did not believe the crews when they came back, because they said they had seen the sun to the north at noon, and wool growing on trees. He tried to cut a canal from the Nile to the Red Sea; and wishing to check the power of Babylon, he brought an army by sea to make war upon Assyria, landing at Acre under Mount Carmel, and intending to march through Gilead. Josiah, being a tributary of Babylon, thought it his duty to endeavour to stop him, and going out to battle with him at Megiddo, was there mortally wounded, and died on his way home, in the year 611. The mourning of the Jews over their good king was so bitter, that it was a proverb long after; and they had indeed reason to lament, for he was the last who stood between them and their sin and their punishment.

Jehoahaz, or Shallum, his third son, a wicked young man, only reigned while Necho was fighting a battle with the Babylonians on the Euphrates, and then was carried off in chains to Egypt, while Necho set up Eliakim, or Jehoiakim, another brother, in his stead. Jehoiakim was idolatrous, cruel, and violent; he persecuted the prophets, and did everything to draw on himself the punishment of Heaven. Necho, making another invasion, was defeated by the great Nebuchadnezzar of Babylon, and hunted back by him into Egypt. On his way Nebuchadnezzar seized Jerusalem, in the year 606, and carried off some of the treasures of the Temple, and many of the royal family, to Babylon, among them the four holy children, but he let Jehoiakim continue to reign as his vassal. Jeremiah prophesied that the time of captivity and desolation should last seventy years from this time, but the worst was not yet come. Jehoiakim was bent on trusting for help to the Egyptians, who had made him king, and treated Jeremiah as a traitor for counselling him to be loyal to the Assyrians; he threw Jeremiah into prison, and when Baruch read the roll of his prophecies in the Temple, he caused it to be cut to pieces and destroyed. At last he rebelled, relying on help from Egypt, but it did not come, for Necho was dying; and in the year 598, Nebuchadnezzar himself came up against Jerusalem, and besieged it. Jehoiakim died in the midst of the war, and his equally wicked son, Jehoiachin, Coniah, or Jeconiah, was soon forced to come out, and surrender to Nebuchadnezzar, who dishonoured his father's corpse, and carried him away to Babylon, with the chief treasures of the Temple, and a great multitude of warriors and mechanics. Among them was the prophet Ezekiel, who, on the banks of the Chebar, saw mighty visions of the chariot of God borne up by the Cherubim; and while he rebuked the present Jews for their crimes, promised restoration, and beheld the new and more perfect Building of God measured out by the angel. A marble cylinder with most of this prophecy engraven on it in Assyrian characters, has lately been found in the ruins near the Tigris.

The last son of Josiah, Mattanias, or Zedekiah, was set up as king, and reigned for eleven years; like his brothers, wavering and sinning, and trusting to false prophets, instead of Jeremiah, who gave him hopes of rest, if he would only bear his present fallen state meekly, and not trust to Egypt. The counsellors who loved Egypt, however, persuaded him to rebel, as Pharaoh Hophra was actually coming out to his assistance; and he put Jeremiah into prison for prophesying that he would bring ruin on himself, Nebuchadnezzar soon marched upon him, and besieged Jerusalem; and his friend, Pharaoh Hophra, left him to his fate, showing himself the broken reed that Jeremiah had said he would prove. The siege of Jerusalem lasted a year, and no one suffered more than the prophet, who was thrown into a noisome prison, and afterwards lowered into a pit, where he nearly died; but not for all this did he cease to denounce the judgments of God on the rebellious city. Horrible famine prevailed, and the streets were full of dead; but Jeremiah told the king, that if he would go out and make terms with Nebuchadnezzar all might yet be saved. But Zedekiah would not listen, and at last broke out with his men of war to cut his way through the enemy. His self-will met its deserts; he was taken by Nebuzaradan, the captain who had been left to carry on the siege, and brought a prisoner to Babylon, after his sons had been slain in his very sight, and his eyes then put out, according to a prophecy of Ezekiel, which he is said to have thought impossible; namely, that he should die at Babylon, and yet never see it.

The Temple was stripped of the last remains of its glory, and utterly over-thrown, the walls were broken down, and the place left desolate; the Edomites who were in the conqueror's army savagely exulting in the fall of their kindred nation; but both Psalm cxxxvii. and the Prophet Obadiah spoke of vengeance in store for them likewise. All the Jews of high rank were carried away, and none left but the poorer sort, who were to till the ground under a ruler named Gedaliah. Jeremiah, who was offered his choice of going to Babylon or remaining in Judea, preferred to continue near the once glorious city, whose solitude and ruin he bewailed in the mournful Book of Lamentations; and he did his utmost to persuade the remaining Jews to rest quietly under the dominion of Assyria. Had they done so, there would yet have been peace; but Ishmael, a prince of the seed royal, who had fled to the Ammonites during the invasion, came back, and in the hope of making himself king murdered Gedaliah at a harvest feast, with many Jews and Chaldeans, and was on his way to his friend, the King of Ammon, when Johanan, a friend of Gedaliah, came upon him and slew many of his party, so that he escaped with only eight men to the Ammonites. So shocked were the Jews at this murder of Gedaliah, that they ever after kept a fast on the anniversary. Johanan now asked counsel from Jeremiah, who still enjoined him to submit to the Assyrians, but assured him that if he went to Egypt it would only be to share the ruin of that country; but Johanan and his friends would not listen, and carried all the remnant of Judah, and Jeremiah himself, off by force into Egypt. All this happened in the miserable year 588, and Jerusalem remained utterly waste, the land enjoying a long sabbath of desolation, What became of Jeremiah afterwards is not known; he is said to have been stoned in Egypt, but this is not at all certain. He left behind him the promise that a Deliverer should come--the Lord our Righteousness--and that the former redemption out of bondage in Egypt should be as nothing in comparison with the ingathering of the New Covenant from the north country and from all countries; also that the New Covenant should be within, written upon the hearts and minds of the faithful.

LESSON XI.
BABYLON.

"By the waters of Babylon we sat down and wept, when we remembered thee, O Sion."--Psalm cxxxvii, 1.

Babylon, the city which was to be the place of captivity of the Jews, was the home of the Chaldeans, who are believed not to have been the sons of Gush, like the Assyrians whom they had conquered at Nineveh, but to have been at first a wandering tribe of the north, and to have descended from Japhet. They had nearly the same gods as the Ninevites, but thought the special protector of their city was Bel-Merodach, the name by which they called the planet Jupiter. They were such great observers of the courses of the stars, that astronomy is said to have begun with them; but this was chiefly because they fancied that the heavenly bodies would help them to foretel coming events, for they put great faith in soothsayers. They settled upon the bank of the Euphrates, near the ruins of the Tower of Babel, round which a city arose, sometimes free, sometimes under the power of the King of Nineveh.

In the time of the weak and luxurious Saracus, Nabopolassar was governor of Babylon. He joined himself to the Medea, giving his son, Nebuchadnezzar, in marriage to the Median Princess Amytis; and as has already been said, the two nations together destroyed Nineveh, after which, Babylon became the head of the Assyrian Empire, and Nebuchadnezzar was the king.

He made the city exceedingly grand and beautiful. It was fifty five miles in circuit, square, surrounded by a wall eighty-seven feet thick, and three hundred and fifty high, with houses and a street on the top, and an enormous ditch filled with water all round, another lesser wall some way within. There were one hundred brazen gates in the wall, besides two larger gateways upon the Euphrates, which ran through the middle, dividing the city into two parts. It was full of streets and houses, with such fields and vineyards, that it was like a whole country walled in; and the soil was exceedingly rich, being all brought down from the Armenian hills by the Euphrates. As this river rose in the mountains of Armenia, it used to overflow in the spring, when the snows melted and swelled the stream; but to prevent mischief, the country was covered with a network of canals, to draw off the water in safety. The pride of the city was the Temple of Bel, which is thought to have been built on a fragment of the Tower of Babel. It was a pile of enormous height, with seven stages in honour of the seven planets then known, and with a winding ascent leading from one to the other. On the top was the shrine, where stood Bel's golden image, twelve cubits high, and before it a golden table where meats and wine were served up to him. On either side of the river were two palaces, joined together by a bridge, and the nearer one, four miles round, with wonderful grounds, containing what were called the hanging gardens, namely, a hill which Nebuchadnezzar had caused to be raised by heaping up earth, and planted with trees, to please his Median queen, whose eye pined for her native mountains in the flats of Babylon.

There must have been other eyes at Babylon wearying for their own free heights, for there the captives of Judah bore the punishment of their fathers' sins and their own, and repented so completely, that they never returned to their idolatry. When in 606, Nebuchadnezzar carried to Babylon Jehoiachin and the nobles of Judah, he commanded that some of the royal children should be brought up as slaves to serve in his palace, and gave them new names after his gods. Daniel, Ananias, Azarias, and Misael, gave their first proof of their obedience to the Law of their God in their exile and slavery, by denying themselves the choice meats set before them, lest they should eat of some forbidden thing, and living only on dry beans and water. So blessed was their abstinence, that they excelled all the other youths both in beauty and in wisdom, and were soon promoted above them. Soon after, Daniel was shown to be a prophet, for God inspired him, not merely with the meaning of Nebuchadnezzar's perplexing dream, but revealed to him the dream itself, which the king had forgotten. That dream was the emblematic history of the world. It was an image with a head of gold, shoulders of silver, thighs of brass, legs of iron, feet partly of iron, partly of clay, all overthrown together by a stone cut out without hands from a mountain. Great Babylon was the head, soon to give way to the less splendid Persian power, then again to the Greek dominion, and lastly to the iron rule of Rome, which would grow weak and mixed with miry clay, till at last all would be overthrown and subdued by the Stone which the builders rejected.

After this wonderful interpretation, Daniel became a chief ruler under Nebuchadnezzar, and even in his youth, his name was a very proverb for wisdom and holiness. He judged among the Jews, and confuted the two wicked elders who sought to bring about the death of Susanna; and he probably stood too high to be accused, when, soon after the taking of Zedekiah, Nebuchadnezzar threw the three other princes into the fiery furnace, for refusing to bow down to the golden image on the plains of Dura. Then the fiery blast was to them as a moist whistling wind, and even the tyrant beheld the Form like the Son of God, walking with them in the midst of the flame, while they sung that hymn which calls every created thing to praise the Lord. The miracle seems not to have been witnessed by a heart hardened against belief Nebuchadnezzar proclaimed the glory of the God who could work such miracles, and whose instrument of vengeance he himself was. Edom was soon after conquered by Nebuchadnezzar, thus fulfilling many prophecies.

Another great work which was set for him to do, was to give the first great overthrow to the Phoenicians, and fulfil the prophecies of Isaiah and Ezekiel, by destroying Tyre. The siege lasted thirteen years, and the besiegers suffered as much as the besieged, till, as Ezekiel had foretold, every head was bald, every shoulder peeled with the burdens that were carried; but at last it was taken in the year 573, and so utterly destroyed, that not a trace was left of it. It had been said by Isaiah, that after seventy years Tyre should take her harp and sing again, and return for a time to her former splendour and corruption; and thus it happened, for a new Tyre arose upon a little island at some little distance from the shore.

Ezekiel had promised the Chaldeans that the toils of Tyre should be repaid by the spoil of Egypt, the land that was henceforth to be a slave for ever; and in 574, Nebuchadnezzar marched thither, and conquered it with the utmost ease, there being at that time a quarrel among the Egyptians, which weakened their hands; Hophra, the last of the Pharaohs, was slain by a rebel, and Egypt has never more been free, or under native rulers. The Ammonites too, were put down for ever by Nebuchadnezzar, and he came home puffed up with the pride of conquest. Then came another warning dream, of a tree, great and spreading, the rest and stay of bird and beast, till a watcher and a holy one came down and bade that it should be cut down, and only a stump to be left, to be wet with the dew of Heaven until it should recover. It was no wonder that Daniel was astonished for one hour ere he explained the vision, which bore that the great conqueror should lose his reason, be chased from the haunts of men, and live like the beasts, with hair like eagle's feathers, and nails like eagle's claws. Nebuchadnezzar does not seem to have punished him for thus revealing the will of God; and time went on, while the city grew more magnificent under the builder's hand, till at last, in the pride of his heart, the king made his boast, "Is not this great Babylon that I have builded, for the house of the kingdom, and for the honour of my majesty?"

That moment, the watcher cried from Heaven, and sense and strength fled from the mighty Nebuchadnezzar. He was driven from men, and lived seven years among the beasts of the field, till for one year, reason was mercifully restored to him, and he made the best use of it in publishing to all the world the story of his pride and of his fall, and with all his heart honouring the King of Heaven, whose works are truth, and His ways are judgment.

This humbled conqueror died in 563, and was succeeded by his son, Evil-Merodach, who released the captive Jehoiachin, and made him eat at his own table until his death. Two more kings succeeded, each reigning but a few years, and then came Belshazzar, in the first year of whose reign Daniel had a vision, where the like events as were shown by the dream of Nebuchadnezzar, were foreshadowed under the form of animals, typifying the several empires. Four beasts came from the sea: the lion with eagle's wings was his own Assyria, but was set aside by the devouring bear of Persia; then followed the flying four-headed leopard of Greece; and lastly, the dreadful and terrible destroying creature, meaning Rome, which ground with iron teeth, and brake all in pieces. It had ten horns, which are believed to mean the kingdoms into which Rome was divided in later times, and one which destroyed some of the others, and became blasphemous, till all was lost in an awful manifestation of the Ancient of Days coming to judgment. This little horn is thought to mean the spirit of Antichrist, and the great falling away which is to prevail in the latter days, but the end is not yet.

A second vision was sent two years after, likewise of emblematic beasts, and was likewise explained by an angel. A ram, pushing west, north, and southwards, was Persia, whose victory was already nigh, even at the door; but in his full power came from the west the Grecian he-goat, who overthrew the ram, and stamped on him, and waxed great; but then his one great horn was broken, and four others rose up, four lesser kings instead of one great conqueror; and one of these produced a lesser horn, which wrought woe and ruin to the pleasant land. This horn was not meant, like the first, to typify the sinful one of the latter Christian days, but a terrible foe, who was to try the faith of the Jews; and all these visions seem to have been intended to show, that though prophecy, and God's visible dealings with His people, were so nearly over, yet all kingdoms and empires are His, and are founded, flourish, and decay at His will.

LESSON XII.
CYRUS.

"When the Lord turned again the captivity of Sion, then were we like unto them that dream."--Psalm cxxvi. 1.

The Persian power, prefigured by the silver shoulders, the bear and the ram, was indeed nigh. The ram had two horns, because two nations were joined together, the Medes, who had revolted from Nineveh, and the Persians. The Medes lived in the slopes towards the Tigris, and had learnt to be luxurious and indolent from their Assyrian neighbours; but the Persians, who lived in the mountains to the eastward, were much more spirited and simpler, and purer in life. They are thought to be sons of Japhet, and their religion had not lost all remains of truth, for they believed in but one God, and had no idols, except that they adored the sun as the emblem of divine power, and kept horses in his honour, because they thought he drove his car of light round the sky. They worshipped fire likewise as the sign of the light-giving and consuming Godhead; and this notion is not entirely gone yet, so that there are many Parsees, or fireworshippers, still in the East. Their priests were called Magi, and their faith was therefore termed Magian. Though it went astray in adoring these created things, yet it did not teach wickedness, as did the religions of the sons of Ham; and the Persians were a brave, upright race, who loved hardy, simple ways, and said the chief things their sons ought to learn were, to ride, to draw the bow, and speak the truth.

Cyrus was the son of a Persian king and Median princess, and had been so well brought up at home, that when as a little boy he visited his grandfather at Echatana, in Media, he was very much shocked to see the court drinking to intoxication, and said wine must be poison, since it made people lose their senses; and he was much puzzled by the hosts of slaves who would not let people do anything for themselves. He thought only those who were old and helpless could like being waited on, and he kept these hardy, simple ways, even after he was a great king over both nations.

When he was about forty years old one of the kings in Asia Minor made war on him, and he not only overthrew this monarch, but won that whole country, which was kept by the Persians for many years. Afterwards, in the year 540, he marched against Assyria, which had insulted him in the time of Evil-Merodach. He beat Belshazzar in battle, and then besieged him in his city; but the Babylonians had no fears; they trusted to their walls and brazen gates, and knew that he could not starve them out, as they had so much corn growing within the walls. For two years they remained in security, and laughed at the Persian army outside; but at last Cyrus devised a new plan, and set his men to dig trenches to draw off the water of the Euphrates, and leave the bed of the river dry. Still there were the great gates upon the river, which he expected to have to break down; but on the very day his trenches were ready, Belshazzar was giving a great feast in his palace, and drinking wine out of the golden vessels that Nebuchadnezzar had brought from the Temple.

Full in the midst of his revelry appeared a strange sight. Near the seven-branched Candlestick that once had burnt in the Holy Place, came forth a bodiless hand, and the fingers wrote upon the wall in characters such as no man knew. The hearts of the revellers failed them for fear, and the king's knees smote together! Then Nitocris, his mother, a brave and wise woman, bethought her of all that Daniel had done in the days of Nebuchadnezzar, and at her advice he was called for. He knew the words; they were in the Hebrew tongue, the language of his own Scriptures, the same in which the Finger of God revealed the Commandments. He read them, and they signified, "God hath numbered thy kingdom, and finished it. Thou art weighed in the balances, and found wanting. Thy kingdom is divided, and given to the Medes and Persians!"

At that moment Cyrus and his Persians were entering by the river gates, which had been left open in that time of careless festivity. One end of the city knew not that the other was taken; and ere the night was past Belshazzar lay dead in his palace, and the Assyrian empire was over for ever.

It was 170 years since, by the mouth of Isaiah, God had called Cyrus by name, had said He would give the nations as dust to his sword, and stubble to his bow; had said of him that he was His anointed and His shepherd, and that he would build up the Holy City and Temple, and let the captives go free without money or price. Moreover, it was seventy years since Daniel himself had been carried away from the pleasant land, and well had he counted the weary days prophesied of by Jeremiah; till now he hoped the time was come, and most earnestly did he pray, looking towards Jerusalem, as Solomon had entreated, when his people should turn to God in the land of their captivity, pleading God's goodness and mercy, though owning that Judah had done wickedly. Even while he was yet speaking came the answer by the mouth of the Angel Gabriel; and not only was it the present deliverance that it announced, but that from the building of the street and wall in troublous times, seventy weeks of years were appointed to bring the Anointed, so long promised, the real Deliverer.

Daniel's prayers had won, and in the first year of Cyrus, 536, forth went the joyful decree that Judah should return, build up the city and Temple, and receive back their sacred vessels and treasure from the king, to aid them in their work. Daniel being nearly ninety years old, did not go with them, but remained to protect them at the court of Babylon. Cyrus set up his uncle, who is commonly called Darius, to be king in Babylon, while he returned to Persia; and Daniel, though so old a man, was made one of the chief rulers under him, one of the three presidents over the hundred and twenty satraps or princes over the provinces of the great Persian empire. The envy of the Medes caused them to persuade Darius by foolish flattery to say that whoever for a month should make request of god or man, save of the king, should be cast into a den of lions, and Daniel, who was not likely in his old age to cease from prayer to his God for any terror of man, endured the penalty, much against the king's will; but only that again God's power might be known among the heathen, and His glory proclaimed by the shutting the mouths of the hungry lions. About the same time he seems to have shown Darius, who, though not an idolater himself, was puzzled by seeing that the victuals daily spread on Bel's golden table always disappeared, that after all, the idol was not the consumer. He spread ashes on the floor at night, and in the morning showed the king the tell-tale footmarks of men, women, and children, the priests and their families, the true devourers of the feast. No wonder that after this, the Persians ruined the Temple of Bel, while decay began in Babylon, and the river never being turned back into its proper bed, spread into unwholesome marshes. Daniel, when at Susa, a Median city on the river Ulai, beheld his last vision, when the Angel Gabriel prophesied to him in detail all the wars of the Persians, and afterwards of the Greek kings of Egypt and Syria, who should make Judea their battlefield, and the afflictions of the Jews under the great Syrian persecutor. He ended with a sure promise to Daniel himself, that he should "stand in his lot" when the end of all things should come; and some time after this blessed assurance, died this "man greatly beloved," a prince, a slave, an exile, and a statesman, perhaps the most wonderful of all the sons of David, except the great Anointed One of whom he spoke. His tomb is still deeply reverenced, and no one is allowed to fish near the part of the river where he is said to have seen his vision.

Cyrus died about seven years after Daniel, much loved by his people, who, for many years, would not believe him dead, but trusted he would yet return to rule over them.

LESSON XIII.
THE REBUILDING OF THE TEMPLE.

"The Lord doth build up Jerusalem, and gather together the outcasts of Israel."--Psalm clxxvii. 2.

42,360 was the number of Jews who returned to their own land by the permission of Cyrus. They were under the keeping of Joshua the High Priest, and of Zerubbabel, son of Salathiel, who was either by birth, son of King Jehoiachin, or else had been adopted by him from the line of Nathan, son of David. In either way, he was head of the house of David, and would have been king, had not the crown been taken away because of the sin of his fathers. He had, it is said, won favour at the court of Darius the Mede by his cleverness in a contention of wits, where each man was asked what was the strongest thing in existence. One said it was wine, because it made men lose their senses; another said it was the king, because of his great power; but Zerubbabel said it was woman, and so ingeniously proved how women could sway the minds of men, that the king was delighted, and promised to give him whatever he would ask. What Zerubbabel requested was, that the decree of Cyrus might at once be put in force, so that his people might go home to their own country. Darius consented, and put into his hands orders that the vessels of the Temple, and all the other sacred things, together with a large sum of money, should be given to him; and thus he went forth, praising and blessing God. Some of the dispersed of Israel joined the returning Jews, and were thenceforth counted among them; but so many of Judah itself had become settled in the place of their exile, that they never returned, though they sent gifts to assist in rebuilding Jerusalem. It used to be said that only the bran, or coarse sort of people, returned, the fine flour remained; but it must have in truth been in general the lovers of ease who stayed, the faithful who loved poverty in the Promised Land better than wealth at Babylon.

Zerubbabel was called Tirshatha, or governor. His kingdom was gone, but his right remained to the fields of Boaz and Jesse at Bethlehem; and thence should "He come forth Whose goings are from everlasting." The true birthright was not lost by this son of Solomon, whom God blessed by the lips of Zechariah for having laid the foundation of His Temple, and not having despised the day of small things. The blessings to the Priest, Joshua, were foreshadowings of Him Whose Name he bore, and Whose office he represented.

All was ruin and desolation; heaps of stones lay where beauteous buildings had been, and the fields and vineyards lay waste; but glad promises came by the mouth of Zechariah, that these empty streets should yet be filled with merry children at play, and with aged men leaning on their staves, at peace and at ease.

The first thing done by these faithful men, was to set up an Altar among the ruins, where they might offer the daily sacrifice once more. Then they began the Temple, in the second year after their return; the trumpeters blew with silver trumpets, the Levites sang, and the people shouted; but what was joy to the young, whose hope was fulfilled, was grief to the old, who had seen Solomon's Temple in its glory. Where was the Ark? where the manna? where the Urim and Thummim? where the Light upon the Mercy-seat? Gone for ever, and heaps of ruins around! The old men wept as the youths cried out for joy, and the shout of rejoicing could barely be heard for the sound of wailing. But Haggai was sent to console them with the promise, that though this House was as nothing in their eyes, its glory should exceed that of the former one, for the Desire of all nations should come and fill this House with glory. Haggai had likewise to rebuke the people for their slackness in the work, and for building their own houses instead of the Temple, and soon they fell into trouble. The men of Samaria, children of those whom Esarhaddon had planted there, came, saying that they worshipped the God of the Jews, and wished to be one with them; but these half idolaters would soon have corrupted the Jews, so Zerubbabel and Joshua refused their offers. This made them bitter foes to the Jewish nation, and they wrote to the Persian court, saying that these newly returned exiles were no better than a set of rebels, who would destroy the king's power, if they were allowed to rebuild their city. Cyrus was dead, and his son, Cambyses, (called also Ahasuerus) who was a cruel selfish tyrant, at once forbade the work to go on, so that it was at a standstill for many years.

The wealth and luxury of Babylon were fast spoiling the Persians, who were losing their hardy ways, and with them their honour, mercy, and truth; and Cambyses was a very savage wretch, almost mad. He made war on Egypt, where he gained a battle by putting a number of cows, dogs, and cats, in front of his army, and as the Egyptians thought these creatures sacred, they dared not throw their darts at them, and so fled away. He won the whole country; and he afterwards marched into Ethiopia, where he nearly lost his whole army by thirst in a desert. The Egyptians hated him because he struck his sword into their sacred bull Apis, in his anger at their feasting in honour of this creature, when he himself had just met with such misfortunes. He had but one brother, named Smerdis, whom he caused to be secretly put to death; and when his sister wept for him, he kicked her so that she died. No one grieved when he was killed by a chance wound from his own sword, in the year 522; but a young Magian priest, pretending to be Smerdis, whose death was not generally known, became king. However, some of the nobles suspected the deceit; and one of them, whose daughter was among the many wives of the king, sent word to her to find out whether the king were the real Smerdis. She could not tell, having never seen the Prince Smerdis; but her father, who knew that the young Magian had had his ears cut off for some offence, told her to examine. She Answered that the king was earless; and the fraud being thus detected, seven of the great lords combined and slew him. One daughter of Cyrus still remained and the seven agreed that one of them should marry her and reign. The rest should have the right of visiting him whenever they pleased, and wearing the same sort of tiara, or high cap, with the point upright, instead of having it turned back like the rest of the Persians. The choice was to be settled by Heaven, as they thought; namely, by seeing whose horse would first neigh at the rise of their god, the sun. Darius Hystaspes, who thus became king in 521, was a good and upright man, in whose reign the Jews ventured to go on with the Temple. When the Samaritans came and stopped them, they wrote to beg that search might be made among the records of the kingdom for Cyrus's decree in their favour, which no one could change, because the laws of the Medes and Persians could not be altered. The decree was found, and Darius gave the Jews farther help, and forbade anyone to molest them; but they were very poor, and the restoration went on but feebly.

In Darius's reign Babylon revolted, and he laid siege to it. So determined were the inhabitants to hold out, that they killed their wives and children in order that the provisions might last longer, and thus they fulfilled what Isaiah had foretold-- that in one day the loss of children and widowhood would come on them. The place was at last betrayed by a friend of Darius, who cut off his own nose and ears, and showed himself bleeding, at the gates, pretending the king had done him this cruel injury. The Babylonians received and trusted him, and he soon opened the gates to his master, who terribly punished the rebels, destroyed as much as he could of the Temple of Bel, and left the city to go to decay, so that she never again was the Lady of Kingdoms. Darius was a great King, and records of his history are still to be read, cut out in the face of the rocks; but he tried two conquests that were far beyond his strength. He led an army into the bare and dreary country of the Scythians, the wild sons of Japhet, near the mouth of the Danube, and there would have been almost starved to death, but that a faithful camel loaded with provisions kept close to him. He also sent a large fleet and army to subdue the brave and wise Greeks, who lived in the isles and peninsulas opposite to Asia Minor, thinking he should easily bring them under his dominion, but they met his troops at Marathon, and gained a great victory, driving the Persians home with great loss.

Darius died in 485, and his son, Xerxes, who Daniel had said should stir up all the east against Grecia, led a huge army to conquer that brave little country. All the nations of the east were there, and Xerxes made a bridge of boats chained together over the Hellespont, for them to cross over. So proud and hasty was he, that when a storm destroyed his works, he caused the waves to be scourged, and fetters to be thrown into the sea, to punish it for having dared to resist him. He sat on his throne to see the army pass over the bridge, and as he saw the multitudes, he wept to think how soon they must all be dead, but he did not cease from sending them to their death. Though they were so many, the Greeks were much braver, and though they overran all the north part of the country, after they had killed the few brave defenders of the little pass of Thermopylae, they could not keep what they had taken; they were beaten both by land and sea, and a very small remnant came home to Persia in a wretched state. Xerxes was a weak vain boaster, and was very angry; he wanted to make another attempt, but never did so; he stayed at home feasting with his wives and living in luxury, till he was murdered, in the year 464.

LESSON XIV.
THE WALL REBUILT.

"They that be of thee shall build the old waste places; thou shall raise up the foundations of many generations, and thou shalt be called the repairer of the breach."--Isaiah, lviii. 12.

There is great difficulty as to what the Persian kings were called; their real names were very hard to pronounce, and they are commonly known by words that mean a king, instead of by their real names. This makes people uncertain whether the king who is called Ahasuerus in the Book of Esther be the same with him whom the Greeks call Xerxes, or with Artaxerxes the Long-armed, his son. It was one or other of these kings who made a great banquet at his palace at Shuahan or Susa, where the remains of the pillars that supported the many-coloured hangings of his palace are still to be seen. After seven days' feasting, he sent in his pride for Vashti, his queen, to show her beauty to his companions. It was, as it is still in Persia and most eastern countries, a shame and disgrace for a woman's face to be seen by any man save her husband; and Vashti refused this insulting command of the king. He was persuaded by the satraps that her example would teach all other ladies to think for themselves, which did not suit these self-ish men, who did not care to have a wife for a help-meet, but only for a slave and toy; so that poor Vashti was set aside and degraded for being a modest woman; and the tyrant sent and swept away every beautiful girl from her home, to be brought to his palace on trial, and if she did not become queen, to be a slave for ever. Thus the young Benjamite orphan, Esther, whom her kinsman, Mordecai, had tenderly trained in the right way, was taken away, never to see his face again, but to live in the multitude of slavish heathen women, who were taught no kind of employment, and thought even spinning and embroidery unworthy of a queen. But even the king's passion was made to serve God's ends. It was for no vain purpose that the noble beauty of the family of Saul had come down to Esther, and though she alone demanded no ornaments to set her off to advantage, she was the only maiden who took the king's fancy. Mordecai, her cousin, soon after found out a plot against the king's life, and sending her warning, she told the king, and he was thus saved. Mordecai daily sat at the palace gate to hear of his beloved cousin, and there daily saw the king's new counsellor pass by--Haman, an Agagite, descended from that hateful Amalekite nation, whom Saul ought to have totally destroyed. Mordecai would not bow before the man whom his law had taught him to loathe; and Haman, taking offence, and remembering the old enmity between the two nations, that had begun at the battle of Rephidim, promised the king 10,000 talents of silver for permission to let their enemies loose upon the Jews in their still unwalled city, and destroy them everywhere by a general slaughter. The king actually granted this horrible request, though without taking the bribe; and Haman, setting the royal seal to his decree, made it one of the unalterable Persian laws. The day was fixed for the massacre, and Haman prepared an enormous gallows on which to hang Mordecai, or as is supposed, to nail him up alive. But Mordecai contrived to warn Esther, and order her to persuade the king to save their lives. She was in a great strait, for it was death to enter the king's presence unbidden, unless he were in the mood to show mercy, and should hold out his golden sceptre; but in her extremity she took courage, arrayed herself royally, and came before him, fainting with fear. The Power above stirred his heart, and he held out the sceptre; but she dared not accuse his favourite, and only asked him and Haman together to a banquet in her apartments. Twice she received them before she took courage to speak; but at last she told the king that she and her people were sold to utter destruction. He demanded in anger who had dared to do this. "The adversary and enemy is this wicked Haman," she said: and when the king found how horrible a decree had been surprised from him, and that the gallows had been made ready for the queen's cousin, the man who had saved his life, he flew into such a rage, that he caused Haman to be hung on his own gallows at once, and all his sons to be slain with him. Still the order to destroy the Jews had gone forth, and could not be repealed, but Mordecai obtained that the Jews should be allowed to arm themselves; and having due notice, they defended themselves so well that they killed 800 of their enemies at Susa, and 75,000 of the spiteful Samaritans and other foes who had come upon them at Jerusalem.

Esther's power with the king seems to have done more for the Jews, and a new gift was sent from the treasury to Jerusalem, under the care of Ezra, a man of the seed of Aaron, and very learned in the Law. He gave himself up to the work, which had sadly languished since Zerubbabel's time; and he began in the right way, for ere entering the Glorious Land, he halted all the companions of his pilgrimage, and fasted three days, entreating the Lord for forgiveness, and protection from their enemies. It is from this time, about 458, that the seventy weeks of years, mentioned by Daniel, began to be counted, perhaps because till this time the work hardly proceeded in earnest. Another great helper soon followed Ezra, namely Nehemiah, one of the palace slaves, who, hearing of the miserable state of Jerusalem, prayed with all his heart, weeping so bitterly that when he went to wait upon the king and Queen Esther at their meal, they remarked his trouble; and on their asking the cause, he told them, with secret prayers, how his heart was grieved that his city and his fathers' sepulchres lay waste, and begged for permission to go with authority to Jerusalem, to assist in the rebuilding. His request was granted, authority was given to him, and he set off with a train of servants and guards, for he was a very rich man; but when he came near, he left them all, and rode on by night to examine the state of the city. Most sad was the sight; the gates broken and burnt, and the walls lying in ruins, the streets blocked up so that no one could pass! Nehemiah at once encouraged the Jews to set to work, and build up the breaches; and they heartily began, while he kept open house at his own expense for all his poor brethren. Down upon them came the Samaritans again, scoffing at those "feeble Jews," saying that a fox could break down their wall, and then attacking them; so that Nehemiah was forced to set a constant watch, and the workmen built with their swords ever ready for use. When the walls once more girded around the city built upon the hill, the inhabitants were no longer easily molested by their foes; and a great assembly was held, when Ezra read and explained the Law, for seven days, at the feast of the Tabernacles, after which there was a great fast and confession of sin, and the Covenant was solemnly renewed. Still a great purification was needed; the Sabbath had become ill observed, many of the people, even priests and Levites, had married heathen wives, and one of the sons of the High Priest was son-in-law to Sanballat, the worst enemy of the Jews. Ezra and Nehemiah brought many to a sense of their sin: no burdens were allowed to be touched on the Sabbath, and the heathen wives were put away; but this priest refusing to part with his wife, was thrust out from the priesthood, and was received by the Samaritans, who afterwards built a schismatical temple upon Gerizim, the Mount of Blessing.

At this time lived Malachi, the last of the prophets, who left the promise of the coming of the Prophet Elijah, as the forerunner of the Messiah, and of the rising of the Sun of Righteousness. Ezra is believed to have composed the Books of Kings from older writings, under the guidance of inspiration, to have collected the latter part of the book of Psalms, and to have been taught to discern which histories, and which books of the Prophets to keep, and which to cast aside. The Scriptures were all put under the keeping of scribes, who wrote the copies out with the utmost care, and were held guilty if the smallest point or mark failed; and a roll was placed under the care of the priests, besides many others which were dispersed through the country, that they might never be forgotten again. Ezra likewise arranged, that in places too far from Jerusalem for people to come weekly to worship at the Temple, there should be synagogues, or places of meeting for prayer, though of course not for sacrifice. There, every Sabbath day, eighteen prayers were appointed to be said, and lessons from the Scripture were read aloud and explained. In their exile, the Jews had forgotten their Hebrew tongue, and learnt to speak Chaldean, so that after the Law was read in their own language, a scribe stood up to translate and explain it, and thus they were saved from forgetting the Scripture, as they had done in the time of Josiah, and from resorting to groves and high places for worship. Idolatry was so thoroughly purged out of them, that they never returned to it; and their hope of the Messiah was kept alive, though they had no new prophets.

They enjoyed quiet and peace for many years; and most of the Jews who were settled in other countries--in Persia, Babylon, and Egypt--came from time to time to keep the feasts, and make offerings; while those settled near enough kept the three yearly pilgrimages to Jerusalem, singing, as it is believed, the beautiful psalms called in the Bible the Songs of Degrees, as the parties from towns and villages went up together in procession towards the Hill of Sion.

In the meantime, their masters, the Persian kings, grew worse and worse; brother killed brother, son rose against father, and the women even committed horrible crimes. They invented tortures too horrid to mention, and lived between savage cruelty and vain luxury, till there was no strength nor courage in them, and in less than 200 years from the time that Cyrus had conquered Babylon, their realm was rotten, and their time of ruin was come. All through this time, the Jews were chiefly ruled by the high priests, though paying tribute to the Persian king, and sometimes visited by the Satrap of the Province of Syria, to which Palestine belonged.

LESSON XV.
ALEXANDER.

"Ships shall come from Chittim, and shall afflict Eber, and shall afflict Assur."--Num. xxiv. 24.

Mountain lands, small islets, and peninsulas broken into by deep bays and gulfs, rise to the northward of the east end of the Mediterranean, and were known to the Jews as the Isles of the Gentiles. The people who dwelt in them have been named Greeks; they were sons of Japhet, and were the race whom God endowed, above all others, with gifts of the body and mind, though without bestowing on them the light of His truth. They had many idols, of whom Zeus, the Thunderer, was the chief; but they did not worship them with cruel rites like the Phoenicians, and some of their beautiful stories about them were full of traces of better things. Their best and wisest men were always straining their minds to feel after more satisfying knowledge of Him, Who, they felt sure, must rule and govern all things; and sometimes these philosophers, as they were called, came very near the truth. Every work of the Greeks was well done, whether poems, history, speeches, buildings, statues, or painting; and the remains have served for patterns ever since. At first there were many separate little states, but all held together as one nation, and used to meet for great feasts, especially for games. There were the Olympian games, by which they reckoned the years, and the Isthmean, which were held at the Isthmus of Corinth. Everyone came to see the wrestling, boxing, racing, and throwing heavy weights, and to hear the poems sung or recited; and the men who excelled all the rest were carried high in air with shouts of joy, and crowned with wreaths of laurel, bay, oak, or parsley, one of the greatest honours a Greek could obtain. Of all the cities, Athens had the ablest men, and Sparta the most hardy; and these two had been the foremost in beating and turning back the great Persian armies of Darius and Xerxes; but since that time there had been quarrels between these two powers, and they grew weak, so that Philip, King of Macedon, who had a kingdom to the north of them, and was but half a real Greek, contrived to conquer them all, and make them his subjects.

The ensign of Macedon was a he-goat, the rough goat that Daniel had seen in his vision; and the time was come for the fall of the Ram of Persia. Philip's son, Alexander, set his heart on conquering the old enemy of Greece; and as soon as he came to the crown, in the year 333, though he was but twenty years of age, he led his army across the Hellespont into Asia Minor. His army was very brave, and excellently trained by his father, and he himself was one of the most highly-gifted men who ever lived, brave and prudent, seldom cruel, and trying to do good to all who fell under his power. The poor weak luxurious Persian King, Darius, could do little against such a man, and indeed did not come out to battle in the way to conquer; for he carried with him all the luxuries of his palace, his mother, and all his wives and slaves. Before his army marched a number of men carrying silver altars, on which burnt the sacred fire; then came three hundred and sixty-five youths in scarlet dresses, to represent the days of the year; then the Magi, and the gilded chariot and white horses of the Sun; and next, the king's favourite soldiers, called the Immortal Band, whose robes were white, their breastplates set with jewels, and the handles of their spears golden. They had small chance with the bold active Greeks; and at the Battle of the Issus they were routed, and Darius fled away, leaving all his women to the mercy of the conqueror. The poor old Persian Queen, his mother, had never met with such gentle respect and courtesy as Alexander showed to her old age; he always called her mother, never sat down before her but at her request, and never grieved her but once, and that was by showing her a robe that his mother and sisters had spun, woven, and embroidered for him, and offering to have her grandchildren taught the like works. She fancied this meant that he was treating them like slaves, and he could hardly make her understand that the Greeks deemed such works an honour to the highest ladies, and indeed thought their goddess of wisdom presided over them.

While Darius fled away, Alexander came south to Palestine, and laid siege to Tyre upon the little isle, to which he began to build a causeway across the water.

The Tyrians had an image of the Greek god Apollo, which they had stolen from a temple in Greece, and they chained this up to the statue of Moloch, their own god, to hinder Apollo from going over to help the Greeks; but neither this precaution nor their bravery could prevent them from being overcome, as the prophet Zechariah had foretold, "The Lord will cast her out, and will smite her power in the sea, and she shall be devoured with fire."

"Gaza also shall see it, and shall be very sorrowful." Alexander took this brave Philistine city after a siege of two months, and behaved more cruelly there than was his wont. It was the turn of Jerusalem next; but the Lord had promised to "encamp about His House, because of him that passeth by;" and in answer to the prayers and sacrifices offered up by the Jews, God appeared to the High Priest, Jaddua, in a dream, and bade him adorn the city, and go out to meet the conqueror in his beautiful garments, with all his priests in their ephods. They obeyed, and as Alexander came up the hill Sapha, in front of the city, be beheld the long ranks of priests and Levites in their white array, headed by the High Priest with his robes bordered with bells and pomegranates, and the fair mitre on his head, inscribed with the words "Holiness unto the Lord." One moment, and Alexander was down from his horse, adoring upon his knees. His friends were amazed, but he told them he adored not the man, but Him who had given him the priesthood, and that just before he had left home, the same figure had stood by his bed, and told him that he should cross the sea, and win all the chief lands of Asia. He then took Jaddua by the hand, and was led by him into the Temple, where he attended a sacrifice, and was shown Daniel's prophecies of him as the brazen thighs, the he-goat and the leopard; he was much pleased, and promised all Jaddua asked, that the Jews might follow their own laws, and pay no tribute on the Sabbath years, when the land lay fallow.

Alexander next passed on to Egypt, where he built, at the mouth of the Nile, the famous city that still is called by his name, Alexandria; indeed he founded cities everywhere, and made more lasting changes than ever did conqueror in the short space of twelve years. He then hunted Darius into the mountain parts of the north of Persia, and after two more victories, the Greeks found the poor Persian king dying on the ground, from wounds given by his own subjects. So the soft silver of Persia yielded to the brazen might of Greece. After this, Alexander called himself King of Persia, and wore the tiara like an eastern king. He took his men on to the borders of India, but they thought they were getting beyond the end of the world, and grew so frightened that he had to turn back. All that the Medes and Persians had possessed now belonged to him, and he wanted to make Babylon his capital; he made his court there, and received messengers who paid him honour from all quarters; but he was hurt by so much success; he grew proud and passionate; he feasted and drank too much, and did violent and hasty things, but worst of all, he fancied himself a god, and insisted that at home, in Greece, sacrifices should be offered to him. He tried to restore Babylon to what it had been, and set multitudes to work to clear away the rubbish, and build up the Temple of Bel; but when he ordered the Jews to share in the work, they answered that it was contrary to their Law to labour at an idol temple, and he listened to them, releasing them from the command. He wished to turn the waters of the Euphrates back into their stream, and drain the swamps into which they had spread; but Babylon was under the curse of God, and was never to recover. Alexander caught a fever while going about surveying the unwholesome swamps, and after trying to hold out against it for nine days, his strength gave way. He said there would be a mighty strife at his funeral, perhaps recollecting how the prophecy had said that his kingdom should not continue; and instead of trying to choose an heir, he put his ring on the finger of his friend, and very soon died. He was but thirty-two, and had not reigned quite twelve years; but perhaps no one ever did greater things in so short a time. He died in the year 323; and so the great horn of the goat was broken when it was at the strongest. No one hated him; for though sometimes violent, he had generally been kind; he was frank, open, and free-handed, warm-hearted to his friends, and seldom harsh to his enemies, and he had done his best to educate and improve all the people whom he conquered. It was owing to him that Greek manners and habits prevailed, and the Greek tongue was spoken everywhere around the eastern end of the Mediterranean, though Persia itself soon fell back into the old eastern ways. Babylon became almost deserted after his death; the swamps grew worse, till no one could live there, and at last, the only use of the great walls was to serve as an enclosure for a hunting ground, where the wild beasts had their home, and kept court for ever.

LESSON XVI.
THE GREEK KINGS OF EGYPT.

"Why hast Thou then broken down her hedge, that all they that go by pluck off her grapes?"--Ps. lxxx. 12.

The leopard of Daniel's vision had four heads--the great horn of the rough goat gave place to four horns; so when Alexander was taken away so suddenly from the midst of his conquests, leaving no one in his room, his great officers divided them between themselves; and after much violence and bloodshed, four Greek kingdoms were formed out of the fragments of his conquests, Thrace, Macedon, Egypt, and Syria. It is only the two last of which we have to speak. The angel who spake to Daniel called their princes the Kings of the North and South. The north, or second kingdom of Syria, was very large, and went from Asia Minor to the borders of India, and it had two great capital cities, Antioch in Syria, and Seleucia upon the Tigris, where the Babylonians went to live when their city became deserted and uninhabitable. Both these places were named after the Greek Kings of Syria, who were by turns called Seleucus and Antiochus.

It would have seemed natural for Palestine to have belonged to Syria, but the Greek King of Egypt, whose name was Ptolemy Lagos, contrived to secure it. He entered Jerusalem on the Sabbath-day, when the Jews thought it wrong to fight, and so he gained the city without a blow; but this was no great misfortune to them, for the first Ptolemies were milder masters than the Seleucidae, and did not oppress their subjects. Ptolemy, however, brought a colony of Jews and Samaritans to live in Lybia and Cyrene, parts of Egypt, and so fulfilled Isaiah's prophecy, that five cities in Egypt should speak the language of Canaan. They were treated with much favour, for he saw that they were the most trustworthy of all his people. Indeed, the Greeks respected them much; and one of Ptolemy's soldiers tells this story: he says that while travelling in a large company by the Red Sea, he fell in with a very brave strong Jew, called Masollam. Presently the whole company came to a halt. Masollam asked why; and a soothsayer, pointing to a bird, told him that if the bird stopped, it would be lucky for them to stop; if it flew on, they might go on; if it went back, so must they. All the answer Masollam made, was to fit an arrow to his bow-string, and shoot the bird dead; and when the Greeks cried out at him, he rebuked them for thinking the poor bird could know their future, when he could not even save himself from the arrow.

At this time the High Priest was Simon the Just, son of Onias, the same who is so highly praised in the fiftieth chapter of the Book of Ecclesiasticus, and compared to the morning star, and to a young cedar of Libanus, when he stood before the Altar in his beautiful robes, and turned round and blessed the people. He was the last of the hundred and twenty great prophets, or wise men, whom the Jews called the great Synagogue; and it was he who sealed up the Old Testament, adding to the former collection the books of Ezra, Nehemiah, and Malachi; and it is thought, compiling the books of Chronicles from older writings, for the genealogy of the house of David there given, comes down to about the year 300, when he was alive, since he died in 292. The Jews thought nothing went so well with them after his time, and were alarmed when the scape-goat, with the band of scarlet wool on his brow, instead of rushing down a precipice, as usual, and being killed at once, ran off into the desert, and was eaten by the Arabs. They enjoyed tolerable peace for the whole of the time they were under the Greeks of Egypt. Ptolemy Lagos wanted to make his new city of Alexandria as much famed for learning as Athens; and for this purpose he founded a great library there, collecting, from every quarter, books written either on parchment, or on the paper rush of Egypt. When he died, in the year 284, his son, Ptolemy Philadelphus, or lover of his brethren, went on still more eagerly seeking for curious writings; and among those for which he wished were the Holy Scriptures. As they were in Hebrew, he caused them to be translated into Greek; and the Jews believe that this was done by seventy-two elders, who were shut up all day, two and two, in thirty-six little cells in a palace on a little island in the Nile, each pair taking one book of the Bible, and going back every evening to sup with the king. This history does not seem likely to be true, but it is quite certain that a version of the Old Testament from the Hebrew into Greek was made about this time, and is called the Septuagint, from this tradition about the seventy. It came more and more into use, as Greek was considered the language of all learned men in the east. Most of the quotations in the New Testament are taken from it, and it is of great value in helping to show the exact meaning of the old Hebrew.

But if Ptolemy did desire to have the Scriptures in his own tongue, it was only for curiosity, not for edification, for he was a great idolater; and when his wife died he tried to build a temple to her at Alexandria, which was to have a loadstone arch, with a steel statue of her in the middle, where he hoped the equal attraction would keep it as if flying in the air; but of course the fancy could not be carried out. He had a quarrel with Antiochus Theos, King of Syria, but it was made up by his giving his daughter Berenice in marriage to the Syrian, as Daniel had foretold: "The king's daughter of the South, came to make an agreement with the King of the North." But Antiochus had another wife before, whom he loved better; so when, in 246, Ptolemy Philadelphus died, he put Berenice away, and took her back. She requited him by poisoning him for fear her favour should not last, and her son, Seleucus, became king, and taking Berenice prisoner, put her to death.

"But out of a branch of her roots shall one stand up in his estate, which shall come with an army, and shall enter into the fortress of the King of the North." This was the brother of Berenice, Ptolemy Euergetes, or the Benefactor, who came out of Egypt, overran Syria, and killed the murderess, carrying home much spoil and many of the Egyptian gods, which had been taken from the temples there in the time of Cambyses. Ptolemy Euergetes himself came to Jerusalem, and attended a sacrifice in the Temple; but Greek learning was doing the Jews no good, and some began to reason like the heathen philosophers. A man named Joseph taught that people ought to be holy for the love of goodness, and not for the sake of a reward after death; and his follower, Zadok, or Sadoc, went still farther, saying that there was no promise of any reward. His disciples, who were called Sadducees, declared that the soul was not separate from the body, but died with it; that there were no angels, nor spirits, and that only the five books of Moses were the real Word of God, thus casting aside all the prophecies. Such Jews as abhorred this falling away, kept themselves apart, and were called Pharisees, from a word meaning separate; and these grew the more strict in the observance of all that had come down to them from their fathers, adding to it much that had gradually been put into the explanations and interpretations of the Law which were read on the Sabbath in the Synagogue.

Ptolemy the Benefactor was the last brave man of his family; his son, Ptolemy Philopator, or lover of his father, was weak and violent, and had a disastrous war with Antiochus the Great of Syria. In the course of the conflict he came to Jerusalem, and tried to force his way into the Holy of Holies, though the High Priest and all the priests and Levites withstood him, and prayed aloud that the profanation might be hindered. When he came to the court of the priests, such a strange horror and terror fell on him, that he reeled and fell, and was carried out half dead; but he was only hardened by this great wonder, and on his return revenged himself by collecting the Jews at Alexandria, and insisting that they should be marked with the ivy leaf, the sign of the Greek god of wine, or else be made slaves, or put to death. Out of many thousands, only three hundred submitted to this disgraceful badge; so in his rage, he collected all the others in the theatre, and caused elephants to be made drunken with wine and frankincense, so that when driven in on them, they might trample them to death. But for two days following the king was too drunk himself to be present at the horrible spectacle, and the Jews had all that time for prayer; and when, on the third day, the execution was to take place, the beasts ran upon the spectators instead of upon the martyrs, so that though numbers of Greeks were killed, not one Jew was hurt, and Ptolemy gave up his attempt; though he did afterwards commit one savage massacre on his Jewish subjects. He died when only thirty-seven years of age, worn out by drunkenness; and the Jews, who had learnt to hate the Egyptian dominion, gladly received the soldiers of his enemy, Antiochus the Great, into Jerusalem, deserting his young son, who was only five years old; and thus, in the year 197, Jerusalem came to belong to the Seleucidae of Syria, instead of to the Ptolemies of Egypt. The history of Ptolemy Philopator in predicted from the 10th to the 13th verse of the 11th chapter of Daniel's prophecy. The Jews suffered terribly all through these wars, which were usually fought out on their soil. Each sovereign robbed them in turn, while they were too few to guard themselves, and could do no otherwise than fall to the strongest.

LESSON XVII.
THE SYRIAN PERSECUTION.

"The dead bodies of Thy servants have they given to be meat unto the fowls of the air, and the flesh of Thy saints unto the beasts of the land."--Ps. lxxix. 2.

The history of Antiochus the Great is foretold in the 11th chapter of the prophet Daniel, from the 14th to the 19th verse. On the death of Ptolemy Philopator, this king entered Palestine with a great army, and easily obtained from the time-serving Jews the surrender of Jerusalem. Some of them who had forsaken their Law to gain the favour of Ptolemy, were punished by Antiochus, because he knew that no trust could be placed in men who cared for their own profit more than for their God. He then laid siege to Gaza and to Sidon, and won great victories, ravaging and consuming the adjoining lands with his armies; and afterwards made peace with young Ptolemy Epiphanes, giving him his daughter in marriage, hoping that she would betray her husband to him. She, however, entirely forsook him, and made common cause with her husband. "After this," the prophecy declared that he would "turn his face to the isles and take many." This meant that he should make an expedition to Greece, where he gained a good deal of land; but here he came in contact with the iron power, shadowed out by the great and terrible beast of Daniel's second vision.

Some four hundred years before this time, the city of Rome had begun to grow up on some of the seven hills on the banks of the Tiber in Italy. The inhabitants were a stern, earnest, brave, honest set of men; not great thinkers like the Greeks, but great doers, and caring for nothing so much as for their city and her honour. They thought their own lives and happiness as nothing in comparison with Rome;

and all the free citizens had a share in the government, so that their city's concerns were their own. Their religion seems in early times to have been more solemn and grave than that of the Greeks. Jupiter was their chief god, the King of gods and men, who held thunderbolts in his hand, and they had eleven other principal gods; but by the time they had learnt to write books, they had begun to think these were the same gods as the Greeks worshipped under other names; they said Jupiter was the same as Zeus, and told of him all the foolish stories which the worse sort of Greeks had invented of Zeus, and as their religion grew worse, they became more selfish, proud, and cruel. At first, their neighbours in Italy were always fighting with them, and their wars were for life or death; but after nearly three hundred years of hard struggling, without one year's peace, the Romans had conquered them all, and had safety at home. But they had grown too fond of war to rest quietly, so they built ships and attacked countries farther off, beginning with the great Phoenician city of Carthage in Africa, which it is said was settled by Canaanites who fled away from Joshua, and whose first queen was Dido, Jezebel's niece. A great Carthaginian general, named Hannibal, who had been banished from home, came to Antiochus, and offered to help him in his war upon Greece. This Hannibal did chiefly out of hatred to the Romans, who were pretending to assist the Greeks, only that they might become their masters. If Antiochus had taken the advice of Hannibal, he might have succeeded better, but he was self-willed; the Romans gave him a terrible defeat, and he was obliged to promise to pay a great sum of money, and a heavy tribute afterwards; to keep no elephants to be used in war, and to give up his younger son, Antiochus, as security for his performance of the conditions. The tribute he had to pay to Rome quite ruined him; and while he was trying to rob an idol temple at Elymais, the people rose on him and slew him, in the year 187.

His son, Seleucus, called by. Daniel "a raiser of taxes," was very poor in consequence of the tribute, and therefore greedy. He tried to raise money by sending his servant, Heliodorus, to rob the temple at Jerusalem Onias, the High Priest, and all the people, were in great distress, and made most earnest entreaties to God to deliver them from such profanation. Heliodorus came, however, to the temple, and was pressing on to the treasury, when suddenly a horse, with a terrible rider, appeared in armour like gold, and cast the spoiler to the ground, while two young men, of marvellous beauty, scourged him on either side, so that when the heavenly champions had vanished, he lay as one dead. Onias prayed for him, and he was restored; the same beings who had struck him down coming to reveal to him that his life was granted at the intercession of the High Priest. When he returned to his master, and was consulted as to who might be a fit man to send to Jerusalem, he answered, "If thou hast any enemy or traitor, send him thither, and thou shalt receive him well scourged." So little impression did such a revelation of glory make on that hard selfish heart! The man who had been smitten by a visible angel could jest about it, and soon went on to greater crime. He poisoned his master in the hope of becoming king, as Seleucus's son was a hostage at Rome, that is, he had been given as a pledge that the tribute should be paid; but Seleucus's brother, Antiochus, who was on his way home from captivity at Rome, flattered the adjoining kings into helping him, drove Heliodorus away, and became king in 178. He was the little horn of the Grecian goat, "the vile person to whom they should not give the honour of the kingdom," so much was it fallen since the time of his father, Antiochus the Great. Vile indeed he was, nearly mad with violence and excess, going drunk about the streets of Antioch crowned with roses, and pelting with stones those who followed him, so that the Greeks laughed at him for calling himself Antiochus Epiphanes, or the Illustrious, and said he was really Antiochus the madman. He cared little for the old Greek gods; but the Roman Jupiter, "a god whom his fathers knew not," was his chief object of devotion, and in his honour, he instituted games like those of Greece. Some of the Jews had begun to weary of their perfect Law, and fancy it narrow and vulgar, and the brothers of the good Onias were among the worst; Joshua, the next in age, changed his glorious prophetic name to the Greek Jason, and going to Antioch, offered a great sum of money to be made High Priest, and for leave to set up at Jerusalem a place for the practice of the heathenish games of strength, where men fought naked. Antiochus was but too glad of the offer; so the good High Priest was carried off to die a prisoner at Antioch, and the apostate was set up in his room in order to pervert the Jewish youth to idolatry. However, he was soon overthrown by his apostate brother, Menelaus, whom he had sent to pay the tribute at Antioch, and who, when there, promised the king a larger revenue, and to bring all the Jews to embrace the heathen worship. Jason fled to the Ammonites, and Menelaus and his brother sold the gold vessels of the Temple to the Phoenicians. The Jews sent complaints to the king at Tyre, but instead of attending, he murdered the messengers, so much to the horror of the Tyrians, that they gave them honourable burial.

Antiochus now began a war with Egypt, (Dan. xi. 25,) and while he was there, Jason came back from the Ammonites and regained Jerusalem; but the news brought the king back in the utmost rage, Jason fled to Greece, and Antiochus, coming to Jerusalem, cruelly treated the people, robbed the treasury, himself went into the holy place, led by that horrible traitor, Menelaus; and uttering blasphemy, he sacrificed a hog upon the altar, and boiling the flesh, sprinkled the Temple with the broth, carried off the candlestick and all the rest of the gold, and when he went away to continue his wars, he left a captain and garrison to oppress the Jews, and an old man to teach them the worship of Jupiter. A little altar for sacrifice to Jupiter was raised on the true altar, the Temple was dedicated to Jupiter, as was also that of the Samaritans on Mount Gerizim, the Sabbath was abolished, so was circumcision, and on the day of the king's birth, in each month, the Jews were forced to eat swine's flesh, and partake of idol sacrifices, and, at the feast of the god of wine, to carry ivy in the mad drunken processions in his honour.

It was the most utter misery that had yet befallen the Jews. Temple, Priesthood, all gone! "We see not our tokens; there is not one prophet more;" and yet that was the great time of glorious Jewish martyrdoms. Numbers of the faithful were burnt to death together in a cave, where they had met to keep the Sabbath day; two women who had circumcised their babes, had them hung round their necks, and were then pitched from the highest part of the wall of Jerusalem; and the aged scribe, Eleazar, who was ninety years old, when swine's flesh was forced into his mouth, spat it out again, and was scourged to death, saying with his last breath that he bore all this suffering because he feared the Lord. A mother and her seven sons were taken, and as each refused to share in the idol rite and break the Law, they were put to death, one by one, with horrible tortures, each before the eyes of his remaining brethren; but the parting words of all were full of high hope and constancy. "The Lord looketh on us, and hath comfort in us," said one. "The King of the world shall raise us up who have died for His laws unto everlasting life," was spoken by another. "Think not our nation is forsaken of God, but abide awhile and behold His great power, how He will torment thee and thy seed," said another, (for they were as yet only faithful Jews, hope and forgiveness for their persecutors was for the Christian.) The mother stood firmly by while each son's limbs were cut off, and he was roasted to death over a fire; and all her words were to exhort them to be stedfast, and to assure them their Creator could raise them if they died for Him. When the turn of the last son came, the persecutors, pitying his youth, entreated him to change his resolution, promising him riches and prosperity if he would adore the idol, and even calling his mother to plead with him. Then the noble woman laughed the tyrant to scorn. "Have pity on me, my son," she began; but it was not by saving his life, but by losing it, that she bade him show pity on her, so that she might receive him again with his brethren. He made a still fuller confession than the rest--he was slain by a still more savage torture; and then his mother, blessing God, died gloriously like her sons. Others fled, and lived in the mountains, lurking in caves, and feeding on wild roots and herbs. Of such St. Paul says, "They were tempted, were slain with the sword; they wandered about in sheep-skins and goat-skins, being destitute, afflicted, tormented: of whom the world was not worthy."

LESSON XVIII.
THE MACCABEES.

"In that day will I make Jerusalem a burdensome stone for all people; all that burden themselves with it shall be cut in pieces."--Zechariah, xii. 3.

Never was there a time when God left Himself without a witness; and in these darkest times of the Jewish history, He raised up a defender of His Name. There was a small town, named Modin, near the sea shore, whither a Greek officer called Apelles was sent to force the people into idolatry. He set up an altar to one of his gods, and having ordered all the inhabitants to assemble, insisted on their doing sacrifice. Among them came a family of priests, who, from their ancestor, Hasmon, were known as the Asmoneans. The father, Mattathias, declared with a loud voice that he would permit no such dishonour to his God, and the first Jew who approached to offer incense, was by him struck down and slain. Then with his five brave sons, and others emboldened by his example, he fell upon Apelles, drove him away, and pulled down the idolatrous altar. He then fled away to the hills, where so many people joined him, that he had a force sufficient to defend themselves from their enemies; and he went round Judea, circumcising the children, and rescuing the copies of the Law which the Greeks had seized from the synagogues. Some of these holy books, which had been defiled by paintings of the heathen idols, were destroyed, by order of Mattathias, after the writing had been carefully copied. It was at this time that the Jews began to read Lessons from the Prophets in the synagogue, because Antiochus had only forbidden reading the Law, without specifying the prophetic books. Mattathias, who was already an old man, soon fell sick; and gathering his sons about him, reminded them of the deeds that God had wrought by the holy men of old, and exhorting them to do boldly in defence of His Covenant. He appointed as their leader his third son, Judas, who for his warlike might was called Maccabaeus, or the Hammerer; and the second, Simon, surnamed Thassi, (one who increases,) was to be his chief adviser.

In the year 166, Judas Maccabaeus set up his standard, with the motto, "Who is like unto Thee, O Lord, among the gods?" the first letters of which words in Hebrew made his surname, Maccabee. He went through the land, enforcing the Law, and putting the cities in a state of defence. Antiochus, meantime, was holding a mad and hateful festival at Daphne; but on hearing of the revolt of the Jews, he went into a great rage, and sent a huge army to punish them. Maccabaeus defeated this force, drove it back to Antioch, and then marched to Jerusalem, and forced the Greek garrison to take refuge in a fortress called Akra, on Mount Zion. The courts of the Temple were overgrown with shrubs which stood like a forest, the priests' chambers had been pulled down, and the Sanctuary lay desolate. These brave men rent their clothes and wept at the sight; and then set at once to repair the holy place, their priest-leader choosing out the most spotless among them for the work. They pulled down the Altar that had been defiled, and setting aside its stones, built a new one, and out of the spoil that was in their hands, renewed the Candlestick, the shew-bread table, and the Altar of incense; and then they newly dedicated the Temple, after three years of desolation. The anniversary was ever after kept with gladness, and was called the winter feast of dedication. Still Judas was not strong enough to take the castle on Mount Zion; but he built strong walls round the Temple, so that it too became a fortress, and he then went to Bethshan to defend the south border of Judea against the Edomites.

These tidings terribly enraged Antiochus, who was gone on an expedition to Persia, and he designed to form a league with his neighbours for the utter destruction of the Jews; but "he came to his end, and none could help him," for an overturn of his chariot so much increased an inward disease that had already begun, that he fell into most horrible tortures, and was in such a state of decay that scarcely anyone could bear to come near him. Horrible fears tormented him, and in his remorse he repented of all the evil he had done to the Jews, and sent them a letter assuring them of his favour; but it was now too late, and he died in great misery in 164. His son, Antiochus Eupator, was only nine years old, and his affairs were managed by a governor named Lysias, who continued the persecution, and led an army to the relief of the garrison in Mount Zion. Judas marched out to meet him, but was repulsed with the loss of six hundred men, and of his younger brother, Eleazar, who seeing an elephant of huge size, with a tower of unusual height on its back, thought the king himself must be there, and running beneath it, stabbed it so as to be crushed himself in its fall. Lysias then advanced upon Jerusalem, and laid close siege to it, placing the Jews in extreme peril. Just then another regent rose up against Lysias, and he made a hasty peace with Maccabaeus, and was admitted into the city; but when he saw its strength, he broke his promises, and overthrew the wall. On his return to Antioch, he punished the apostate high-priest, Menelaus, as the author of all these misfortunes, by smothering him in a tower filled with ashes. "Woe to the idol shepherd who had left his flock!" Another half heathen, named Alcimus, was appointed in his place, and when the Jews would not receive him, brought down their enemies upon them again. Judas gained a victory, and wrote to entreat the alliance and protection of the Romans; but ere the answer to his letter arrived, he had, with only 800 men, fallen on a whole army of the Syrians, and was killed in the battle, B.C. 161. His brothers, Jonathan and Simon, took up his body, and buried it at Modin, in the tomb of their fathers; and they continued to lead the faithful Jews, while Alcimus held Jerusalem, and there began to alter the Temple, taking down the wall of separation between the courts of the Jews and that of the Gentiles; but in the midst of the work he was smitten with palsy, and died.

It was the plan of the Romans to take the part of a weak nation against a strong one, because it afforded them an excuse for conquering the mightier of the two, so they gave notice that the quarrels of the Jews were their own; and after much fighting, Jonathan obtained two years of peace, and became high-priest. Onias, the son of the good Onias, whom Jason had set aside, went to Egypt, and ministered in a temple built by the Jews, who had settled there.

Ever since the Syrian kings had begun to misuse the Jews, they had grown weak and miserable. Antiochus Eupator was dethroned and murdered by his cousin Demetrius; but shortly after, a man named Balas came forward, calling himself the son of Antiochus Epiphanes, and begging Jonathan to take his part, sending him a golden crown and purple robe, and naming him commander of the Jewish force. In a battle in the year 153, Demetrius was slain; and Balas became king. Both Balas and his son Antiochus treated Jonathan with great favour, and he fortified Jerusalem, got possession of many other towns, and considerably strengthened the rightful cause: but a wicked rebel named Trypho, who designed the murder of his young master, Antiochus, began his conspiracy by treacherously assassinating Jonathan in the land of Gilead, B.C. 143, and soon after succeeded in killing the young king.

Simon Thassi was the only survivor of the brave Maccabaean brothers, but he finished their work, and obtained from Rome, Egypt, and Syria, an acknowledgment that the Jews were a free people, and that he was their prince and priest. He took the castle on Mount Zion from the Syrians, and so fortified the Temple, that it became like another citadel, and he was honoured by all his neighbours. He built a noble tomb for all his family at Modin, consisting of seven pyramids, in honour of his father and mother, and their five sons; all covered in by a portico, supported on seven pillars, the whole of white marble, and the pediment so high that it served for a mark for sailors at sea. He died, like his brave brethren, by a bloody death, being murdered at Jericho, B.C. 135, by his own son-in-law, who hoped to usurp the government; but his eldest son, John Hyrcanus, was able to punish the murderer, and to obtain the full authority, by giving large presents both to the Romans and Syrians. It is said that he found, laid up in the sepulchre of David, 3000 talents of silver, which he used for this purpose. Hyrcanus was a very powerful and mighty prince, and not only reigned over all Judea, but conquered Edom, with all the curious dwellings in the rocky caves of Petra; he brought the country under subjection, circumcised the inhabitants, and brought them under the Mosaic Law. From that time Idumea decayed, and now has become an utter wilderness, the carved faces of the rocks still witnessing to the truth of prophecy, as they stand forth, lonely and deserted in their grandeur, though glowing freshly with the rosy marblings of the rocks of Seir.

LESSON XIX.
THE ROMAN POWER.

And He shall put a yoke of iron on thy neck until He have destroyed thee.--Deut. xxviii.48.

Aristobulus, the son of Hyrcanus, was called King, as well as High Priest of the Jews; but the mixture of worldly policy with the sacred office did not suit well, and the Asmonean Kings were not like their fathers, the Maccabees. Still their courage and steadiness made the Jews much respected; and the Greeks and Romans around them began to read their books, and there were some few who perceived that the religion, there taught, was purer than idolatry, and wiser than the beat philosophy. The kings were assisted in government by what was called the Sanhedrim, a council of a hundred and twenty of the Scribes and of the chief priests, namely, the heads of the courses of priests. This council met daily in a hall near the great gate of the Temple, and heard cases brought before them for judgment, after the example of the seventy elders appointed by Moses. Alexander Janneus, the son of Aristobulus, reigned from B.C. 104 to B.C. 77, and left his kingdom to his wife, Alexandra, who trusted much to the Pharisees, and raised them to great power. Her eldest son, Hyrcanus, was High Priest, and she left the kingdom to him at her death, B.C. 69; but his brother, Aristobulus, rebelling, with the help of the Sadducees, defeated him, and drove him from his throne.

Hyrcanua was indolent, and was rather glad to be relieved from the trouble of reigning; but his friend, Antipas, an Edomite by birth, and of the Jewish religion, persuaded him that his life would not be safe in Judea, and stirred him up to ask help, first from the Arabs, and when they were beaten, from the Romans, to whom however, Aristobulus had already sent a present of a golden vine, in hopes of winning their support.

The great awfulness of the Roman power was in the sureness of its conquests. It did not fly onward without touching the earth, like the great eastern conquerors; but let it set one claw on a nation, and the doom of that nation was fixed. First the help of the Romans was asked and readily given; then in return a tribute was demanded and paid; then the Romans would meddle with the government, till their interference became intolerable, and there was a rising against it, which they called rebellion; then they sent an army, and ruined the nation for ever. The king, queen, generals, and all the riches, were carried to Rome, where the conqueror came in to enjoy what was called a triumph. He was seated in a chariot drawn by white horses, a laurel wreath round his head, and all his captives and spoils displayed behind him; the senate or council coming out to meet him, and the people shouting for joy as they led him to the Temple of Jupiter to give thanks. The captives were afterwards slain; and, as a farther festival, the people were entertained with shows of gladiators, namely, slaves trained to fight, even to death, with each other or with wild beasts. Then the conquered land became a Roman province. After the magistrates had served a year at Rome, they were allowed to choose which province they would govern; and there they did as they pleased, and laid heavy burthens on the poor inhabitants, for all men, not of Roman birth, they called barbarian, and used like slaves; nor was there any hope of breaking this heavy bondage, for each city was a station of Roman soldiers, who were the bravest and best disciplined in the world. The army was divided into legions, each about 6,000 men strong, with a silver eagle for the standard; these were again subdivided into cohorts, and again into hundreds, each commanded by a centurion, whose helmet had some mark by which his men might know him. No soldier could miss his place, either in battle, on a march, or in the perfect square camps which they set up wherever they halted; they obeyed the least word, and feared nothing; and nothing could hold out against their steady skill, perseverance, and progress. Wherever they went they built fortresses, and made wonderful straight solid roads, some of which remain to this day; and their ships and messengers going for ever from one province to another, made their empire all like one country; where the stern Roman was the lord, and the native was crushed down under his feet,

They had just at this time put down the kingdom of Syria, and conquered nearly all Asia Minor. Their great general, Pompey, was holding a court at Damascus, whither, among ten other suppliant princes, Hyrcanus and Aristobulus came to lay their cause before him, thus asking a heathen who should be the Priest of the Most High. Pompey took the part of the elder, as the rightful heir, and led an army against Jerusalem. The siege lasted three months, and so strong was the place, that it would have held out much longer, but that the Jews would not defend themselves on the Sabbath, at least no more than enough to protect their own lives. They would not disturb any of the operations of the siege, nor keep the engines from the walls on that day; and thus, B.C. 63, the Gentiles again entered Jerusalem on the very day observed as a fast in memory of Nebuchadnezzar's conquest.

Pompey spared the city from plunder, and touched none of the treasure in the Temple; but he would not be withheld from going into every part, even into the Holy of Holies; and though no immediate judgment followed, it was remarked that from that time his prosperity left him. He set up Hyrcanus as High Priest, but not as King--made him pay a tribute, put him under the control of Antipas, and forbade him to extend his domains. Aristobulus and his sons were carried off to appear in Pompey's triumph, but their lives were spared. Thus Judea, by her own fault, fell under the dominion of the fourth power with the teeth of iron.

Rome had hitherto been ruled by two consuls, who were chosen every year, and after their rule at home was over, went to make war in the provinces; but of late this plan had been wearing our, and the great general, Julius Caesar, who had conquered France, then called Gaul, and had visited Britain, was making himself over-powerful. Pompey stood up for the old laws, but Caesar was too strong for him, and at last hunted him to Egypt, where he was murdered by the last of the Ptolemies. Julius Caesar, who was one of the greatest warriors and most able men who ever lived, managed Rome as he chose, and coming to Syria, confirmed Hyrcanus in his rank, and finding him careless and indolent, made Antipas procurator, or governor for the Romans; and thus Antipas and his son, Herod, held all the real power in their hands, though still under the Romans. Going back to Rome, Julius Caesar became so powerful, that it was thought he would make himself king, and after four years, some of the friends of the old laws killed him with their daggers in the Senate House, B. C. 44. After this, there was great confusion; and while Augustus Caesar, the nephew of Julius, gained power in the west, Mark Antony, another Roman general, came to Egypt to attend to the affairs of the East. He was a selfish licentious man, who cared more for Cleopatra, the beautiful sister of the last Ptolemy, and Queen of Egypt, than for Rome or for his duty; and he took bribes from Herod to support his power over the old prince, Hyrcanus, to whose daughter, Mariamne, Herod was betrothed.

The son of the deposed Aristobulus, Antigonus by name, made friends with the Parthians, the descendants of the old Persians, and bursting into Judaea when the nation was unprepared, carried off poor old Hyrcanus as a prisoner, and cut off his ears that such a blemish might prevent him from ministering again as High Priest. Herod escaping, went to Rome, where he represented his case so ably, that Augustus and Antony gave him men and money that he might drive out Antigonus, and promised that he should himself be king under them. The Roman army helped him to win back the country; and as the caves in the hills were full of robbers, he let down soldiers in boxes over the face of the precipices, and thus contrived to destroy them all. After a siege of six months he took Jerusalem, and Antigonus surrendered to the Romans, who kept him prisoner for some time, and then, at Herod's entreaty, put him to death.

Herod thus became King of the Jews, B.C. 37. He married Mariamne, who was very beautiful and amiable, and thus he hoped to please the Jews who were attached to the old line; but as he was an Idumean, and therefore could not be High Priest, he gave the holy office to her brother, until becoming fearful of the young prince's just rights to the crown, he caused his attendants to drown him while bathing, and afterwards appointed High Priests, as he chose, from the chief priests of the Sanhedrim. Indeed Herod lived in constant fear and hatred of every Asmonean, and at last even turned against his own wife, Mariamne. He caused her to be put to death, and then nearly broke his heart with grief for her; and afterwards the same dread of the old royal stock led him to kill the two sons she had left to him.

The seventy weeks of Daniel were drawing to a close, and everyone expected that the long-promised Deliverer and King would appear. Some flatterers said it was Herod himself, the blood-stained Edomite, and he did all in his power to maintain the notion, by repairing the Temple with great care and cost, making restorations there that were forty-six years in progress, and spreading a golden vine over the front of the Sanctuary.

There were others who said the one great King, whom even the heathen expected, was coming to Rome. Augustus Caesar had gained all the power; he had beaten Antony and Cleopatra in a sea-fight, and following them to Egypt, found that they had both killed themselves, Antony with his sword, Cleopatra by the bite of an asp, in order to save themselves from being made prisoners. Augustus was welcomed at Rome with a great triumph, and was called Emperor, the name always given to a victorious general; the Romans gave him all their offices of state, and he ruled over all their great dominions without anyone to dispute his power, any enemy to conquer at home or abroad. There was a great lull and hush all over the world, for the time was come at last. But the King was neither Herod in Judea, nor Augustus at Rome! Nay Herod, as a son of Edom, was but proving that the Sceptre had departed from Judah; and the reign of Augustus was a time when darkness covered the earth, and gross darkness the people, for the Greeks and Romans had lost all the good that had been left in them, and were given up to wicked cruelty and foul self-indulgence; when one of their own heathen oracles was caused to announce to Augustus that the greatest foe of the Roman power should be a child born among the Hebrews.

LESSON XX.
THE GOSPEL.

"It shall bruise thy head, and thou shalt bruise His heel."--Gen. iii. 15.

It was in the 4004th year of the world, the 30th of the empire of Caesar Augustus, the 37th of the reign of Herod the Edomite, that Augustus, wishing to know the number of his subjects, so as to regulate the taxes paid by the conquered countries, to provide corn for the poorer Roman citizens, sent out an edict that each person should enroll his name at his native place, and there pay a piece of money. Thus the Divine Power brought it to pass, that the Blessed Virgin, who was about to bring forth a son, should travel with her betrothed husband to the home of their fathers, Rachel's burial place, Bethlehem, the little city, whence David had once been called away from the sheepfolds.

There the stable of the ox and ass received, the Master of Heaven and earth, when His people considered Him not, and shut their doors when, "Unto us a Child was born, unto us a Son was given." There, the shepherds on the hills heard the angels sing their song of peace on earth, good will to men; there, on the eighth day of His Life on earth, that Child was circumcised, and received the Greek form of the Divine name, Jehovah the Saviour, the same which had been borne before by the Captain and by the Priest, who had led His people to their inheritance. Thence the Desire of all nations was carried to His presentation in the Temple. He was truly the first-born of all creation, but He was only known to the aged Simeon and devout Anna, as the messenger of the covenant, the Lord for whom they had waited. To Bethlehem came the mysterious wise men from the east. They had been led by the star to Jerusalem, and were there directed on by the scribes, learned in the prophecies; but their inquiries had alarmed Herod's jealousy, and he sent forth the savage order, that the babes of Bethlehem should all be murdered, in hopes of cutting off the new-born King of the Jews; but while the mothers wept for the children who should come again to them in a better inheritance, the Holy One was safe in Egypt, whither Joseph had carried Him, by the warning of God.

This massacre was well nigh the last of Herod's cruelties. He was already in failing health, and after having killed his innocent sons because of their Asmonean blood, he was obliged to put to death the son of another of his wives for rebelling against him. A terrible disease came on, and fearing that the Jews would rejoice at his death, he declared they should have something to mourn for; and sending for all the chief men to Jericho, where he lay sick, he shut them all up in the circus, or place for Roman games, and made his sister promise that the moment he expired, soldiers should be sent in to kill them all. In this devil-like frame, Herod died, in the seventieth year of his age, and the thirty-fourth of his reign, the first year of our Lord;[1] and his sister at once released the captives. He had had nine wives, and many children, of whom he had himself put three to death. Archelaus and Herod Antipas were the sons of one mother, Herod Philip of another, and the murdered son of Mariamne had left two children, named Herod Agrippa and Herodias. Archelaus took the kingdom, but had not power to control either the people or the army. Three thousand Jews were massacred by the soldiers in the Temple, and Archelaus went to Rome to beg to be confirmed on his throne, and assisted in keeping his people in order; but his brother, Herod Antipas, was there already, begging for a share in the kingdom, and the Jews sent after Archelaus, saying, "We will not have this man to reign over us!" Augustus thereupon refused to give to either the title of King, but split Palestine into four divisions called tetrarchies, from *tetra*, the Greek word for four, giving to Archelaus Judea, Samaria, and Idumea; to Antipas, Galilee; to Philip, Iturea, the part beyond the Jordan; and to a Greek named Lysanias, Abilene, in the north, near Mount Hermon. After this, Joseph returned from Egypt, but avoided the dominions of the cruel Archelaus, by going to his former abode in Galilee.

Archelaus grew so wicked, that in the year 12 A.D. an accusation against him was sent to Rome by the Jews and Samaritans; and Augustus deposed him, sending him into banishment to Vienne, in Gaul. His brothers did not obtain his domain,

1   From the Birth of our Lord, time is counted onwards, and the years marked as A.D., Anno Domini, Year of the Lord.

but it was joined to the province of Syria, and put under the charge of a Roman procurator or governor, who kept down disturbances by the strong hand; but this made the Pharisees very discontented, as they fancied it was against the Divine Law to pay tribute to strangers. Augustus had been all his life busy in setting his empire in order, and making laws for it. It stretched from the Atlantic Ocean nearly to the river Euphrates, and bordered the Mediterranean Sea on both sides, the Alps shutting it in to the north, and the deserts of Africa to the south. The Roman citizens considered themselves the lords of all this space; and though at first only the true-born Romans were citizens, Augustus gave the honour to many persons of the subject nations. It freed them from being taxed, gave them a right to vote for magistrates, and saved them from being under the authority of the governors of the provinces. Every educated person spoke Latin and Greek, but the latter tongue was most used in the east, as the Romans themselves learnt it as an accomplishment. Augustus died, A.D. 17, leaving his power to his step-son, Tiberius, whom he had adopted as his own son, and thus given him the name of Caesar. Tiberius had not been kindly treated in his youth, and he was gloomy and harsh, and exceedingly disliked by the Romans. Under him, Pontius Pilate was made Procurator of Judea, and took up his abode in Caesarea, a city built by Herod and him son Philip, on the coast, and named after the emperors. Pilate set up shields with idolatrous inscriptions in Jerusalem; but the Jews petitioned Tiberius, who ordered them to be removed, and there was much hatred between the Procurator and the Jews. The thirty years of silent bearing of the common lot of man were now nearly over; and six months ere the Messiah began to make Himself known, His messenger, John, the Desert Priest, began to prepare His way by preaching repentance in the spirit and power of the great Elijah, and then baptizing in the Jordan unto repentance. Such washing was the manner in which the Jews accepted their proselytes, as they called the strangers who embraced the Law. The great purpose of the Old Covenant was accomplished when John, having made his followers feel all the weight of their sins against the Commandments, pointed out Him whom he had already baptized, and said, "Behold the Lamb of God, which taketh away the sin of the world!" A few faithful Galileans followed and believed, and miracles began to testify that here was indeed the Christ, the Prophet like to Moses, giving bread to the hungry, eyes to the blind, feet to the lame. Decreasing as He increased, John offended Herod Antipas by "boldly rebuking vice." This Antipas had forsaken his own wife, the daughter of an Arabian king, and had taken in her stead, his niece Herodias, the wife of his brother Philip; and for bearing witness against this crime, John was thrown into prison, and afterwards beheaded, to gratify the wicked woman and her daughter, Salome. The Arab King avenged his daughter's wrongs by a war, in which Antipas met with a great defeat.

Meanwhile, the Pharisees and Sadducees, their heads full of the prophecies of greatness and deliverance, to which their minds gave a temporal, not a spiritual meaning, grew more and more enraged at every token that the lowly Nazarene was indeed the Saviour, the Hope of the whole world. Each token of perfection, each saying too pure for them, each undoubted miracle, only made them more furious, and for once they made common cause together. The Passover came. Herod Antipas came to Jerusalem to observe the feast, Pilate to keep the peace among the Jews; and Jerusalem saw her King coming, meek, and riding on an ass, and amid the Hosannas of the children, weeping at the vengeance that He foresaw for the favoured city where He had been despised and rejected, and where He was Himself about to become the true Passover, which should purchase everlasting Redemption.

The traitor sold Him to the Sanhedrim, or council, in which the last words of the prophecy through the Priesthood had declared that one man must die for the people; and a band of Roman soldiers was obtained from Pilate. Meanwhile, our blessed Lord instituted the new Passover, the Communion by which all the faithful should be enabled to partake of the great Sacrifice; then He went out to the garden, among the grey olives which still stand beside the brook Kedron, and there, after His night of Agony, He was betrayed by a kiss, and dragged before the High Priest, under an accusation of blasphemy; but as the Sanhedrim had not power of life and death, and such a charge would have mattered little to a Roman, a political offence was invented to bring before Pilate. The procurator perceived the innocence of the Holy One, but feared to befriend Him because of the raging multitude; and after vainly trying to shift the responsibility on Herod Antipas, he washed his hands, to show that it was no affair of his own, and gave the Victim up to the murderers. They chose the most shameful death of Roman slaves, that they might show their hatred and contempt, unwitting that each act and each word had been foretold and foreshown in their own Law and Prophets. For six hours He hung on His Cross, while the sun was dark, and awe crept on the most ignorant hearts. Then came the cry, "It is finished;" and the work was done; the sinless Sacrifice had died; the price of Adam's sin was paid; the veil of the Temple was rent in twain, to show that the way to the true Mercy-Seat was opened. The rich man buried Him--the women watched; and when the Sabbath was over, the Tomb was broken through, and the First-fruits of them that slept arose, wondrously visited His followers for forty days, gave them His last charges, and then ascended into Heaven, carrying manhood to the bosom of the Father. Satan was for ever conquered.

LESSON XXI.
THE FOUNDATION OF THE CHURCH.

"Ten men shall take hold, out of all language of all nations, even shall take hold of the skirt of him that is a Jew, saying, We will go with you, for we have heard that God is with you."--Zech. viii. 23.

By the coming of Him who had been so long promised, in His human Body, and the completion of His sacrifice, all the objects of the old ceremonial Law were fulfilled; the shadows passed away and substance took their place, so that the comers thereunto might be made perfect. Instead of being admitted to the covenant by circumcision, which was only a type of putting away the uncleanness of the flesh, the believers were washed from sin in the now fully revealed Name of the Holy Trinity, in the Fountain of Christ's Blood, open for all sin and uncleanness, and the penitent had a right to be constantly purified in the living cleansing streams of grace and pardon. The one great Passover had been offered, to redeem the chosen from the slavery of Satan, and the highway was opened for the ransomed to pass over with songs of joy, keeping the Resurrection Day instead of the Sabbath. Means had been given of their constantly partaking of that Passover, the Lamb slain from the foundation of the world; and thus tasting of the Eternal Sacrifice, in right of which they prayed to the Father, to whom they were united as members of His Son. The one great Day of Atonement was over, and the true High Priest had entered for ever into the Holy Place, opening a way where all might follow to the Mercy Seat, there offering His own Sacrifice, and presenting their prayers. And even in Heaven, He still was the Shepherd of the little flock, to whom it was His good pleasure to give the Kingdom; feeding them, appointing under shepherds, and guarding them gently from His Throne above. The sealed Book of type and prophecy was open and clear at His touch; and the Old Testament found full explanation and fulfilment in the New; and now it, remained to make known the good tidings, and gather in all nations, Jew and Gentile alike, to the Lord's Flock, the Church or House of the Lord, as it was called.

One hundred and twenty believers in their risen Lord awaited together the coming of the promised Comforter, who should abide with them for ever, to guide them into all truth, and to enable them to proclaim the accomplishment of all the promises. The eleven Apostles, who, as their name[2] implied, had been sent forth by their Lord, added to their number Matthias, in the place of the traitor Judas, laying hands on him in order to carry on the Gift that the Saviour had breathed upon them. Besides these, there were the seventy whom our Lord had sent out in pairs, and whose order was afterwards called the elders, presbyters, or priests.

They were all gathered in the upper room to keep the Feast of Weeks, in memory of the giving the Law, when He came upon them Who could enable that Law to be kept, bringing the Divine Presence, which is the pervading Life of the whole Body. His coming was marked by such open signs, as to draw the attention of all the pilgrim Jews, who had come from their distant homes to keep the feast. St. Peter expounded to them that the time of fulfilment was come, and that Jesus, crucified and risen, was their Salvation. 3,000 at once accepted the New Covenant, and were baptized; and thus, on the day of Pentecost, A.D. 33, the Church of Christ sprang into full life. Many of the converts sold their goods, and brought the price to the Apostles, all living on one common stock, and giving bounteous alms; but the new converts of Greek education, found their poor less well provided than the native Jews, and to supply them, seven deacons, or ministers, were set apart as the serving order of the ministry. Foremost of these was Stephen, who, about two years after the Ascension, bore the first witness through death to the doctrine which he taught, being stoned by the people in a sudden fit of fury, at his showing how the whole course of their history was but a preparation for Him whom they had crucified.

In the year 37, Pilate was recalled to Rome to answer the many charges against him. He was sentenced to banishment in Gaul, and there suffered so much from remorse, that he killed himself. At the time of his deposition, the Caesar, Tiberius, was dying, hated by all, and leaving his empire to his nephew, Caligula, who had

---

2 Apostle--one sent

been a youth of great promise; but he lost his senses in a fever, and did all sorts of strange wild things--made his horse a consul, tried to make him eat gilded oats, and once, at a wild beast show, turned the lions in on the spectators. Shortly before his illness, Herod Agrippa, the son of Herod the Great's murdered son, Aristobulus, while driving in a chariot with him, had said how glad everyone would be to see him reigning. The charioteer reported the speech, and Tiberius punished it by keeping Herod in prison, chained to a soldier; but to make up for his sufferings, Caligula no sooner became emperor than he set him free, gave him a crown, made him King of Trachonitis and Abilene, and presented him with a gold chain of the same weight as the fetters which he had worn in prison. This chain Herod hung up in the Temple, for he was a zealous Jew, although such a friend of heathen princes, and he seems to have been greatly puffed up with admiration of his own good management. His sister Herodias, envious of his crown, persuaded her husband, Herod Antipas, to go and sue for another at Rome; but all he gained by his journey was an inquiry into his conduct, which ended in his being exiled to Gaul, and his domain being given to Herod Agrippa. In A.D. 41, the miserable madman Caligula, was killed, but Herod Agrippa continued in high favour with the next emperor, the moody Claudius, and under him the Jews had again the power of giving sentence of death. They used it to persecute the disciples; and this led to many leaving Jerusalem, and carrying the knowledge of the faith to more distant parts. Saul, or Paul, a Benjamite, born at Tarsus, in Asia Minor, a place where the inhabitants were reckoned as Roman citizens, was learned in Greek philosophy, and deeply versed in the Jewish doctrines: he was a zealous Pharisee, and a vehement persecutor, till he was called by the Lord Himself from Heaven, and told that his special mission should be to the Gentiles; and about the same time, it was revealed to St. Peter in a vision, that the hedge of the ceremonial Law was taken down, and no distinction should henceforth be made between the nations, who had been all alike cleansed by the Blood of Redemption. The Roman soldier, Cornelius, was the first-fruits of a mighty harvest; and the Greeks and Romans in general, gave far more ready audience to the Apostles, than did the Jews.

The hatred of the Jews moved Herod Agrippa to put to death James the son of Zebedee, the first Apostle to drink of his Master's Cup; and he would likewise have slain Peter, had not the Angel delivered that Saint out of prison, in answer to the prayers of the Church. The pride of Herod had come to a height. He celebrated games at Caesarea in honour of the emperor, and in the midst came forth in a robe of cloth of silver, to give audience to an embassy from Tyre and Zidon. At his speech, the people shouted, "It is the voice of a god, not the voice of a man!" But while Herod listened and took the glory to himself, he felt a deadly stroke, which made him cry, "Your god is dying!" and in five days he was dead. His son, Agrippa, was too young to take the government, and a Roman procurator was appointed.

About this time the Apostles departed on their several missions. It is said that ere doing so, they agreed on the Creed or watchword of the Church; but it was not written down till more than three hundred years later, lest the heathen should learn it and blaspheme it. Wherever they went they ordained elders and deacons, and in most cities they left one to whom they had conveyed their own apostolic powers. These were not called Apostles, as that name was kept for those sent by our Lord in person, but sometimes angels or messengers, and usually bishops, or over-lookers of the shepherds. St. James, the cousin of our Lord, remained as Apostle of Jerusalem, while his brothers, Sts. Simon and Jude, went into Mesopotamia, St. Andrew to Arabia, his brother, St. Peter, to the dispersed Jews; St. John and St. Philip to Asia Minor, Sts. Thomas and Bartholomew to India, Sts. Matthew and Matthias to Ethiopia, but not till the former had written his Gospel, which several of the Apostles carried with them, and which has been found in possession of the most ancient Churches by them converted.

Little is known of their labours, as from this time the Acts of the Apostles chiefly dwell on the history of St. Paul; but it seems certain that everywhere they began by preaching to the dispersed Jews; and when these rejected the offer of Salvation, they turned to the heathen, by whom in general it was far more readily received. The Romans, heeding this world's greatness more than any spiritual matter, were not inclined to interfere with any one's religion, and only fancied the Church a sect of the Jews. They usually gave the Apostles their protection if the Jews raged against them; and their ships, their roads, and the universality of their dominion, made the spread of the Gospel much more easy, so that they were made to prepare the way of the Lord, even while seeking only their own grandeur. It was about this time that the Emperor Claudius came to Britain, and his generals won all the southern part of the island, rooting out the cruel worship of the Druids in their groves of oak, and circles of huge stones. He died in the year 55, and was succeeded by his step-son, Nero, a half-mad tyrant, who used to show off like a gladiator; racing in a chariot before all the Romans at the games, collecting them all to listen to his verses, and putting those to death who showed their weariness. He was so jealous and afraid of plots on his life, that he killed almost all his relations, even his mother, for fear they should conspire against him; and all the richer and nobler Romans lived in terror under him, though the common people liked him for being open-handed, and amusing them with the cruel gladiator shows.

LESSON XXII.
THE APOSTLE OF THE GENTILES.

"Of Benjamin he said, The beloved of the Lord shall dwell in safety by him, and the Lord shall cover him all the day long, and he shall dwell between His shoulders."--Deut. xxxiii. 12.

After Saul's marvellous call from Heaven, he spent three years in solitude in Arabia, ere entering on his work. Then returning to Damascus, he began to set forth the Gospel. The Jews were so angry at his change, that they stirred up the soldiers of the Arabian king, Aretas, and he only escaped them by being let down over the wall in a basket. Coming to Jerusalem, the gentle Levite, Barnabas, was the first to welcome him, and present him to the company of the Apostles; but he spent some years in retirement at his home at Tarsus, before Barnabas summoned him to come and aid in his preaching at Antioch. There the Word was heartily received, and the precious title of Christians was first bestowed upon the disciples; there, too, on the occasion of a famine in Judea, the first collection of alms for brethren at a distance was made.

At Antioch, a heavenly revelation signified that Paul and Barnabas were to be set apart for a special mission; and after prayer and consecration they set out on their mission, accompanied by the nephew of Barnabas, John, surnamed Mark. Barnabas had once had great possessions in the isle of Cyprus, and thither they first repaired, preaching in all the chief places; and then going into Asia Minor, where they showed such power from on high, that the rude people of Lycaonia fancied them gods in the likeness of men, and had well-nigh done sacrifice to them, though afterwards the spiteful Jews led the same men to draw Paul out of the city, stone him, and leave him for dead. In such perils, Mark's heart failed him, and he departed from them.

Returning to Antioch, they found the Church in doubt whether the Christians of Greek birth were bound to obey the rites of the Jewish Law. To decide this, Paul and Barnabas went to Jerusalem, after fourteen years' absence, taking with them a Greek, named Titus; and here was held the First General Council of the Church, a meeting of her Apostles and elders, in the full certainty that the Divine grace would inspire a right judgment, according to the promise that Christ would be with those who should meet in His Name. St. James presided, and St. Peter spoke; and it was decided that the whole object of these rites had been fulfilled, therefore that they were among the old things that had passed away; and that no such rule need be imposed on the Gentiles, save that given to Noah ere the parting of the nations. It was agreed that St. Paul should go especially to the Gentiles, and St. Peter and St. John to the scattered Jews, while St. James remained at Jerusalem. Two Jewish Christians, Silas and Barsabas, went back with the two Apostles, to notify the resolution to the Church at Antioch, and St. Peter shortly followed them; but there continued to be a great tendency among the Christians of Jewish blood to avoid their Gentile brethren, and St. Peter was drawn in to do the same, so that St. Paul, always more stedfast, was forced to rebuke him. Paul and Barnabas intended to set out on a second journey, and Barnabas wished again to take his now repentant nephew, but Paul would not trust him a second time; and after a dispute on the subject, Barnabas left him, and took Mark to Cyprus, where it is believed that the "Son of Consolation" was at length martyred.

Paul, taking Silas as his companion, went over the former ground in Asia Minor, and at Iconium ordained a disciple, named Timothy, whose father was a Greek, but whose Jewish mother and grandmother had faithfully bred him up in the knowledge of the Scriptures. A Greek physician, named Luke, likewise at this time joined him; and with these faithful companions, he obeyed a call sent him in a dream, and crossed over into Macedon, where he gained many souls at Philippi and Thessalonica, but the Jews stirred up such persecution, that he was forced to go southward into Greece. Athens was no longer a powerful city, but it served as a sort of college for all the youths of the Roman Empire who wished to be highly educated; and it was full of philosophers, who spent their time in the porticos and groves, arguing on questions of their own--such as whether, this life being all of which they were sure, it was best to live well or to live in pleasure. The Stoics were the philosophers who upheld the love of virtue and honour; the Epicureans said that it was of no use to vex themselves in this life, but that they might as well enjoy themselves while they had time. St. Paul was well learned in all these questions, and set forth to the Athenian students, in glorious words, that the truth was come for which they had so long yearned, and declared to them the Unknown God Whom they already worshipped in ignorance. Some few believed, but the others were too fond of their own empty reasonings, and Athens long continued the stronghold of heathenism. He had better success at Corinth, where he spent eighteen months, working at his trade as a tent-maker, and whence he wrote his two Epistles to his Thessalonian converts, about the time that St. Luke was writing his Gospel, it is thought by direct revelation, since neither he nor St. Paul had been with our Lord. The Jews hunted them away at last; after a short stay at Jerusalem, they went back to Asia Minor, and passed three years at Ephesus, whence were written the Epistle to the Galatians, against the Jewish practices, and the First to the Corinthians, on some disorders in their Church. Ephesus was the chief city in Asia Minor, and contained an image of the Greek goddess of the moon, Diana, placed in a temple so beautiful, that it was esteemed one of the seven wonders of the world, and thither came a great concourse of worshippers. There was a silversmith who made great gain by selling small models of her temple; and he, growing, afraid that his trade would be ruined if idols were deserted, stirred up the mechanics to such a frenzy of rage, that for two hours they shouted, "Great is Diana of the Ephesians!" and they would have torn Paul to pieces, had they not been with much difficulty appeased. He was obliged to leave the city, and go to Macedonia, whence he again wrote to the Corinthians, to console them in their repentance, and he also wrote to the Church at Rome, which he had never yet seen. After visiting the Greek Churches, a Divine summons called him back to keep the feast of Pentecost at Jerusalem, though well knowing that bonds and imprisonment awaited him there; and on his way he had a most touching meeting at Miletus, with the elders of Ephesus, who sorrowed grievously that they should see his face no more. His beloved Timothy was left with them as their bishop.

At Jerusalem, a terrible tumult arose against him for having, as the Jews fancied, brought Greeks into the Temple, and he was only rescued by the Roman garrison, who treated him well on finding that he was a citizen. Then the Jews laid a plot to murder him, and to prevent this he was sent to the seat of government at Caesarea, where he was brought before the procurator, Felix, and his wife, Drusilla, a daughter of Herod Agrippa. His words made Felix tremble, but the time-server put them aside, and neither released him nor sent him to Rome for judgment, but on going out of office left him in prison. Festus, the new procurator, could not understand his case, and asked the young Agrippa and his sister Bernice, to help him to find out under what accusation to send him to Rome. Again St. Paul's speech struck his hearers with awe, and Agrippa declared himself almost persuaded to be a Christian, but he loved too well the favour of the Jews and Romans, and his petty tetrarchy of Trachonitis, to become one of the despised sect. The noble captive would have been set free, but that he had sent his appeal to Rome, and therefore could only be tried there.

On his way, coasting along as sailors did before the compass was known, came his shipwreck at Malta, when the life of his shipmates was granted to him. The Emperor Nero was so much more disposed to amusement than business, that St. Paul's cause was not heard, but he lived in his own hired house, under charge of a soldier seeing the Christians freely, and writing three beautiful epistles, full of hope and encouragement, to his children at Ephesus, Colosse, and Philippi, also a friendly intercession for a runaway slave to Philemon, and letters of pastoral counsel to Timothy at Ephesus, and to Titus, who was Bishop of Crete. It is thought that the Epistle to the Hebrews, which shows how the Old Covenant points throughout to the New, must be also of this date; but we have no longer the inspired pen of St. Luke to tell of St. Paul's history, and it is not certain whether he were ever at liberty again, though some think that he was free for a short time, and went to Spain, Gaul, and even to Britain. St. Peter had likewise come to Rome. He had met with St. Mark, and taken him as his companion, and, as it is believed, assisted in composing his Gospel. St. Peter likewise wrote two epistles to the Jews dispersed abroad. But dark times were coming on the Church. St. James, who left an epistle, was, in his old age, slain by the Jews, who cast him from the top of the Temple, and then beat out his brains. The Emperor Nero had also broken out in sudden rage. In a fit of folly, he set Rome on fire to see how the flames would look, and then persuaded the citizens that it was done by the Christians. St. Peter, who is considered as the first Bishop of Rome, and St. Paul, were thrown into a dungeon; and about that time Paul wrote his last letter, to call to his side Timothy, and also the once weak Mark, now profitable to the ministry, even as the ever faithful Luke. The fight was over, the crown was ready, and on the same day, the two Apostles went to receive it; the Roman citizen by the sword, the Jewish fisherman by the cross, esteemed dishonour by the Romans, but over-much glory by the saint, who begged to suffer with his head downwards, so as not to presume on the very same death as that of his Master. Many Christians likewise perished; thrown to wild beasts, or smeared with grease, and then slowly burnt, to light the Romans at their horrible sports; but to them death was gain, and the Church was only strengthened. St. Timothy went back to his post at Ephesus, and St. Mark founded a Church at Alexandria, where, many years later, he was martyred by being dragged to death through the streets.

LESSON XXIII.
THE FALL OF JERUSALEM.

"The Lord hath accomplished His fury; He hath poured out His fierce anger, and hath kindled a fire in Zion, and it hath devoured the foundations thereof"--Lam. iv. 11.

In His triumphal entry into Jerusalem, oar Lord had wept for the woes of the city which would not own Him, and had foretold that the present generation should not pass away until His mournful words had been fulfilled. One alone of His Apostles was left to tarry until this coming for vengeance; the rest had all gone through the pains of martyrdom to their thrones in Heaven. St. Andrew died in Greece, bound on a cross shaped like the letter X, and preaching to the last. His friend, St. Philip, had likewise received the glory of the Cross in Asia; and the last of the Bethsaida band, St. Bartholomew, was tied to a tree and flayed alive, in Armenia. St. Matthew and St. Matthias died in Ethiopia or Abyssinia, leaving a Church which is still in existence; and St. Thomas was slain by the Brahmins in India, where the Christians of St. Thomas ever after kept up their faith among the heathen around. St. Jude died in Mesopotamia, after writing an epistle to his flock; and his brother, St. Simon Zelotes, also went by the same path to his rest; but their deaths only strengthened the Church, and their successors carried out the same work.

The judgments of God were darkening around Jerusalem. A procurator named Florus was more cruel and insulting than usual, and a tumult broke out against him. Agrippa tried to appease it, but the Jews pelted him with stones, and drove him out of Jerusalem; they afterwards burnt down his palace, and rose in rebellion all over Judea, imagining that the prophesied time of deliverance was come, and that the warlike Messiah of their imagination was at hand. Nero was much enraged at the tidings, and sent an army, under a plain blunt general, named Vespasian, to punish the revolt. This army subdued Galilee and Samaria, and was already surrounding Jerusalem, when Vespasian heard that there had been a great rebellion at home, and that Nero had been killed. He therefore turned back from the siege, to wait and see what would happen, having thus given the token promised by our Lord, of the time when the desolation of Jerusalem should be at hand, when the faithful were to flee. Accordingly, in this pause, all the Christians, marking well the signs of coming wrath, took refuge in the hills while the way was still open. Armies were seen fighting in the clouds; a voice was heard in the Holy of Holies saying, "Let us depart hence!" the heavily-barred gate of the Temple flew open of its own accord; and a man wandered up and down the streets day and night, crying, "Woe to Jerusalem! Woe! woe!" The Jews were hardened against all warning; they had no lawful head, but there were three parties under different chiefs, who equally hated the Romans and one another. They fought in the streets, so that the city was full of blood; and fires consumed a great quantity of the food laid up against the siege; yet still the blind Jews came pressing into it in multitudes, to keep the now unmeaning Feast of the Passover, even at the time when Vespasian's son, Titus, was leading his forces to the siege.

It was the year 70, thirty-seven years since that true Passover, when the Jews had slain the true Lamb, and had cried, "His Blood be on us and our children!" What a Passover was that, when one raging multitude pursued another into the Temple, and stained the courts with the blood of numbers! Meanwhile, Titus came up to the valleys around the crowned hill, and shut the city in on every side, digging a trench, and guarding it closely, that no food might be carried in, and hunger might waste away the strength of those within. Then began the utmost fulfilment of the curses laid up in the Law for the miserable race. The chiefs and their parties tore each other to pieces whenever they were not fighting with the enemy; blood flowed everywhere, and robbers rushed through the streets, snatching away every fragment of food from the weak. The famine was so deadly, that the miserable creatures preyed on the carcases of the dead; nay, "the tender and delicate woman" was found who, in the straits of hunger, killed her own babe, roasted, and fed upon him. So many corpses were thrown over the walls, that the narrow valleys were choked, and Titus, in horror, cried out that the Jews, not himself, must be accountable for this destruction.

For the sake of the Christian fugitives in the mountains, these dreadful days were shortened, and were not in the winter; and in August Titus's soldiers were enabled to make an entrance into the Temple. For the sake of its glorious beauty, he bade that the building should be spared; but it was under the sentence of our Lord, and his command was in vain. A soldier threw a torch through a golden window, and the flames spread fast while the fight raged; the space round the Altar was heaped with corpses, and streams of blood flowed like rivers. Ere the flames reached the Sanctuary, Titus went into it, and was so much struck with its beauty, that he did his utmost to save it, but all in vain; and the whole was burnt, with 6,000 poor creatures, whom a false prophet had led to the Temple, promising that a wonder should there be worked for their deliverance. The city still held out for twenty more days of untold misery; but at last the Romans broke in amid flames quenched in blood, and slaughter raged everywhere. Yet it was a still sadder sight to find the upper rooms of the houses filled with corpses of women and children, dead of hunger; and indeed, no less than a million of persons had perished in the siege, while there were 97,000 miserable captives, 12,000 of whom died at once from hunger. As Titus looked at the walls and towers, he cried out that God Himself must have been against the Jews, since he himself could never have driven them from such fortresses. He commanded the whole, especially the Temple, to be leveled with the ground, no two stones left standing, and the foundation to be sown with salt; and he carried off the Candlestick, Shewbread Table, and other sacred ornaments, to be displayed in his triumph. An arch was set up at Rome in honour of his victory, with the likeness of these treasures sculptured on it. It is still standing, and the figures there carved are the chief means we have of knowing what these holy ornaments were really like. He gave the Jews, some to work in the Egyptian mines, some to fight with wild beasts to amuse the Romans, and many more to be sold as slaves. Other people thus dispersed had become fused into other nations; but it was not so with the Jews. "Slay them not, lest my people forget it, but scatter them abroad among the heathen," had been the prophecy of the Psalmist; and thus it has remained even to the present day. The piteous words of Moses have been literally fulfilled, and among the nations they have found no ease, neither has the sole of their foot found any rest; but the trembling heart, and failing eye, and sorrowful mind, have always been theirs. They have ever been loathed and persecuted by the nations where their lot has been cast, ever craving for their lost home, ever hoping for the Messiah of their own fancy. Still they keep their Sabbath on the seventh day; still they follow the rules of clean and unclean; and on each Friday, such as still live at Jerusalem sit with their faces to the wall, and lift up their voice in mournful wailing for their desolation. Their goodly land lies waste, the sky above like brass, the earth beneath like iron; her fruitfulness is over, and from end to end she is a country of ruins, a sign to all nations! Some there are who read in the prophecies hopes for the Jews, that they may yet return and learn Who is the Saviour. Others doubt whether this means that they will ever be restored as a nation; and still the Jews stand as a witness that God keeps His word in wrath as well as in mercy--a warning that the children of the free New Covenant must fear while they are thankful.

LESSON XXIV.
THE PRIMITIVE CHURCH.

"I will also take of the highest branch of the high cedar, and will
set it; I will crop off from the top of his young twigs a tender
one, and will plant it on a high mountain and eminent."--Ezekiel,
xvii. 22.

In the year 70, the same in which Jerusalem was destroyed, happened the first great eruption of the volcano, Mount Vesuvius, in which was killed Drusilla, the wife of Felix. Her brother, Agrippa, ruled by favour of the Romans for many years in the little domain of Chalcis. Titus was emperor after his father. He was a very kind-hearted man, and used to say he had lost a day whenever he had spent one without doing a good action; but he was soon poisoned by his wicked brother, Domitian, who succeeded to his throne in 81. Domitian was a savage tyrant, cruel to all, because he was afraid of all. He hated the Jews; and hearing that some persons of royal blood still existed among them, he caused search to be made for them, and two sons of St. Jude were brought before him. They owned that they came of the line of David; but they told him they were poor simple men, and showed him their hands hardened with toil; and he thought they could do him so little harm, that he let them go. He also laid hands on the aged St. John, and caused him to be put into a caldron of boiling oil; but the martyr in will, though not in deed, felt no hurt, and was thereupon banished to the little Greek Isle of Patmos. Here was vouchsafed to him a wonderful vision, answering to those of Daniel, his likeness among the prophets. He saw the true heavenly courts, such as Moses had shadowed in the Tabernacle, and which Ezekiel had described so minutely; he saw the same fourfold Cherubim, and listened to the same threefold chant of praise, as

Isaiah had heard; he saw the seven lamps of fire, and the rainbow of mercy round about the Throne; and in the midst, in the eternal glory of His priestly robes, he beheld Him on Whose bosom be had lain, and Who had called him beloved. From His lips he wrote messages of counsel and warning to the angels, or Bishops, of the Seven Churches of Asia Minor; and then came a succession of wonderful visions, each opening with the Church in Heaven and in earth constantly glorifying Him that sitteth on the Throne, and the Lamb, for ever and ever; but going on to show the crimes in the world beneath, and the judgments one after another poured out by the Angels; the true remnant of the Church persecuted; and the world partly curbed by, partly corrupting, the visible Church; then the destruction of the wicked world, under the type of Babylon; the last judgment; the eternal punishment of the sinful; the final union of Christ and His Church; and the eternal blessedness of the faithful in the heavenly Jerusalem, with the Tree of Life restored.

When Domitian was killed, in 86, St. John went back to Ephesus, and there wrote his Gospel, to fill up what had been left out by the other three Evangelists, and especially dwelling on the discourses of the Lord of Life and Love. That same sweet sound of love rings through his three Epistles; and yet that heart-whole love of his Master made him severe, for he started away from a house he had entered, and would not go near it while it contained a former believer who had blasphemed Christ. A young man whom he had once converted fell into evil courses in his absence, and even became a tobber. St. John, like the Good Shepherd, himself went out into the wilderness to find him, and was taken by the thieves When his convert saw him, he would have fled in shame and terror; but St. John held out his arms, called him back, and rested not till he had won him to repentance. So gentle was he to all living things, that he was seen nursing a partridge in his hands, and when he became too old to preach to the people, he used to hold out his hands in blessing, and say, "Little children, love one another." He died in the year 100, just before the first great storm which was to try the Church.

The Emperor Trajan had found out that the iron of the Roman temper had become mixed with miry clay, and that the men of his time were very different from their fathers, and much less brave and public spirited. He fancied this was the fault of new ways, and that Christianity was one of these. There were Christians everywhere, in every town of every province, nobles, soldiers, women, slaves, rich and poor; all feeling themselves members of one body, all with the same faith, the same prayers and Sacraments. All day they did their daily tasks, only refusing to show any honour to idols, such as pouring out wine to the gods before partaking of food, or paying adoration to the figures of the Caesars, which were carried with the eagle standards of the army; and so close was the brotherhood between them, that the heathen used to say, "See how these Christians love one another!" At night they endeavoured to meet in some secret chamber, or underground cave. At Rome, the usual place was the Catacombs, great vaults, whence the soft stone for building the city had been dug out, and where the quarry-men alone knew the way through the long winding passages. Here, in the very early morning of Lord's Day, the Christians made every effort to assemble, for they were sure of meeting their Bishop, and of receiving the Holy Communion to strengthen them for the trials of the week. The Christian men and women stood on opposite sides; a little further off were the learners, as yet unbaptized, who might only hear the prayers and instructions; and beyond them was any person who had been forbidden to receive the Holy Eucharist on account of some sin, and who was waiting to be taken back again. The heathen knew nothing of what happened in these meetings, and fancied that a great deal that was shocking was done there; and Trajan ordered that Christians should be put to the torture, if they would not confess what were their ceremonies. Very few would betray anything, and what they said, the heathen could not understand; but the emperor imagining that these rites would destroy the old Roman spirit, forbade them, and persecuted the Christians, because they obeyed God rather than man. The Bishop of Antioch was an old man named Ignatius, who is believed to have been the little child whom our blessed Lord had set in the midst of His disciples as an example of lowliness. He had been St. John's pupil, and always walked in his steps, and he is the first Father of the Church, that is, the first of the great wise men in those early days, whose writings have come down to us. As Trajan was going through Antioch, he saw this holy man, and sentenced him to be carried to Rome, there to be thrown to the lions for the amusement of the bloody-minded Romans. As has been said, from early days the favourite sport of this nation had been to sit round on galleries, built up within a round building called an amphitheatre, to watch the gladiators fight with each other, or with savage beasts. Many of these buildings are still to be found ruined in different parts of the empire, and one in especial at Rome, named the Coliseum, where it is most likely that the death of St. Ignatius took place, when, as he said, he was the wheat of Christ, ground by the teeth of the lions. He is reckoned as one of the Fathers of the Church. His great friend was Polycarp, Bishop or Angel of Smyrna, the same, as it is believed, to whom St. John had written in the Revelation, "Be thou faithful unto death, and I will give thee a crown of life."

The Emperor Antoninus began a persecution, which was carried on by his successor, Marcus Aurelius; and in 167, St. Polycarp, who was a very aged man, and had ruled the Church of Smyrna towards seventy years, was led before the tribunal. The governor had pity on his grey hairs, and entreated him to save his life by swearing by the fortunes of Caesar, and denying Christ. "Eighty and six years have I served Him, and He has never done me a wrong; how could I then blaspheme my King, who hath saved me?" said Polycarp; and all the threats of the governor did but make him glad to be so near glorifying God by his death. He was taken out to be burnt alive, and as he stood bound to the stake, he cried aloud, "Lord God Almighty, Father of the blessed and well-beloved Son, Jesus Christ, by Whom we have received the grace to know Thee; God of angels and of powers, God of all creatures, and of the just who live in Thy Presence, I thank Thee that Thou hast brought me to this day and hour, when I may take part in the number of the martyrs in the Cup of Thy Christ, to rise to the eternal life of soul and body in the incorruption of the Holy Spirit. May I be received into Thy Presence with them as an acceptable offering, as Thou hast prepared and foretold, Thou the true God Who canst not lie. Therefore I praise Thee, I bless Thee, I glorify Thee by the eternal and heavenly High Priest, Jesus Christ, Thy beloved Son, to Whom, with Thee and the Holy Ghost, be glory now and for ever and ever. Amen." The fire was kindled, and to the wonder of the beholders, it rose into a bright vault of flame, like a glory around the martyr, without touching him; whereupon the governor became impatient, and caused him to be slain with the sword. He was the last of the companions of the Apostles; but there was no lessening of the grace bestowed on the Church. Even when Aurelius's army was suffering from a terrible drought in an expedition to Germany, a legion who were nearly all Christians, prayed aloud for rain, a shower descended in floods of refreshment. The emperor said that his god Jupiter sent it, and caused his triumphal arch to be carved with figures of soldiers, some praying, others catching rain in their helmets and shields; but the band was ever afterwards called the Thundering Legion. This unbelieving emperor persecuted frightfully, and great numbers suffered at Vienne in Gaul, many dying of the damp of their prison, and many more tortured to death. Of these was the Bishop Pothinus of Lyons, ninety years old, who died of the torments; and those who lived through them were thrown to wild beasts, till the animals were so glutted as to turn from the prey; but no pain was so great as not to be counted joy by the Christians; and the more they were slain, the more persons were convinced that the hope must be precious for which they endured so much; and the more the Word of God prevailed. Aurelius Caesar died in 180, and the Church was left at rest for a little while,

LESSON XXV.
THE PERSECUTIONS.

"Blessed are they which are persecuted for righteousness' sake, for theirs is the Kingdom of heaven."--Matt v. 10

It had been revealed to St. John that the Church should have tribulation for ten days; and accordingly, in her first three hundred years, ten emperors tried to put out her light. Nero, Domitian, Trajan, Antoninus, and Aurelius, have been mentioned; and the next persecutor was Severus, an emperor who went to Britain, firmly established the Roman power over England, and built the great wall to keep the Scots from injuring the northern settlers.

In his time died the glorious band of martyrs of Carthage--five young converts, two men, named Satur and Saturninus, a noble young married lady, called Perpetua, who had a young infant, and two slaves, Revocatus and Felicitas, the last of whom gave birth to a daughter in the prison. But not even love to their babes could lead these faithful women to dissemble their belief; Perpetua left her child with her family; Felicitas gave hers to a Christian woman to bring up; and the lady and the slave went out singing, hand in hand, to the amphitheatre, where they were to be torn by beasts. A wild cow was let loose on them, and threw down the two women; but Perpetua at once sat up again, covered herself with her garments, and helped up Felicitas, but as if in a dream, for she did not remember that the cow had been loosed on her. Satur had an especial horror of a bear, which was intended to be the means of his death, and a good soldier named Pudens put meat in front of the den, that the beast might not come out. A leopard then flew at him, and tore him; Satur asked the soldier for his ring, dipped it in his own blood, and gave it back as a memorial, just before he died under the teeth and claws of the animal. The others were all killed by soldiers in the middle of the amphitheatre, Perpetua guiding the sword to her own throat.

The persecution of the Emperor Decius was one of the worst of all, for the heathen grew more ingenious by practice in inventing horrible deaths.

Under the Emperor Valerian died St. Lawrence, a young deacon at Rome, whom the judge commanded to produce the treasures of the Church. He called together all the aged widows and poor cripples who were maintained by the alms of the faithful, "These," he said, "are the treasures of the Church." In the rage of the persecutors, he was roasted to death on bars of iron over a fire. St. Cyprian, the great Bishop of Carthage, was beheaded; and one hundred and fifty martyrs at Utica were thrown alive into a pit of quick-lime. At Antioch one man failed; Sapricius, a priest, was being led out to die, when a Christian named Nicephorus, with whom he had a quarrel, came to beg his forgiveness ere his death. Sapricius would not pardon, and Nicephorus went on humbly entreating, amid the mockery of the guards, until the spot of execution was reached, and the prisoner was bidden to kneel down to have his bead cut off. Then it appeared that he who had not the heart to forgive, had not the heart to die; Sapricius's courage failed him, and he promised to sacrifice to the idols; and Nicephorus was put to death, receiving the crown of martyrdom in his stead. The persecuting Valerian himself came to a miserable end, for he was made prisoner in a battle, in 258, with the Persians, and their king for many years forced the unhappy captive to bow down on his hands and knees so as to be a step by which to climb on his elephant, and when he died, his skin was taken off, dyed red, and hung up in a temple. After his captivity, the Church enjoyed greater tranquillity; many more persons ventured to avow themselves Christians, and their worship was carried on without so much concealment as formerly.

But the troublous times were not yet over, and the rage of the prince of this world moved the Romans to make a yet more violent effort than any before to put down the kingdom of the Prince of Peace. Two emperors began to reign together, named Diocletian and Maximian, dividing the whole empire between them into two parts, the East and the West. After a few years' rule, they both of them fell savagely upon the Christians. In Switzerland, a whole division of the army, called the Theban Legion, 6,000 in number, with the leader, St. Maurice, all were cut to pieces together rather than deny their faith. In Egypt the Christians were mangled with potsherds, and every torture was invented that could shake their constancy. Each tribunal was provided with a little altar to some idol, and if the Christians would but scatter a few grains of incense upon it, they were free; but this was a denying of their Lord, and the few who yielded in the fear of them who could kill the body, grieved all their lives afterwards for the act, and were not restored to their place in the Church until after long years of penance, or until they had atoned for their fall by witnessing a good confession. Sometimes they were not allowed to receive the Holy Communion again till they were on their dying beds. But these were the exceptions; in general, God's strength was made perfect in weakness, and not only grown men, but timid women, tender maidens, and little children, would bear the utmost torture with glad faith, and trust that it was working for them an exceeding 'weight of glory. St. Margaret of Antioch was but fifteen years old, St. Agnes of Rome only twelve, and at Merida, in Spain, Eulalia, at the same age, went out in search of martyrdom, insulting the idols, until she was seized and put to death full of joy; but in general, the Christians were advised not needlessly to run into the way of danger.

This was the first persecution that reached to Britain, There a kind-hearted Roman soldier, named Alban, received into his house a priest who was fleeing from his persecutors, and while he was there, learnt from him the true faith. When search was made for his guest, Alban threw on the dress of the priest, and was taken in his stead; he was carried to the tribunal, and there declaring himself a Christian, was sentenced to be beheaded. The city where he suffered is called after him St. Alban's, and a beautiful church was afterwards built in memory of him. These cruelties did not long continue in Britain, for the governor, Constantius, had married a Christian British lady, named Helena; and as soon as he ventured to interfere, he stopped the persecution.

Diocletian became tired of reigning, and persuaded his comrade, Maximian, to resign their thrones to Constantius and to another prince named Galerius. Constantius forbade all persecution in the West, but Galerius and his son-in-law, Maximin, were very violent in the East; and Maximin is counted as the last of the ten persecuting emperors. Under him a great many Christians were blinded, scarred with hot iron, or had their fingers and ears cut off. Some were sent to the deserts to keep the emperor's cattle; some were driven in chains to work in the mines. These, who suffered bravely everything except death, were called confessors instead of martyrs. Galerius died in great misery in 311, of the same horrible disease as the persecutor of the Jews, Antiochus Epiphanes; and like him, he at last owned too late the God whom he had rejected, and sent entreaties that prayers might be offered up for him.

LESSON XXVI.
THE CONVERSION OF CONSTANTINE.

"The kingdoms of this world are become the kingdoms of our Lord, and of his Christ."--Rev. xi, 15.

The son of Constantius, Constantine, became emperor in 307. He was in doubt between the two religions; he saw that Christianity made people good, and yet he could not quite leave off believing in the heathen gods, and was afraid of neglecting them. As he was passing the Alps to put down a very powerful and cruel tyrant, who had made himself master of Italy, he and all his army suddenly beheld in the sky, at mid-day, a bright light shaped like a cross, and in glorious letters round it, the Latin words meaning, "In this sign thou shalt conquer." This wonderful sight made Constantine believe that the cross was truly the sign of salvation, and that He who could show such marvels in heaven, must be the true God. He set the cross on his standards instead of the Roman Eagle; and such great victories were vouchsafed to him, that by-and-by he became the only emperor, and put down all his enemies.

He was not as yet baptized, but he was a hearty believer, and he tried in everything to make the Church prosperous, and to govern by Christian rules. From that time all the chief powers of this world have professed to be Christian, and the Church has been owned as the great means appointed by God of leading His people to Himself. Constantine's mother, Helena, though in her eightieth year, set off to the ruins of Jerusalem to try to trace out the places hallowed by our Saviour's suffering. All was waste and desolate, and no one lived there save a few very poor Jews and Christians in wretched huts. The latter had never lost the memory of the places where the holy events of the Passion had taken place; and the empress set men to dig among the ruins on Mount Calvary, till she found the Holy Sepulchre, and not far from it, three crosses, and the nails belonging to them. She built a most beautiful church, so large as to cover the whole of Golgotha. The sepulchre itself formed a round vault within, crusted over with marble, and lighted with silver lamps. The true Cross was kept in the church, but the nails she brought home as the most precious gift she could carry to her son. She also beautified and made into a church the cave of the Nativity at Bethlehem, and she built another church on Mount Carmel in memory of Elijah. From her time it became a habit with devout persons to go on pilgrimage, to worship at the holy tomb and in the Cave of Bethlehem; and a new city of Jerusalem rose upon the ruins of the old one, though, of course, without a Temple. Rome was so fall of the tokens of heathenism, that Constantine feared that his court would never be heartily Christian till he took it to a fresh place; so he resolved to build a new capital city for his empire. This was the city called after him, Constantinople, the city of Constantine, on the banks of the Bosphorus, just where Europe and Asia nearly meet. The chief building there was a most beautiful church, dedicated to the holy Wisdom of God, and named in Greek St. Sophia. The Bishop there was termed the Patriarch of Constantinople. There were already five patriarchs, or great Father Bishops, to rule over divisions of the Church at Jerusalem, Antioch, Alexandria, and Rome. The Patriarch of Rome was called the Pope. All was peace and prosperity, and the Christians were so much at their ease, that some finding that they missed the life of hardness, which they used to think a great blessing, went apart from men, and lived in caves, quite alone, working hard for very scanty food, and praying constantly. These were called hermits. But there soon were troubles enough rising up within the Church herself, for a man named Arius, a priest at Alexandria, began wickedly to teach that our blessed Lord was not from all eternity, nor equal with God the Father. So many persons were led away by this blasphemous heresy, (which means a denial of the faith,) that it was resolved to call together as many Bishops as possible from the entire Church, to hold a General Council, and declare the truth.

The emperor came to Nicea, in Asia Minor, in the year 325, and there met three hundred and eighteen bishops from every quarter, many of them still scarred by the injuries they had received in the persecutions, and many learned priests and deacons, among whom the most noted was Athanasius of Alexandria. Together, they drew up the two first paragraphs of the confession of faith called the Nicene Creed, and three hundred of the bishops set their sign and seal to it, declaring it was the truth, as they had been charged to hold and teach it fast, the Catholic or universal faith. Arius was put out of the Communion of the Church, and all his followers with him. But they were many and powerful; and in after times, Constantine became confused by their representations. He ought to have seen that he who was not even baptized ought not to interfere in Church matters; but instead of this, he wrote to Athanasius, who had just been made Patriarch of Alexandria, telling him to preserve peace by receiving Arius back to Communion. Athanasius refused to do what would have tainted the whole Church, so Constantine banished him, and allowed Arius to come to Constantinople. There the heretic deceived him so completely, that he desired that he should be received back on the next Sunday. While the faithful clergy wept and prayed that the Church might be kept clear from the man who denied honour to the Lord who bought him, Arius went through the streets in triumph; but in the midst he was smitten by a sudden disease, and died in a few moments. This judgment convinced Constantine, and he held to the Catholic faith for the rest of his life. He was baptized, and received his first Communion on his death-bed, when sixty-four years old, and is remembered as the first believing monarch.

After him came worse times, for his son, Constantius, was an Arian, and persecuted the Catholics, though not to the death. St. Athanasius was driven to hide among the hermits in Egypt, and a great part of the Eastern Church fell into the heresy. Then, in 361, reigned his cousin, Julian the Apostate, who, from being a Christian, had turned back to be a heathen, and wanted to have the old gods worshipped. In hopes to show that the prophecies were untrue, he tried to build up the Temple at Jerusalem, and the foundations were being dug out, when balls of fire came bursting out of the ground; and thus God's will and power were made known, so that the workmen were forced to leave off. Julian was very severe towards the Catholics, and it seemed as though the old times of persecution were coming back; but after three years he was killed in battle, and the next emperor brought back better days. St. Athanasius finished this life in peace, and left behind him writings, whence was taken the glorious Creed that bears his name.

LESSON XXVII.
THEODOSIUS.

"The sons also of them that afflicted thee shall come bending unto thee; and all they that despised thee shall bow themselves down at the soles of thy feet; and they shall call thee the City of the Lord, the Zion of the Holy One of Israel"--Isa. lx. 14.

The empire was again divided into two parts, which were held by two brothers. Valentinian, who had the eastern half, was an Arian; and Valens, who ruled at Rome, was a Catholic. Though all the empire was Christian, still there were sad disputes; for many had fallen away into the heresy, and there was so great a love of arguing in a light careless manner in market-places, baths, feasts, and places of common resort, that it was a great distress to the truly devout to hear the most sacred mysteries discoursed of so freely.

The great and learned Saint Jerome hid himself away from this strife of tongues, to pray and study in a hermitage at Bethlehem. By the desire of the Pope, he did the same work for the New Testament as Simon the Great had done for the Old Testament: he examined into the history of all the writings that professed to have come down from the Apostles' time, and proved clearly which had been really written under the inspiration of God, and had been always held as Holy Scriptures by the Church. Then he translated the whole Bible into Latin, and wrote an account of each book, setting apart those old writings of the Jews that are called the Apocrypha, and are read as wise instruction, though they be not certainly known to be the Word of God, in the same manner as the Holy Scriptures themselves. St. Jerome is counted as one of the chief Fathers or doctors of the Church.

Another great Father of the Church who lived at the same time, was Ambrose.

He was the Governor of the Italian city of Milan; and though a devout believer, was still unbaptized, when the clergy and the people, as was then the custom, met to choose their Bishop. A little child in the crowd cried out, "Ambrose Bishop!" and everyone took up the cry with one voice, and thought that the choice was inspired by the Holy Spirit. Ambrose was very unwilling to accept the office, but at last he submitted; he was baptized, and a week after was first confirmed, and then ordained priest, and consecrated Bishop. He was one of the most kind and gentle of men, but he had a hard struggle to fight for the truth. The Emperor, Valens, died, and his widow, Justina, who ruled for her little son, was an Arian. She wanted a church for her friends, but Ambrose would allow none to be profaned by a service where the blessed Saviour would be robbed of His honour. He knew his duty as a subject too well to lift a hand against the empress, but he filled up the Church with his faithful flock, and there they prayed, and sang psalms and hymns without ceasing; and when Justina sent soldiers to turn them out, they were so firm, that only one woman ran away. Instead of offering violence, the soldiers joined and prayed with them, and thus Justina was obliged to give up her attempt in despair.

A very good emperor named Theodosius had begun to reign in the east, and assisted Justina's young son to govern the west. He was a thorough Catholic, and loved the Church with all his heart. Some fresh heretics had risen up, who taught falsehoods respecting the Third Person of the most Holy Trinity; and to put them down, Theodosius called another General Council to meet at Constantinople, and there the following addition was made to the Nicene Creed: "I believe in the Holy Ghost, the Lord and Giver of Life, Who proceedeth from the Father, Who with the Father and the Son together is worshipped and glorified--" and so on to the end. Thus each heresy was made the occasion of giving the faithful a beautiful watch-word.

Though good and religious, Theodosius was hasty and violent by nature, and could be very severe. He had laid a tax on the people of Antioch, which made them so angry that they rose up in a rage, knocked down the statues of the emperor and his wife which adorned their public places, and dragged them about the streets; but as soon as they came to their senses, they were dreadfully alarmed, knowing that this was an act of high treason. They, therefore, sent off messengers to entreat the emperor's pardon; and in the meantime they met constantly in the churches, fasting and praying that his wrath might be turned away. John, called Chrysostom, or Golden Mouth, from his beautiful language, was a Deacon of Antioch, and he preached to the people every day during this time of suspense, telling them of the sins that had moved God to give them up to their foolish passion, so as to put them in fear, and lead them to repentance. One of these sins was vanity, and love of finery and pleasure; and another was their irreverent behaviour at church. They did repent heartily; and before the emperor's men had time to do more than begin to try some of the ringleaders, there came other messengers at full speed, bringing his promise of pardon.

Love of the sight of chariot races was a great snare to the Greeks. At Thessalonica, one of the favourite drivers behaved ill, and was imprisoned by the governor, upon which the people flew out in a fury, and actually stoned the magistrate to death. In his passion at their crime, Theodosius sent off soldiers with orders to put them all to death; and when he grew cool, and despatched orders to stop the execution of his terrible command, they came too late--the city was in flames, and the unhappy people, innocent and guilty alike, all lay slain in the streets. Theodosius was at Milan; and St. Ambrose thought it right to shut him out from the congregation while he was so deeply stained with blood. The emperor came to the church door and begged to be admitted; but the Bishop met him sternly, and turned him back. Theodosius pleaded that David had sinned, and had been forgiven. "If you have been like him in sin, be like him in repentance!" said the Bishop; and this great prince turned humbly away, and went weeping home. Easter was the regular time for reconciling penitents; and at Christmas the emperor stayed praying and weeping in his palace till a courtier advised him to try whether the Bishop would relent. He came to the church, but Ambrose told him that he could not transgress the laws in his behalf. At last, however, when he saw the emperor so truly contrite and broken-hearted, he gave him leave to come in again; and there the first thing Theodosius did was to fall down on his face, weeping bitterly, and crying out in David's words, "My soul cleaveth to the dust, quicken Thou me according to Thy word!" He lay thus humbly through all the service; nor did he once wear his crown and purple robes till after several months of patient penitence he was admitted to the blessed Feast of Pardon. He made a decree that no sentence of death should be executed till thirty days after it was spoken, so that no more deeds of hasty passion might be done.

One great happiness of St. Ambrose's life was the conversion of Augustine. This youth was the son of a good and holy mother, St. Monica; but he had not been baptized, and he grew up wise in his own conceit, and loving idle follies and vicious pleasures. For many years he was led astray by heretical and heathenish fancies; but his faithful mother prayed for him all the time, and at last had the joy of seeing him repent with all his heart. He was baptized at Milan; and it is said that the glorious hymn *Te Deum* was written by St. Ambrose, and first sung at his baptism. The hymn, "Veni Creator," which is sung in the Ordination Service, is also said to be by St. Ambrose. Monica and her son spent a short and peaceful space together; and then she died in great thankfulness that he had been given to her prayers. He spent many years as Bishop of Hippo, in Africa, and wrote numerous books, which have come down to our day. One is called the City of God, so as exactly to fulfil the prophecy of Isaiah, that the Church should so be called by the descendants of those who had afflicted her. St. Martin, a soldier, who once gave half his cloak to a beggar, and afterwards became a Bishop, completed the conversion of Gaul at this time, and was buried at Tours. St. Chrysostom likewise left many sermons and comments on the Holy Scripture. He was made Patriarch of Constantinople, but he suffered many things there, for the wife of the Emperor Arcadius, son of the good Theodosius, hated him for rebuking her love of finery, and her passion for racing shows, and persuaded her husband to send him into exile in his old age, to a climate so cold, that he died in consequence. The beautiful collect called by his name comes from the Liturgy which was used in his time in his Church at Constantinople; but it is not certain whether he actually was the author thereof.

LESSON XXVIII.
THE TEUTON NATIONS.

"The Kingdom of Heaven is like unto a leaven, which a woman took and hid in three measures of meal till the whole was leavened."--Matt. xiii. 33.

The miry clay which Nebuchadnezzar saw mixed with the iron of Rome, had by the end of the fourth century nearly overcome the strong metal, and the time had come when the great horn of the devouring beast was to be broken off, and give place to ten others. The Romans for the last two hundred years had been growing more and more selfish and easy in their habits; and instead of fighting their own battles, had called in strangers to fight for them, till these strangers became too strong for them. The nations to whom these hired soldiers belonged, were the forefathers of most of the present people of Europe. They were called Teutons altogether, and lived in the northern parts of Europe. They were tall, fair, large people, very brave and spirited, with much honour and truth, though apt to be savage and violent; and they showed more respect to their women than any of the heathens did. They had many gods, of whom Odin, who left his name to the fourth day of the week, was the chief and father. Freya, the Earth, was his wife, and Thor was Thunder. There was a story of Baldur, a good and perfect one, who died by the craft of Lok the Destroyer, and yet still lived. This seemed like a copy of the truth; and so did the story of Lok himself, the power of evil, with a serpent on his brow, who lay chained, and yet could walk forth over the earth, and whose pale daughter, Hela, was the gaoler of the unworthy dead. They thought the brave who died in battle had the happiest lot their rude fancies could devise; they lived in the Hall of Odin, hunting all day, feasting all night, and drinking mead from the skulls of their conquered enemies.

The tribe called Goths, who lived near the Romans, and who took their pay and entered their armies, learnt the Christian faith readily; but unfortunately, it was through Arians that they received it, and those farther off continued to worship Odin. The great Theodosius left his empire parted between his two sons, Arcadius in the east, Honorius in the west. Both were young, weak, and foolish. They quarrelled with the great Gothic chief, Alaric, who began to overrun their dominions, and at last threatened Rome so much, that Honorius was forced to call home all his soldiers to protect himself.

The first province thus left bare of troops, was Britain, which remained a prey to the savage Scots, and then was conquered by the Saxons and Angles, two of the heathen tribes of Teutons, who seemed for a time quite to have put out the light of Christianity in their part of the island. The Britons in the Welsh hills, however, still continued a free and Christian people; and Patrick, a noble young Roman, who had once been made captive by the wild Irish, and set to feed their sheep, no sooner grew up than he went back to preach the Gospel to them, and deliver them from a worse bondage than they had made him suffer. So many did he convert, and such zealous Christians were they, that Ireland used to be called the Isle of Saints; and it has never forgotten the trefoil, or shamrock leaf, by which St. Patrick taught his converts to enter into the great mystery, how Three could yet be One.

In the meantime Alaric marched against Rome. Once he was beaten back, and Honorius celebrated the victory by the last Roman triumph ever held, and after it, by the last of the shows of righting slaves. A monk sprung into the amphitheatre while it was going on, and, in the name of Christ, forbade the death of a gladiator who had been wounded, and was to have been killed. The people, in a rage, stoned the good man; but they were so much ashamed, that these shocking entertainments were given up for ever. Rome never won another victory. Alaric came on again; and though he honoured the noble city so much, that he could not bear to let loose his wild troops on it, the false dealing of Honorius at last made him so angry, that he led his Goths into the city; but he was very merciful, he ordered that no one should be killed, and no church injured nor plundered; and he led his army out again at the end of six days. Honorius had fled to Ravenna, and though a few more weak and foolish men called themselves Emperors of the West, the very title soon passed away, and the chief part of Italy was held by the Goths and other Teuton tribes; but they seldom came to Rome, where the chief power gradually fell into the hands of the Pope.

Gaul was conquered by another Teuton race called Franks, who were very fierce heathen at first, but were afterwards converted. Their great leader, Clovis, married a Teuton lady named Clotilda, a Catholic Christian. She was very anxious to lead him to the truth; and at last, in a great battle, he called out in prayer to Clotilda's God; and when the victory was given to him, he took it as a sign from Heaven, and on coming home was baptized, and built the Church of Notre Dame at Paris, which is said to be just as long as the distance to which King Clovis could pitch an axe.

Spain was conquered by a set of Arian Goths; but a Frank princess, great grandchild to Clotilda, brought her husband, the young prince, to a better way of thinking; and though they were persecuted, even to the death, their influence told upon the rest of the family; and the younger brother, who came to the throne afterwards, brought all Spain to be Catholic.

It was something like this with England, where Bertha, another Frank princess, worked upon her husband, Ethelbert, King of Kent, to listen to Augustin, whom Pope Gregory the Great had sent to preach the Word to the Saxons, recollecting how he had once been struck by the angel faces of the little Angle children, whom he had found waiting to be sold for slaves in the marketplace. From Kent, the sound of the Gospel spread out throughout England; and before one hundred years had passed, all the Saxons and Angles were hearty Christians, and sent out the missionary, St. Boniface, who first converted the Teutons in Germany. So, though it would have seemed that the great rush of heathen savages must have stifled the Christian faith, it came working up through them, till at last it moulded their whole state and guided their laws; but this was long in coming to pass, and for many centuries they were very savage and fierce.

St. Gregory the Great was one of the very best of the Popes, very self-denying, and earnestly pious, and doing his utmost to train the Romans in self-discipline, and to soften the Teutons. He put together a book of seven services, to be used by devout people in the course of each day; and he arranged the chants which are still called by his name, though both they and the services are much older. A little before his time, St. Benedict had made rules for the persons who wished to serve God, and to live apart from the world. They lived in buildings named monasteries, or convents; the men, who were called monks, under the rule of an abbot, the women, nuns, under an abbess. They took a vow of poverty, chastity, and obedience; lived and worked as hard as possible, and spent much time in prayer and doing good, teaching the young, giving medicine to the sick, and feeding the poor. They would fix their home in a waste land, and bring it into good order, and they went out preaching and convening the heathen near. Everyone honoured them; and in the worst times, they were left unhurt; their lands were not robbed, and in those savage days, little that was gentle or good would have been safe but for the honour paid to the Church.

LESSON XXIX.
MAHOMET.

"God shall send them strong delusion that they should believe a lie."--2 *Thess*. ii. 11.

The Eastern Empire was not broken up like the Western. The emperors reigned at Constantinople in great state and splendour, in palaces lined with porphyry and hung with purple, and filled with gold and silver. The Greeks of the east had faults the very contrary to those of the Teutons of the west. Instead of being ignorant, rude, and savage, they were learned, courtly, and keen-witted; but their sharpness was a snare to them, for what they were afraid to do by force, they did by fraud, and their word was not to be trusted. In matters of faith too, they were too fond of talking philosophy, and explaining away the hidden mysteries of God; so there sprang up sad heresies among them, chiefly respecting the two Natures of our blessed Lord; and though there were councils of the Church held, and the truth was plainly set forth, yet great numbers were led away from Catholic truth.

Long ago, the Lord of the Church had warned the Churches of Asia by His last Apostle, that if they should fall from their first faith, He would remove their candlestick--that is, take away the light of His Gospel. The first warning they had was, when the Persians broke out in great force, came to the Holy Land, robbed the churches at Jerusalem, and carried away the true Cross, which had been put in a gold case, and buried under ground in hopes of preserving it. They afterwards went on to the very banks of the Bosphorus, and seemed likely to take Constantinople itself; but the emperor, Heraclius, who had hitherto been very dull and sleepy, suddenly woke up to a sense of the danger, and proved himself an able warrior, hunting the Persians back into their own country, and rescuing the Cross, which he carried up the hill of Calvary again upon his own shoulders.

But a worse foe was growing up among the wild sons of Ishmael in Arabia. Nobody can tell what kind of religion these wandering tribes had in the old times, except that they honoured their father, Abraham, still circumcised their sons, and believed in one God, though they paid some sort of worship to a black stone, which was kept at Mecca. Some bad learnt a little Christianity, some had picked up some notions from the Jews; but they cared for hardly anything, except their camels, horses, and tents, and had small thought beyond this life. Among these men there arose, about the year 600, a person named Mahomet. He had at first been servant to a rich widow, whom he afterwards married. Either he fancied, or persuaded others that he believed, that the angel Gabriel spoke to him in a trance, and told him that he was chosen as a great prophet, to announce the will of God, and restore the faith to what it had been in Abraham's days. He caused all that he pretended to have been told by the angel, to be set down in writings, which were called the Koran, meaning the Book, the first sentence of which was, "There is no God but one God, and Mahomet is His prophet." Mahomet blasphemously pretended to be as much greater a prophet than our Lord, as our Lord was than Moses. He ordered prayers and fastings and washings at set times, forbade the least drop of wine to be touched, and commanded that not only no image should be adored, but that no likeness of any created thing should exist, promising that all who strictly obeyed all these rules, should be led safely over a bridge, consisting of a single hair, and enter into a delicious garden, full of fruits, flowers, and fountains, there to be waited on by beautiful women. He gave men leave to have four wives, and did nothing to teach them real love, purity, or devotion; and thus his religion suited the bad side of their nature, and he persuaded great numbers to join him. Indeed no unbeliever is so hard to convert as a Mahometan.

Some of the Arabs being offended at the new teaching, wanted to put him to death; and he fled from his home at Mecca. On his way he was so closely pursued as to be forced to hide in a cave. His enemies were just going to search the cave, when they saw a spider's web over the mouth, and fancied this was a sign that no one could have lately entered it, so they passed by and left him safely concealed. In his anger at this persecution, be declared that the duty of a true Mahometan was to spread his religion with the sword; and calling his friends round him, they fought so bravely that he won back Mecca, and conquered the whole of Arabia. They did not persecute Christians, but they kept them down and despised them; and any Mahometan who changed his religion, was always put to death. Mahomet called himself Khalif, and ruled for ten years at Mecca, where he died and was buried. Mahometans go on pilgrimage to Mecca, and always turn their faces thither when they pray at sunrise or sunset, throwing water over themselves, or sand if they cannot get water.

The Khalifs who came after Mahomet, went on conquering. The chief tribe of the Arabs was called Saracens; and this was the name given to the whole race whom God had sent to punish the Christian world. The Holy City itself, and all the sacred spots, were permitted to fall into their hands; and though they did not profane the churches, the Khalif Omar built a great mosque, or Mahometan place of worship, where the Temple had once been, so as quite to overshadow the Church of the Holy Sepulchre.

They conquered Persia, and spread their religion through that country, putting down the fire worshippers; they seized almost all Asia Minor, where the heretical Christians too easily became Mahometans, and they obtained possession of Egypt, and the great library at Alexandria, where they burnt all the collection of books, because they said, "If they taught the same as the Koran, they were useless, if otherwise, they were mischievous." Then from Egypt they spread all along the north coast of Africa, where the Roman dominion had once been, and were only grieved that the waves of the Atlantic Ocean kept them from going further to the west.

In Spain the Gothic king, Rodrigo, mortally offended one of his nobles, who, in revenge, called in the Saracens to punish him; and the whole kingdom fell a prey to these Mahometan conquerors, except one little mountainous strip in the north, where the brave Christians drew together, and fought gallantly for their Church and their freedom through many centuries. It almost seemed as if these terrible Saracens, who bore everything down before them, were intended to conquer all Europe, and crush down the Church there as they had done in the east; but God was with His people, and He raised up a great warrior among the Christian Franks. Charles Martel, or Charles of the Hammer, so called, because he always went into battle with a heavy iron hammer, led the Franks against the Saracens, when they came up into the South of France; and in the year 732 gave them at Tours the first real defeat they had yet met with. It turned them back completely, and they never came north of the Pyrenees again; but all over the west of Asia and north of Africa, the first places where Christianity had spread, the heavy dark cloud of Mahometanism settled down, and has never been removed.

LESSON XXX.
THE FIRST SCHISM.

"While men slept, his enemy came and sowed tares among the wheat." --St. Matt. xiii. 25

I s the West there was no heresy as there was in the East. The simple Teutons believed what they were taught, and grew softened by little and little, as their clergy gained more influence over them. The clergy were usually bred up in the convents, and there read the good old books which had come down from learned times, St. Jerome's Latin Bible, and the writings of the holy Fathers of the Church, from St. Clement, the friend of St. Paul, down to St. Gregory the Great. Each monastery had a few of such books, as well as of the Liturgy, or Communion Service, and Breviary, or Daily Service; and they were worth much more than their weight in gold. The monks used to copy them out, and adorn the borders and first letters of the chapters with beautiful colours and gilding; but such writing took a long time, and when it was done, few but the clergy could read. Except the clergy, only such persons as were partly Roman by birth had any notion of Latin, or cared to read at all; and so changed were things now that the new race were the conquerors, that to be a Roman was thought quite contemptible, and in France there was a less heavy punishment for killing a Roman than for killing a Frank. The fierce Teuton nobles thought nothing but war worth their attention, and yet they were very devout, and would weep bitterly over their sins. They gave richly to churches, founded convents, and paid great honour to clergymen, and to everything belonging to religion.

Sometimes this honour began to run into idolatry. They treated relics, that is, remains, or things that had belonged to holy persons, as having some sacredness of their own, and fancied that they would save him who carried them from harm. And when they glorified God for His saints in Heaven, and thought of the Communion of saints, they began to entreat their prayers, and the more ignorant would even pray to the saints themselves, as if they could by their own power grant the things that were asked. The blessed Virgin was more sought in this manner than any other saint. The pictures and images of saints, and the crucifix or figure of our blessed Lord on His Cross, which stood in all the churches, often had lights burning before them, and people kneeling round in prayer, till there was danger that, in their ignorance, they might be bowing down to the likeness, and breaking the Second Commandment.

One of the Greek emperors named Leo, was much displeased at this practice, and tried to put a stop to it. There was a great uproar at Constantinople, and many profane things were done and said, which shocked the western branch of the Church. At last the Greeks made a rule that there might be pictures of sacred subjects in their churches, but no images, and to this they have kept ever since. The Latins would not agree to this, and kept both images and pictures; and thus began a feeling of distrust between the two branches.

The great Frank king, Charles le Magne, grandson of Charles Martel, was a very religious man, and did a great deal to convert the heathens in Germany, and spread the power of the Church. He saved Rome from some dangerous enemies, and made the Pope a sort of prince over the city; and the Pope, in return, crowned him Emperor of Rome, though without any right to give away that title. He died in 814, and after his time all the Christian west suffered horribly from the Teuton heathens, who lived in Norway and Denmark, and who used to come down in their ships and ruin and ravage all the countries round, especially England and France. They loved nothing so well as burning a convent; and such a number of learned monks and their books perished under their hands, that the world was growing more ignorant than ever, when our good King Alfred rose up in 880, taught himself first, and then his people; and though he died early, left such good seed behind him, that at last his Saxons converted their enemies themselves, and Norway and Denmark became Christian too, through kings who had learnt the faith in England. But all the errors grew the faster from the ignorance of the people; and at Rome, where there was plenty of learning, the power the Pope enjoyed had done little good, for it made ambitious men covet the appointment, and they ruled their branch of the Church so as to ensure their own gain, more than for the sake of what was right. The Patriarchs of Constantinople greatly disapproved of this, and made the most of all the differences of opinion and practice. When the Council of Constantinople had added to the Nicene Creed the sentence which asserts the Godhead of the Third Holy Person of the Ever Blessed Trinity, the third clause had been "Who proceedeth from the Father." Of late the Western Church had added the words "and the Son." Now though the Greeks believed with all their hearts that the blessed Spirit doth come forth from the Father and the Son, yet they said that the Latins ought not to put words into the Creed that no Council had yet authorized; and thus a great dispute arose. Besides, the Popes had begun to think themselves universal Bishops, heads over all other Patriarchs; and to this the Patriarch of Constantinople would not submit, and rightly said that from the old times all Patriarchs had been equal, and had no right to take authority over one another. At last matters ran so high, that the Pope sent three legates or messengers, who laid on the altar of St. Sophia an act breaking the communion between the two Churches, and then shook off the dust from their feet. This was in the year 1056, a very sad one, for here was the first great rent in the Church, the first breach, and one that has never been repaired, for the Greeks will not, to this day, hold communion with anyone belonging to the Western Church, nor will the Roman Church with them; and after the first happy thousand years when the Church was one outwardly as well as inwardly, thus began the time when her unity has become a matter of faith, and not of sight. But it is our duty to believe that all good Christians are joined together, because they are joined to our blessed Lord, as the boughs of a tree belong to one another by their union with the root, though they may grow apart on different branches.

There were many other differences. The Greeks and Latins reckoned the time of keeping Easter in different ways, and had not the same way of shaving the heads of their clergy. Besides, the Greeks thought that when St. Paul said an elder might be the husband of one wife, he meant that a parish priest *must* be married; so if a clergyman's wife died, they put him into a convent, and took away his parish. The Roman Catholics said, on the contrary, that the clergy were better unmarried; and by-and-by they forbade even those who were not monks to have wives; and in process of time a far more serious evil gradually arose in the Western Church.

The clergy said that there was no need for the people to partake of the Cup at the Holy Eucharist, so they were cut off from that privilege, though our Lord had said, "Drink ye ALL." The clergy said it was all the same whether the people drank of it or not, since Flesh and Blood were one; but this was thinking for themselves, and over explaining, and so by-and-by they lost the real spiritual devout way in which they ought to have reverently spoken of that great and holy mystery, and thought of it in a manner that answered better to their mere human understanding.

LESSON XXXI.
THE MIDDLE AGES.

"Surely the isles shall wait for Me."--Isaiah, ix. 9.

It is not easy to make out exactly the ten kingdoms to which the Roman dominion was said in Daniel to give place, because sometimes one flourished, sometimes another; sometimes one was swallowed up, sometimes a fresh one sprang forth; but there can be no doubt that the ten horns mean the powers of Europe, which have always been somewhere about that number ever since the conquest by the Teuton nations.

By the time the first thousand years had past, the "little leaven" had thoroughly "leavened the whole lump;" and the ways of thinking, the habits, laws, and fashions, of the western people, were all moulded by Christian notions. The notions were not always really Christian, nor did the people always act up to them; but they meant so to do; and though there was some error, yet there was also the sincere saving Truth, which made those who followed it holy, and led them to salvation. Perhaps the greatest mistake was the craving to see, instead of only to believe; and this led to peoples' putting their trust in many things besides the Merits of our blessed Lord--in relics, in images of saints, in the intercessions of the blessed Virgin, and above all, in the Pope's promises.

The Popes were Patriarchs of Rome, and had thus some right over the Churches founded from thence. They used to send the Primate, or chief Archbishop, of each country, a pall or scarf, woven of the wool of lambs which they had blessed on St. Agnes's Day. Many questions were sent to them to be decided. At first the right way of choosing a bishop was, that the clergy and people of the place should elect him, and the king give his consent; but when the Pope's power increased, ambitious men used to bribe the people to elect them; and affairs grew so bad, that at last the Emperor Otho, of Germany, came to Rome, put down the wicked Popes, and took the choice quite into his own hands. This was wrong the other way; and after two or three reigns, the great Pope, Gregory VII., after a fierce struggle with the emperor, Henry IV., set matters in order again, and obtained that, as the Roman people were not to be trusted with the choice, it should be put into the hands of the clergy of the parish churches at Rome, who were called Cardinals, and have ever since had the election of the Pope in their hands. They wear purple and crimson robes and hats, in memory of the old Roman purple of the emperors.

It had been thought by almost the whole of the Western Church, ever since they had lost their communion with the eastern branch, which might have kept them right, that the Pope stood visibly in our Lord's place as Head of the Church, and that he was infallible, namely, so inspired by the Holy Spirit, that he could no more fall into error than a General Council could. So he stood at the head of all the Archbishops and Bishops, Abbots and clergy, of the west; and whenever a difficulty arose, it was sent to him to be settled. He ruled likewise over the consciences of all men and women. If they sinned, the being cut off from the Church, excommunicated, as it was called, was the most terrible punishment that could befall them; and if a king or country were very wicked indeed, the Pope could lay them under an interdict, namely, deprive them of every office of religion, shut up the church doors, and forbid all service.

Sometimes these threats were of great benefit. It was good for the kings to be forced to think of what was right, to be stopped from making cruel wars, from misusing their people, or living in sinful pleasure; but the Popes did not always use their power rightly; they would become angry, and excommunicate people for opposing them, and not for doing what was wrong, and they did not bethink them of our Lord's saying, that His Kingdom is not of this world. Still the Church was working great good. Holy people were bred up, some in convents, some in the world: St. Margaret, Queen of Scotland, who taught her people to say grace at their meals; St. Richard, the good humble Bishop of Chichester; and that glorious French monk, St. Bernard, whose holy life and beautiful preaching made him everywhere honoured.

Great alms were given to the poor, and almost all our most beautiful churches and cathedrals were built by devout kings, nobles, or bishops, who gave their wealth for God's glory. These were built so as to be almost as symbolical as the Temple had been. They were usually in the shape of a cross, in honour of the token of our Salvation; the body was called the nave, or ship, because of the Ark of Christ's Church; the doors stood for repentance, as the entrance; the Font, just within, showed that none could enter save by the Laver of Regeneration; the holiest part was to the east, as looking for the Sun of Righteousness. This portion is called the chancel, and belongs to the clergy, as the Sanctuary did to the priests of old; but the people are not as of old cut off, but draw near in faith, to taste of the great Sacrifice commemorated upon the Altar. The eagle desk for the Holy Scripture, shows forth one Gospel emblem; the Litany desk is for times of repentance, when the Priest may mourn between porch and altar. The dead rested within and around, in the shadow of their church, and constant services were celebrated, that so the gates might ever be open.

Even warriors sought to have their alms blessed by the Church; they bound themselves not to fight on holy-days, such as Fridays and Sundays; and before they could be made knights, they were obliged to vow before God that they would always help the weak, never fight in a bad cause, and always speak the truth. So that all would have been like perfect fulfilment of Isaiah's promises of the glory of the Church, save that man will still follow the devices of his own heart; and there were shrines and altars where undue honour was paid to the Saints, and too many superstitious observances were carried on before their images. Prayers and alms were offered for departed souls, in the notion that they were gone to Purgatory, a place where it was said their sins would be purged away by suffering before the Day of Judgment, and whence their friends might, as they imagined, assist them by their offerings.

People used to go on pilgrimage, and especially such as had fallen into any great sin, would go through everything to pray at the Holy Sepulchre for forgiveness. The Saracens, who had not been unkind to the pilgrims, were subdued by a much fiercer set of Mahometans, the Turcomans, who did everything to profane the holy places, and robbed and misused the Christians who came to worship there. The news of this profanation stirred up all Europe to deliver the Sanctuary from the unbeliever. Monks went about preaching the holy war, and multitudes took the cross, that is, fastened on their shoulder one cut out in cloth, and vowed to win back Jerusalem. The Pope took upon himself to say that whoever was killed in such a cause, would have all his sins forgiven, and be in no danger of purgatory; and this be called an indulgence. These wars were called Crusades. In the first, in 1098, Jerusalem was conquered, and a very good and pious man, named Godfrey, set up to be king, though he would not be crowned, saying he would never wear a crown of gold where his Master had worn a crown of thorns. But as the Greek Christians who already lived there, would not own the Pope, but held to their own Patriarch, a Latin Patriarch was thrust in and was in subjection to the Pope; and thus the unhappy schism grew wider. After Godfrey's death, the Christians in Palestine did not behave well, nor show themselves worthy to have the keeping of Jerusalem; and though St. Bernard preached a second Crusade, and the Emperor of Germany and King of France came to help them, their affairs only grew worse and worse.

In 1186, after they had possessed the Holy City only eighty-eight years, they were deprived of it; it was taken again by the Saracens, and they retained only a few towns on the coast. All devout people mourned that the unbeliever should again be defiling the sanctuary; but the Pope had a great quarrel with the Emperor of Germany, and told the poor credulous people that fighting his battles was as good as a Crusade; and they began to forsake the Holy Land, and leave it to its fate. Our own Richard the Lion Heart did his best, and so did the excellent French king, St. Louis, who died in Africa on his way to the Crusade, but all in vain; and finally the Christians were driven out of Acre, their last town, and Palestine became Mahometan again with only a few oppressed Christians here and there. Then came a much more rude, dull, and violent race of Mahometans, the Turks, who burst out of the East, conquered the Saracens, gained all Asia Minor, and at last, in the year 1453, they took the city of Constantinople, killed the last emperor, Constantine, in the assault, and won all the country we now call Turkey, where they sadly oppressed the Greeks, though they could not make them turn from their true Catholic faith. It was then that the light of truth faded entirely away from Ephesus and the Churches of Asia; a blight fell wherever the Turks went, and cities, once prosperous, were deserted and ruined. Tyre was one of these; and she has now become a mere rock, where fishermen spread their nets to dry upon the sea-shore, as Ezekiel had foretold. However, it was only forty years afterwards, that the last remains of the Mahometan conquerors were chased out of Spain, so that it became again an entirely Christian country.

LESSON XXXII.
THE REFORMATION.

"The Kingdom of Heaven is like unto a treasure hid in a field."--Matt. xiii. 44.

When the Services of the Church were first drawn up, almost every-one in the East spoke Greek, and most people in the West under-stood Latin; and when the Teutons learnt Christianity, they also, with it, learnt a little Latin. Thus the Prayers and the Scriptures remained in that tongue, but the people themselves spoke each their own language. German, English, French, Spanish, and Italian are mixtures in different degrees of Latin and Teuton, and only learned persons who understood the old language, could follow the Prayers, or read the Bible. So the people missed more and more of the real truth and meaning of sacred things; and some of the clergy who had grown corrupt, took advantage of their ignorance and deceived them. Whereas the Pope had once declared that those who went on a Crusade were sure of dying in a state of salvation, he now declared, that to give alms for building the great Church of St. Peter at Rome, would answer the same purpose; and indulgences, namely, prom-ises of so many years less of purgatory, used to be absolutely sold; and it was very difficult to set these errors right, for anyone who was thought to speak against the doctrine of the Church, was liable to be punished by being burnt to death. This was quite contrary to the ways of the early Church, which, however bad a heretic might have been, never attempted to harm his person, but only separated him from her Communion.

As the Holy Spirit within the Church is ever cleansing and sanctifying it, wit-nesses against these errors began to be raised up. The way to print books, instead of writing them out, had been discovered in the fifteenth century; and as this art made them much more cheap and common, many more people began to read and to think. In the year 1517, a German monk, named Martin Luther, began to declare how far the selling of indulgences was from the doctrine of the Apostles; and he spoke such plain truth, that he convinced a great number of Germans, and there was a great longing for the cleansing of the Church, especially after Luther had translated the Bible into his own tongue, and everyone could see how unlike the teaching there was to what had been so long believed.

In England, King Henry VIII. separated from the Roman Church because the Pope would not please him by breaking a marriage, which certainly never ought to have been sanctioned; but which having been permitted by the Pope, and having continued twenty years, it was very wrong to dissolve. He called himself Head of the Church in England; and though he believed all the later errors, he allowed the Lessons to be read from a new English translation of the Bible. He pretended to reform the convents, some of which were in a very bad state, and had forgotten their rules; but instead of setting them to rights, he seized their wealth, and turned all the monks and nuns adrift.

The new notions were favoured by his break with the Pope. The whole Western Church was in a ferment; the reformers were constantly writing and preaching against the many errors of the Roman Church, and were rejoicing over the real treasure of true faith they had found hidden within her. Many other sincere and good men were shocked at such disobedience to what they had once respected; and unhappily, almost all the Italian clergy and cardinals were so food of the riches and power in which they were maintained by misleading the people, that they dreaded nothing so much as having them set right.

The Emperor, Charles V., strove hard to bring about a General Council of the Church, as the only hope of making matters right, but he was much hindered by his wars with the King of France, and by the double dealing of the Pope; and in the meantime Luther and his friends drew up a protest against the false doctrines of Rome, and were, for that reason, called Protestants. In Switzerland and France, another reformer, named John Calvin, was preaching against the doctrine of the Pope; and though he neglected what the Church of old pure times had decided, and thus threw away much that was good, as well as much that was untrue, great numbers followed him; but unfortunately, none of the higher clergy on the Continent would listen to these views, and there seemed no choice but to accept falsehood, or to break into a schism. After many trials, Charles V. got together some Italian, Spanish, and German clergy at Trent, in the Tyrol, and called them a council; but this was far from being a true General Council, as there was nobody from the Eastern Church, nor from many branches of the Western. The Protestants knew they should not be fairly treated, and that if these Italians should decide that they were heretics, they might very probably be burnt; so, instead of coming to it, they acted as the early Christians never did, they took up arms and fought, and this attempt at a council broke up in confusion.

Things were happier in England. After the death of Henry VIII., Archbishop Cranmer, and the other guardians of his little son, Edward VI., set to work to clear away the corruptions from the Church in England, so as to make it as like as they could to what it had been in the Apostles' time. The Bible had been translated, and they put the whole Prayer-Book into English, leaving out all that savoured of idolatry, all the notions about purgatory, and everything of error, and keeping the real old precious services of the early Church, restoring to the people the blessed privilege of the Cup, while the Bishops, Priests, and Deacons, went on in an uninterrupted line, as from the beginning. On Edward's early death, his sister, Queen Mary, who was married to Philip II., the son of the Emperor, thought all these changes very wicked, and endeavoured to put them down. Four Bishops, Cranmer, Latimer, Ridley, and Hooper, were burnt for their share in them, with many other persons, and England was again reconciled to Rome; but Mary only reigned five years, and her sister Elizabeth was a sound Churchwoman, and held fast by the Catholic English Church in her reformed state.

Philip II., the son of Charles V., managed to accomplish another sitting of the Council of Trent, and the Church of Rome considers it a true council, though there were only two hundred and fifty-five Bishops, and they condemned the Protestants without hearing their defence. It did some good to the Romish Church by putting down the sale of indulgences, and some bad practices of the clergy; but it bound her to all the errors renounced by the Reformers, and put her into a state of schism from the Catholic Church.

The Lutheran Protestants in Germany, and the Calvinists in France, Holland,

and Scotland, as they could have no bishops, made up their minds that none were needed, though this was quite contrary to Scripture, and to the ways of the Apostles. There was a sad time of warfare through all the centre of Europe; and the Spaniards and French horribly persecuted the Protestants and Calvinists, thinking in their blindness that they were thus doing God service; but Queen Elizabeth stood up as the firm friend of all the distressed Reformers; and at last matters settled down again, though not till all Christianity had been grievously shattered and rent, and there was no more outward unity.

There were four branches of the Church Catholic keeping their Bishops, the Greek, the Roman, the English, the Swedish; but none of these were in outward communion the one with the other, though still owning one Lord, one Faith, one Baptism, and waging the same fight with the Devil and his works. The Roman Church was spread over all Italy, Spain, France, and great part of Germany, and tried to force down all differences of opinion by cruel and bloody means, caring more for unity than for truth, and boasting of being the only Catholic Church, instead of only one branch of it. The Lutheran doctrine was taught in Norway, Denmark, and many parts of Germany, and the Calvinist teaching gained a great hold in Holland, Scotland, and on such French as were not Roman Catholic. The Greek Church meanwhile stood fast through much tribulation in the Turkish dominions, and had gradually won the whole great Russian Empire, where, as the people ceased to be barbarous, they became most devout members of the ancient unchanging Greek Catholic Church.

LESSON XXXIII.
COLONIZATION.

"Enlarge the place of thy tent, and let them stretch forth the curtains of thy habitations; spare not, lengthen thy cords, and strengthen thy stakes."--Isaiah, liv. 2.

Just as the Reformation was beginning, fresh lands were being found beyond the Atlantic Ocean, where the knowledge of the Gospel might reach. Christopher Columbus, a gallant Genoese mariner, and deeply religious man, was full of the notion that by sailing westwards he might come round to India, and thence make a way for winning back the Holy Land. After much weary waiting, and many entreaties, he obtained three little ships from Queen Isabel of Spain; and with them, in the year 1492, came to the islands which he named the West Indies, lovely places, full of gentle natives with skins of a dark ruddy colour, wearing, for their misfortune, golden ornaments. To get gold was the great longing of the Spaniards, and they did not care what cruelties they used so that they could obtain it. The Pope, finding in the prophecies that the isles of the sea should belong to the Church, considered that this gave him a right to give them away to whomsoever he pleased; so he made a grant of all to the west to the Spaniards, all to the east to the Portuguese. Thereupon great numbers of the Spaniards went over to America; they conquered the two great empires of Mexico and Peru, and settled in the West-Indian Islands, robbing the poor natives of their gold and silver, making slaves of them, and hunting them with blood-hounds when they tried to run away. Many good priests who went out as missionaries did all they could to hinder these horrors, but in vain; and when at last the poor delicate Indians began to dwindle away and die off, the plan was resorted to of bringing negroes from Africa to work in their stead.

Though it was a good man who thought of it, in the hope of saving the Indians and making the negroes Christians, it came to most horrible cruelty, and was a disgrace to Christian Europe. However, these faithful priests worked hard in teaching and converting the Indians all over South America. One brotherhood, called the Jesuits, had great establishments, where they trained up large villages of Indiana in Christian habits, and taught them to be very faithful and industrious. But at home, in Europe, these Jesuits did harm by stepping out of their work as ministers, interfering with governments more than was right, and trying to keep up the authority of the Pope more than real Catholic truth. They taught so many false stories as articles of faith, that at last clever people, wise in their own conceit, began to believe nothing, and became like the fool who said in his heart, "There is no God." So there came to be a bad feeling against all the clergy, and the Jesuits, who had made themselves very meddling and troublesome, were put down at the entreaty of several kings. When they were taken away from their converts in South America, it turned out that the poor Indians had not steadfastness enough to take care of themselves; so all their well-ordered establishments were broken up, and the people ran wild again. All the Spanish settlers, of whom there were many, still held fast to their Church, and all the coast of the Continent of South America is Roman Catholic.

The English and Dutch had not been slow to find their way to the West, but they went to the colder North instead of to the South, and sought good land more than gold. Some of the English had, during Queen Mary's reign, made friends with some of the Dutch and German Calvinists, who fancied that whatever Roman Catholics had done must be wrong, instead of only a part, and who cared nothing for the ways of the Apostolic Primitive Church. So when the true Catholic faith was upheld by Queen Elizabeth; by James I., who caused our translation of the Bible to be made by forty-eight learned Hebrew and Greek scholars; and by Charles I., who gave Bishops and a Prayer-Book to Scotland, there were many persons who grew impatient and angry that more changes were not made. These broke away from the Church, calling themselves Puritans and Independants, and living in a state of schism. Some, too, thought the king had too much power; and in Charles's time a great many went away and settled in North America, that they might have freedom, and worship in their own way. Those who stayed at home went on to that rebellion against Church and King, which ended in the Scottish Calvinists betraying King Charles, and the English Independants putting him to death for upholding the Bishops, after Archbishop Laud had been beheaded. For nearly eleven years the Bishops were put down, the clergy persecuted, and the use of the Prayer-Book forbidden in England, while all sorts of sects rose up and explained the Bible as they pleased. When, at length, Charles II. came back, and the Church was re-established in England, many more went to the colonies; and though there was a Church settlement in Virginia, the great mass of the North American colonists were Calvinists or Presbyterians, as they are called, because presbyters are their highest order of their ministry, though they cannot be really commissioned priests, never having been ordained by Bishops come down from the Apostles.

The English began to spread fast on every side, as their nation grew stronger and more numerous. They conquered several of the West-Indian Isles, and the Church was there established; but, to their disgrace, they carried on the slave-trade, to supply the settlers with workmen. In the East-Indies, too, they began to acquire large tracts by conquest and by treaty, and a few churches were built there; but they had not tried to convert the great number of heathens who became subject to them, fearing that, should they take offence, they would shake off their dominion. Such clergy as did go out were ordained in England. There was as yet no Bishop to overlook the colonial Churches, so that they could not take deep root.

Still the English Church was living as a witness of the truth at home, with many a great and holy man within her, such as Bishop Taylor, whose beautiful writings are loved by all; Bishop Ken, whose loyalty to Church and King witnessed a good confession, and whose hymns are like part of the Prayer-Book; Bishop Wilson, whose devotions for home and at the Holy Eucharist are our great guide, with more good and humble men and women than the world will ever know of; and this, under God's mercy, saved the nation from falling into the unbelieving state of France, where people thought it fine to laugh at all religion. There, in the end of the eighteenth century, a terrible outbreak took place against all authority, human or Divine; the King and Queen perished by the hands of their subjects; quantities of blood was shed, and for a time it seemed as if the country was given up to demons; the faithful clergy fled or remained hidden; and though at last people began to return to their senses, the shock to loyalty and religion has never been entirely recovered in that country.

LESSON XXXIV.
THE SPREAD OF THE GOSPEL.

The fearful effects of infidelity in France roused good men everywhere; and the Church began to show that power of reviving and purifying herself, which proves that the Lord abideth with her for ever.

Some time before things had come to this pass, an English clergyman, named John Wesley, had been striving to awaken people to a more religious life; but he did not sufficiently heed the authority of the Church; and his followers, after his death, quite separated themselves from her, and became absolute schismatics, with meeting-houses and ministers of their own, calling themselves Methodists. Still his fervour and earnestness stirred up many within the Church; and from that time there was much more desire to fulfil the mission of Christians by bringing others to the knowledge of the truth. Sunday-schools began to be set up to assist the catechizing in Church enjoined in the Prayer-Book, and often instead of it; and there was a growing eagerness to convert the heathen abroad. The great possessions and wide trade of England seemed to mark her as especially intended for this work. Some persons went about it by giving their money to any Missionary Society that made fair promises, without heeding whether it were schismatic or not; others had more patience, and trusted their alms to the Society for the Propagation of the Gospel, which was managed by the English Bishops.

The American colonies had, by this time, grown impatient of the English Government, and had shaken it off, calling themselves the United States. The Church people among them obtained some Bishops from the Scottish branch of the Church, which the Calvinists had never been able to put down; and every one of the many United States has now a Bishop of its own.

Calcutta was the first English colony to receive a Bishop, in the year 1814. The second Bishop was Reginald Heber, whose beautiful hymns seem the birthright of our Church, like those of Bishop Ken, one hundred and fifty years before. Still very little was done with the natives of India; they were attached to their foul old religion, and Government forbade any open measures against it, though here and there was a conversion; and there have at length come to be three Bishops' Sees, and in the south of the peninsula, in the See of Madras, there are a hopeful number of Christians. The work would everywhere proceed better if there were no schism, so that all Christians could work together. Ceylon also has a Bishop, and many are there gathered in. On the borders of China likewise there is an English Bishopric; and within that empire the French Roman Catholics have been working steadily for many years to win a few of those obstinate heathen to the faith, but with little success, and often receiving the crown of martyrdom.

The French are very ardent missionaries, bearing joyously all kinds of privations, and forming their stations wherever they see any hope of gaining converts. The Sisters of Charity--good women under a vow to spend their lives in nursing and teaching--do much to show what the real fruit of Christianity is; and they are to be found wherever there is trouble or distress. There is a great college at Rome, called the *Propaganda*, where every language under the sun is taught, in order to fit persons for missionary work,

Our own St. Augustine's College at Canterbury is intended to prepare young men to become English missionaries; and north, south, east, and west, are the good tidings spreading, now that the days are come of which Daniel said: "Many shall run to and fro, and knowledge shall be increased."

The English West Indies were first forbidden to import slaves; next, all the slaves were set free; and there are now four Bishoprics for their black and white population. All negroes seized in the ships of other nations, on their way to be made slaves, are brought back to Sierra Leone, on the coast of Africa, there set free, and taught to be Christians under a Bishop of our Church; and the Christian blacks are beginning to carry the message of salvation into the other parts of Africa, where the climate is so hurtful to Englishmen, that only the negro race could there do the work.

South Africa has three Bishops to rule their English settlers, win the Dutch farmers to the Church, and convert the Hottentots and Zulus. And from them a Missionary Bishop has been sent out to the heathen tribes in the interior of the continent.

North America contains nine great Bishops' Sees, and the huge Island of Australia six. New Zealand, scarcely discovered till within the last fifty years, has three Bishops of her own, ruling over a population of English, and of Christian natives, men whose fathers were cannibals, but who are now hearty Christians; and it is the centre whence a Mission Bishop is seeking to gain to the Church the inhabitants of the beautiful islands that thickly dot the Pacific Ocean. Many of these islanders have become Christian, under the teaching of missionaries from the other Societies; and though great numbers still remain savage heathens, yet the light of the Gospel is in the course of shining upon all the islands far away. Everywhere the Creed, the Lord's Prayer, and the Ten Commandments, in the vulgar tongue, are being taught, and each convert is gathered in by baptism and fed by the Holy Eucharist, as when the apostles first went forth; and no one can mark the great spread of the Church within the last fifty years, without feeling that the blessing of God is with her. The Greek Church has done less; but though still enslaved in Turkey, in Greece she is free, and the yoke of the Mahometan is there shaken off, after her long patience and constancy.

There are dark spots in all this brightness, for Rome still teaches the same errors mixed up with the truth, and the spirit of unbelief is to be found far and wide, questioning and explaining away all the mysteries it cannot understand.

We know that it must be so, for it was to fight with sin that Christ came into the world, and left His Church there; and St. Paul prophesied that evil men and seducers should wax worse and worse, deceiving and being deceived. Daniel too, foresaw that the little horn should spring up, and do very wickedly; and all the tenor of prophecy in the Epistles declares that times of trouble and temptation must try the Church.

It seems that there has been, even from the Apostles' times, an evil spirit opposing himself to our Lord, and therefore called by St. John the Anti-Christ. His manifestations have broken out in many ways--in Arianism, in Mahometanism, perhaps in the great errors of Rome, and more lately, in Infidelity, and in Mormonism; and it would seem that there is to be some much more dreadful development of "that wicked one" exalting himself against Christ, and severely trying the elect. But we have a certain promise, that come what may, Christ will never forsake His chosen flock; and those who try to hold fast the faith once delivered to the Saints, and to keep the law of love, clinging to their own true branch of the Church, may be sure that He Who has redeemed them, will guard them from all evil, and that they will share in His glory when He shall come with all His holy angels to put all enemies under His feet. Then He shall sit on His great white Throne, and gather His elect from the four winds to dwell in the eternal Jerusalem, which needs neither sun nor moon, for the Lamb is the light thereof.

QUESTIONS.

LESSON I.

1. In what state was the Earth when first created?

2. To what trial was man subjected?

3. What punishment did the Fall bring on man?

4. How alone could his guilt be atoned for? A. By his punishment being borne by one who was innocent.

5. What was the first promise that there should be such an atonement?--Gen. iii. 15.

6. What were the sacrifices to foreshow?

7. Why was Abel's offering the more acceptable?

8. From which son of Adam was the Seed of the woman to spring?

9. How did Seth's children fall away?

10. What was Enoch's prophecy?--Jude, 14, 15.

11. Who was chosen to be saved out of the descendants of Seth?

12. How was the world punished?

13. In what year was the Flood?

14. Where did the ark first rest?

15. What were the terms of the covenant with Noah?

16. Which of Noah's sons was chosen?

17. What was the prophecy of Noah?--Gen. ix. 25, 26, 27.

18. What lands were peopled by Ham's children?

19. What became of Shem's children?

20. What became of Japhet's children?

LESSON II.

1. Whom did God separate among the sons of Shem?

2. What were the terms of the covenant with Abraham? A. Abraham believed, and God promised that his descendants should have the land of Canaan, and in his seed should all the nations of the earth be blessed.

3. What was the token of the covenant with Abraham?

4. Which son of Abraham inherited the promise?

5. Who were the sons of Ishmael?

6. What measure was taken to keep Isaac from becoming mixed with idolators?

7. Which of Isaac's sons was chosen?

8. Why was Esau rejected?

9. What was the promise to Esau?--Gen. xxvii. 39, 40.

10. By what names were the descendants of Esau called?

11. Where did the Edomites live?

12. What sea was named from them?

13. What were the habits of the Edomites?

14. Who is thought to have been the great prophet of Idumea?

15. What was the prophecy of Job?--Job, xix. 25, 26, 27.

16. How was Jacob's name changed?

17. Who were to be in the covenant after him?

18. What prophecy was there of the Israelites going into Egypt?--Gen. xv. 13.

19. Which son of Jacob was to be father of the promised Seed?

20. What was Jacob's prophecy of the Redeemer?--Gen. xlix. 10.

LESSON III.

1. Who were the Egyptians?

2. What kind of place was Egypt?

3. What remains have we of the ancient Egyptians?

4. What were the idols of Egypt?

5. How long were the Israelites in Egypt?

6. How were they treated in Egypt? 7. What prophetic Psalm is said to have been composed in Egypt?--Ps. I. xxxviii.

8. Who was appointed to lead them out?

9. How was Moses prepared for the work?

10. How did God reveal Himself to Moses?

11. What wonders were wrought on the Egyptians?

12. What token of faith was required of the Israelites at their departure?

13. What feast was appointed in remembrance of the deliverance from Egypt?

LESSON IV.

1. How many Israelites did Moses lead into the wilderness?

2. How were they supported there?

3. What was the difference between the covenant with Abraham, and the covenant on Mount Sinai?

4. How did the Israelites forfeit the covenant?

5. How was God entreated to grant it to them again?

6. What signs of the covenant did they carry with them?

7. How was Moses instructed in their observances?

8. What was the Tabernacle to figure?

9. What did all the ceremonies shadow out?

10. Why were the Israelites to be kept separate from other nations?

11. How were they trained in the wilderness?

12. How long did they wander there?

13. Why did not Moses enter the land of Canaan?

14. What were the two great prophecies of the Redeemer which were given in the wilderness?--Num. xxiv. 17. *Deut*. xviii. 15.

15. What books were written by Moses?

16. What Psalm was written by Moses?--Ps. xc.

LESSON V.

1. In what year did the Israelites enter Canaan?

2. What kind of country was Canaan?

3. Where was the first seat of the Tabernacle in Canaan?

4. How was the inheritance of the tribes arranged?

5. Why did not the Israelites occupy the whole of their territory at once?

6. Who were the Phoenicians?

7. What were the chief cities of the Phoenicians?

8. Who were the chief gods of the Canaanites?

9. How were the Israelites governed?

10. What was the consequence of their falling from the true worship?

11. Who were their chief enemies?

12. In what book in the Bible is this history related?

13. For how long a period did the rule of the Judges last?

14. What crime brought on them the loss of the Ark?

15. How was the Ark sent back?

16. What was the prophecy of the Redeemer during this period? --1 *Sam*. ii. 35.

17. Who was the first of the Prophets and last of the Judges?

LESSON VI.

1. When did the Israelite kingdom begin?

2. Who was the first king of Israel?

3. On what conditions was Saul to reign?

4. What was Saul's great error?

5. Who was chosen in Saul's stead?

6. Of what tribe was David?

7. What was David's great excellence?

8. What were David's exploits?

9. How was David prepared for the throne?

10. What terrible massacre did Saul commit in his hatred of David?

11. What prophecy was thus fulfilled?--1 *Sam*. ii. 32, 33.

12. What was the beginning of David's kingdom?

13. What was the end of Saul?

14. Who reigned over the rest of Israel?

15. What became of Ishbosheth?

16. What were David's conquests?

17. What is the meaning of the name Jerusalem?

18. How did David regulate the service before the Ark?

19. Which are David's chief prophecies of our Lord?--Ps. ii.--xvi.

20. Which Psalm marks David as our Lord's forefather?--lxxxix.

21. Why was not David permitted to build the Temple?

22. How long did David reign?

23. What was the site of the Temple?

24. How was the Divine Presence marked there?

25. For what was Solomon's reign remarkable?

26. How did Solomon fall away?

27. What was to be his punishment?

28. What are the prophecies of Solomon? *A. Prov*. viii. and ix.--where our Lord is spoken of as the Divine Wisdom.--Ps. xlv. The Song of Solomon on the mystical union of Christ and His Church.--Eccles. iv.

LESSON VII.

1. How did Rehoboam bring about the accomplishment of the sentence on Solomon?

2. What tribes were left to him?

3. How was he prevented from making war on Jeroboam?

4. Who was the Egyptian king who invaded Judea?

5. Who succeeded Rehoboam?

6. Who succeeded Abijah?

7. What was Jehoshaphat's great error?

8. Into what danger did Ahab send him?

9. What great deliverances were vouchsafed to Jehoshaphat?

10. How did Jehoram act on coming to the throne?

11. How was he punished?

12. What became of Ahaziah?

13. Who was Athaliah?

14. Why could she not entirely destroy the seed royal?[3]

15. What prophecy was fulfilled by these massacres?--2 Sam. xii. 10.

16. How was Joash preserved?

17. How was he restored to the throne?

---

3   These references are to the Prayer-Book version.

18. How did Joash reign?

19. What was the sin of Amaziah?

20. What was the sin of Uzziah?

21. How was the sin of Uzziah punished?

22. Who reigned in Uzziah's stead?

23. Who began to prophesy in Uzziah's time? A. Isaiah.

24. What was the character of Ahaz?

25. How was the sin of Ahaz punished?

26. What were Isaiah's chief prophecies of our Lord? A. *Isaiah*, vii. 14.--ix. 6.--xi.--xii.--xxxii.--xxxv.--xl.--xlii.--l. 5, 6.--li. 13, 14, 15.--liii.--lxiii.

LESSON VIII.

1. Where had the greatness of Joseph's children been foretold?
A. *Gen*. xlix. 25, 26. *Deut*. xxxiii. 13, 14, 15, 16, 17.

2. How did Jeroboam forfeit these blessings?

3. What warnings did he receive?

4. Who overthrew the house of Jeroboam?

5. What kings reigned next?

6. What city did Omri make his capital?

7. How had the site of Samaria been made remarkable?--Deut, xxvii.

8. What was the difference between the sin of Jeroboam and the sin of Ahab?

9. How was Ahab influenced?

10. What prophet warned him?

11. What proofs were given that the Lord is the only God?

12. Who were the chief enemies of Israel?

13. What was the fate of Ahab?

14. Who became prophet after Elijah? 15. Who executed judgment on the house of Ahab?

16. How long was the house of Jehu to continue?

17. How did Joash disobey Elisha?--2 Kings, xiii. 19.

18. What prophets succeeded Elisha?--A. Hosea and Amos.

19. What was Hosea's prophecy of Redemption?--Hosea, xiii. 14.

20. What was Amos' prophecy of Redemption?--Amos, ix. 11-15.

21. What was the end of the house of Jeroboam?
22. Who were the two allies against Judah?
23. What generous action was done by the Ephraimites?

LESSON IX.
1. Who founded the Assyrian Empire?
2. What is the description of Nineveh?
3. What prophet was sent to warn the Ninevites?
4. How did the Ninevites receive the message?
5. What prophetic book besides Jonah is concerned with Nineveh?
6. Which King of Nineveh was contemporary with Ahaz?
7. Why did Ahaz seek the alliance of Tiglath Pileser?
8. What victories did the Ninevites gain?
9. What was the effect upon Judah?
10. What profanation did Ahaz commit in the Temple?
11. Who was the successor of Ahaz?
12. Who was the last King of Samaria?
13. What partial reformation took place in Israel?
14. What was the punishment of the Israelites?
15. Where were the Israelites placed?
16. What was the next conquest attempted by the Assyrians?
17. How was the danger turned away?
18. What apocryphal book mentions the history of an Israelite captive?
19. What great mercy was vouchsafed to Hezekiah?
20. How did he show that he was uplifted?
21. What was the rebuke for his display? 22. Who was the King of Nineveh after Sennacherib? A. Esarhaddon, also called Sardocheus, and Asnapper.
23. What apocryphal history is supposed to have taken place at this time?
24. How did Esarhaddon fill the empty land of Samaria?
25. What request was made by these heathen colonists?
26. Of what race were they the parents?
27. What additions were made to the Holy Scriptures in Hezekiah's time?
28. What is Micah's chief prophecy?--Micah, v. 2, 3, 4.

29. Who reigned after Hezekiah?
30. How were the crimes of Manasseh punished?
31. What was the end of Nineveh?
32. What is the present state of Nineveh?

LESSON X.

1. What was the character of Amon?
2. What reformation did Josiah make?
3. What discovery was made in cleansing the Temple?
4. Why was the Law of Moses so awful to Josiah?
5. What answer did Huldah make to Josiah's inquiries?
6. What was the great merit of Josiah?
7. What prophecy did Josiah exactly fulfil?--1 *Kings*, xiii. 2. 31, 32,
8. Who were the prophets of Josiah's time? A. Jeremiah, Zephaniah, and a little later, Habbakuk.
9. What was Josiah's situation with regard to his neighbours?
10. Why was he forced to go out to battle?
11. How does Jeremiah speak of Josiah's death?---Jer. xxii. 10.
12. How had Isaiah foretold it?--Isaiah, lvii. 1.
13. What two names had the successor of Josiah?
14. What fate did Jeremiah foretell for him?--Jer. xxii. 11, 12.
15. Whither was Jehoahaz carried captive?
16. Who was set up instead of Jehoahaz?
17. What did Jeremiah predict concerning Jehoiakim? *Jer*. xxii. 18, 19.
18. By whose favour had Jehoiakim been set up?
19. Who was Jehoiakim's enemy?
20. What injury did Nebuchadnezzar inflict in 606?
21. What prophet was then carried captive? *A*. Daniel.
22. What was the promise of Jeremiah?--Jer. xxv. 12.
23. Why was Jeremiah persecuted?
24. What was the great wilfulness of these kings?
25. What was the end of Jehoiakim?
26. By what names was his son called?

27. What does Jeremiah say of Jehoiachin?--Jer. xxii 24 to 30.

28. Was he really childless? *A.* Either he was childless, and Salathiel was his adopted son of another branch of David's family, or else it meant that his son should not reign.

29. What became of Jehoiachin?

30. What prophet was carried off in this captivity?

31. Who was the last King of Judah?

32. What message did Ezekiel send Zedekiah?--Ez. xxii. 25, 26, 27.

33. What was Ezekiel's lamentation for the sons of Josiah? --Ez. xix. I-9.

34. What were Ezekiel's chief prophecies of the Redeemer? --Ez. xxxiv. 23, 24.--xxxvii. 24, 25, 26.

35. What was Zedekiah's duty?

36. How did he show his want of faith?

37. What was the consequence?

38. What was the prophecy of Ezekiel that Zedekiah thought impossible?--Ez. xii. 13.

39. What were the sufferings of Jeremiah in the siege of Jerusalem?

40. What prophecies of Moses had their first fulfilment in this siege?--Deut. xxviii. 52, 53.

41. Who boasted over Jerusalem?

42. What was the desolation of Jerusalem?

43. Which book in the Holy Scripture mourns over it? A. The book of Lamentations of Jeremiah.

44. What became of Jeremiah?

45. How did the remnant act who were left in Judea?

46. Who was the prophet who spoke against Edom? A. Obadiah.

47. What was the great prophecy of Jeremiah?--Jer. xxiii. 5, 6.

48. What was the year of the taking of Jerusalem?

LESSON XI.

1. Who were the Chaldeans?

2. What does Isaiah say of the origin of the Chaldeans?--Is. xxiii. 13.

3. Who was their chief god, and how was he worshipped?

4. Describe Babylon.

5. What were the prophecies of the state of the Jews in captivity?--Lev. xxvi. 33, 34.--38, 39.--Jer. v. 19.

6. What change for the better passed over the Jews?

7. Who were the royal children brought up as slaves?

8. How had their slavery been foretold?--Is. xxxix. 7.

9. What instance of self-denying faith was given by them?

10. How was Daniel's inspiration first made known?

11. What was the first dream of Nebuchadnezzar?

12. What was the interpretation?

13. What judgment is recorded of Daniel in the Apocrypha?

14. What proof did the other princes give of their faith?

15. What is the hymn of praise said to have been sung by them in the furnace?

16. What was the effect on Nebuchadnezzar?

17. Where had Edom's fell been foretold? A. *Numb*. xxiv. 18-21, 22.--Jer. xlix. 7-22.--Obadiah.

18. What other conquest did Nebuchadnezzar effect? 19. Where had the fall of Tyre been predicted? A. *Is*. xxiii.--Ez. xxvi. xxvii. xxviii.

20. How soon was a new Tyre built?

21. What was to be the recompence for the toils of the siege of Tyre?

22. Where is the ruin of Egypt foretold? *A. Is*. xix. 1 to 20.--Jer. xliii. 8 to 13.--xlvi.--Ez. xxx. xxxi. xxxii.

23. What was the end of the Pharaohs?

24. What was Nebuchadnezzar's second dream?

25. What was the meaning and the fulfilment?

26. What acknowledgment did Nebuchadnezzar make?

27. In what year did he die?

28. Who was his successor?

29. What was the first vision of Daniel?

30. What was the interpretation?

31. What was the second vision of Daniel?

32. What was the meaning?

33. How were the visions explained to Daniel?

LESSON XII.

1. What was the power which was to overcome the Assyrian?
2. How had the Persian power been figured in the visions?--Dan. ii. 32.--vii. 5.--viii. 3, 4.
3. What was the meaning of the two horns of the Ram?
4. What was the difference between the Medes and Persians?
5. What was the religion of the Persians?
6. What was the character of Cyrus?
7. Who was the reigning King of Babylon?
8. What was the trust of the Babylonians?
9. But what had been foretold concerning Cyrus?--Is. xlv. I, 2, 3.
10. How did Cyrus attempt to gain an entrance?
11. How were the Babylonians prevented from being on the watch?
12. What awful warning interrupted Belshazzar's feast?
13. Who interrupted the writing?
14. How had Jeremiah foretold the taking of Babylon by the Medes? --Jer. l. 35 to li.
15. How long was the captivity to last?--Jer. xxv. 11.--xxix. 10.
16. What had been the promise of Moses?--Lev. xxvi. 44.
17. What had been the prayer of Solomon?--1 *Kings*, viii. 46 to 50.
18. What had Isaiah said of Cyrus?--Is. xliv. 28.--xlv. 13.
19. Who made intercession for the fulfilment of these prophecies?
20. How was Daniel's prayer answered?
21. What great promise was made to Daniel?--Dan. ix. 24 to 27.
22. In what year was the decree for the restoration of Jerusalem given?
23. Who governed Babylon?
24. What was the proof of Daniel's faith?
25. What story is told of his destroying the worship of Bel?
26. How had Isaiah foretold this overthrow?--Is. xlvi. 1,2.
27. What was revealed to Daniel in his last vision?

28. What was Daniel called? *A*. The man greatly beloved.

LESSON XIII.

1. How many Jews returned from the captivity?

2. Who were the leaders of the return?

3. Who was Zerubbabel?

4. Why is it supposed that his father was only the adopted son of Jehoiachin? *A*. Both because Jeremiah sentenced Coniah to be childless, and in Luke iii. Zerubbabel's descent is derived from David, through Nathan.

5. What story is told of Zerubbabel's gaining favour with Darius?

6. What title did Zerubbabel bear?

7. What was the only inheritance left for him?

8. What was the blessing of God to Zerubbabel for his faith?--Hag. ii. 21 to 23.--Zech. iv, 6 to 10.

9. What were the prophetic blessings to Joshua the priest?--Zech. vi. 11-15.--Hag. ii. 4, 5.

10. Of what typical vision was Joshua the subject?--Zech. iii.

11. What are Zechariah's other remarkable prophecies of Redemption?--Zech. ix. 9 to 12.--xi. 12, 13.--xii. 8-10.--xiii. 1, 6,

12. What was the condition of Jerusalem?

13. What was the promise of restoration?--Zech. viii. 3, 4, 5.

14. What was the first measure of Zerubbabel and Joshua?

15. Where had directions been given for the new Temple?

A. In the latter chapters of Ezekiel, but these were a further prophecy of the New Tabernacle in Heaven.

16. How soon was the Temple begun?

17. What were the feelings of the people?

18. What promise did Haggai give?--Hag. ii. 6, 7-9.

19. What rebuke did Haggai give the Jews?

20. What interference befell the Jews?

21. Why was all intercourse with the Samaritans forbidden?

22. How did the Samaritans revenge themselves?

23. What was the state of the Persian court?

24. What was the end of Cambyses?

25. What was the story of the impostor, Smerdis?

26. Who became King of Persia?

27. What history did Darius's governors send to him?--Ezra, v. 7, &c.

28. How were they answered?--See *Ezra*, vi.

29. What revolt took place in the time of Darius?

30. What prophecies were here fulfilled?--Ps. cxxxvii. 8, 9. *Is*. xlvii. 7, 8, 9.

31. What were Darius's two vain expeditions?

32. What was the great expedition of Xerxes?

33. How had it been predicted?--Dan. xi. 2.

LESSON XIV.

1. Who is Ahasuerus supposed to have been?

2. What was his great act of tyranny?

3. By what means did he try to repair the loss of Vashti?

4. Of what race was Esther?

5. Why would not Mordecai bow down to Haman?

6. What benefit did Mordecai do the king?

7. How did Haman seek revenge for Mordecai's scorn?

8. How did Esther conduct her intercession?

9. What great deliverance was given to the Jews?

10. What fresh aid was given to the building at Jerusalem?

11. What was the date of Ezra's arrival?

12. What is counted from this date?

13. Who was the other assistant who arrived?

14. How had Nehemiah obtained leave to come and assist?

15. In what state did he find the city?

16. What prophecies were' there of her desolation?--Ps. lxxx. *Is*. xxxii. 13, 14.

17. What was Nehemiah's great work?

18. How were the Jews obliged to build?

19. How had this been foretold?--Dan. ix. 25.

20. What blessing had been laid up for Nehemiah?--Is. lviii. 12, 13.

21. What reformations did Ezra and Nehemiah bring about?

22. What became of the schismatical priest?

23. Where was the Samaritan temple?

24. Who was the last of the prophets?

25. What were his great predictions?--Mal. iii. I, 2, 3. --iv. 2, 5, 6.

26. What books are thought to have been compiled by Ezra?

27. What Psalms were collected by Ezra?--From cvii. to the end.

28. What prophetic verse is ascribed to the time of Ezra?--cxviii. 22.

29. What were the songs of degrees?--Ps. cxx. to cxxxiv. 30. Who had the keeping of the Scriptures?

31. In what tongue were the early Scriptures?

32. What tongue was commonly spoken after the captivity?

33. What was therefore done when the Law was read?

34. What arrangement did Ezra make for public worship?

35. What was the synagogue service?

36. How were the Jews dispersed?

37. In what state was the Persian Empire?

LESSON XV.

1. Who were the Greeks?

2. Who was the chief Greek god?

3. What were the Greek philosophers trying to find out?--See *Acts*, xvii. 27, 28.

4. What were the Greek games?--See I *Cor*. ix. 24, &c.

5. Which were the two chief Greek cities?

6. What was the most learned of all cities?

7. Who subdued all the rest of Greece?

8. What was the name of the great King of Macedon?

9. How was Macedon figured in Daniel's visions?--Dan. vii. 6.--viii. 5, 6, 7.

10. What yet older prophecy was there of the Greek invasion?--Num. xxiv. 24.

11. What was Chittim? *A*. The east end of the Mediterranean.

12. In what year did Alexander enter Asia?

13. How was the swiftness of his conquests shown?

14. How did Darius go out to battle with him?

15. What cities did Alexander take in Palestine?

16. What was Zechariah's prophecy about Tyre?--Zech. ix. 2, 3, 4.

17. What was his prophecy about the Philistine cities?--Zech. ix. 5,

18. What about Jerusalem?--Zech. ix. 8.

19. How was Alexander received at Jerusalem?

20. What did he declare that he had seen?

21. What city did Alexander build in Egypt?

22. What became of Darius? 23. How far did Alexander spread his conquests?

24. What city did he wish to make his capital?

25. How did the Jews at Babylon show their constancy?

26. What befell Alexander at Babylon?

27. How had this been foreshown?--Dan, viii. 8.--xi. 3,4.

28. What was the year of Alexander's death?

29. What difference did his conquest make to the East?

30. What language was much learnt from his time?

31. What became of Babylon after his death?

32. How had the ruinous waste of Babylon been fore- told?--Isaiah, xiii. 19 to 22.--Jer. li. 43.

LESSON XVI.

1. How was the division of Alexander's empire foreshown?--Dan. vii. 6.--viii. 8.

2. What were the four horns?

3. What was the Greek power in Nebuchadnezzar's dream?

4. Which of the Greek princes came in contact with Palestine?

5. What did the Angel call them in Dan. xi.?

6. What was the name of all the Greek kings of Egypt?

7. What were the names of the Greek kings of Syria?

8. To which of them did the Jews belong at first?

9. What colony did Ptolemy Lagus bring into Egypt?

10. What prophecy was thus fulfilled?--Isaiah, xix. 18.

11. How were the Jews treated?

12. Who was the high priest?

13. How is he spoken of in Ecclesiasticus?--Ecclus. I.

14. What was Simon's work with regard to the Holy Scripture?

15. What translation was made in the time of Ptolemy Philadelphus?

16. What is the Greek translation called?

17. By how many persons was it made?

18. What marriage took place between the royal families of Egypt and Syria?

19. How had it been foretold?--Dan. xi. 6.

20. What revenge was taken for the murder of Berenice?

21. How was the expedition of Euergetes foretold?--Dan. xi. 7, 8.

22. How were the Jews becoming corrupted?

23. What had been the doctrine of Joseph?

24. What did Sadoc declare after him?

25. What were the disciples of Sadoc called?

26. What were the doctrines of the Sadducees?

27. What were those called who held aloof from them?

28. What kind of kings followed Ptolemy Euergetes?

29. What attempt was made by Ptolemy Philopator?

30. How was it frustrated?

31. What was the prophecy of Philopator's invasion?--Dan. xi. 10.

32. What cruelty was attempted by him on his return to Egypt?

33. How were the Jews saved?

34. To whom did Judea give itself up?

35. How was the treason of the Jews predicted?--Dan, xi. 14.

36. In what year did the Jews pass from the Egyptian to the Syrian power?

LESSON XVII.

1. How was Antiochus's punishment of the traitors foretold?--Dan. xi. 14.

2. What were the conquests predicted in the 15th verse?

3. How did he treat Judea?--verse 16th.

4. What alliance did he make?

5. What was the prophecy of this marriage?--verse 17th.

6. What expedition was predicted in the 18th verse?

7. What checked him in this expedition?

8. What became of Antiochus the Great?

9. How was this predicted?--verse 19.

10. Who were the Romans?

11. What were they in Nebuchadnezzar's dream?--Dan. ii. 33.

12. What were they in Daniel's vision?--Dan, vii. 7.

13. Why were they like iron?

14. To what were they most devoted?

15. What great Phoenician city had they conquered?

16. What yoke did the Romans impose on Syria?

17. What was the name of the successor of Antiochus?

18. How does Daniel describe him?--Dan. xi. 20.

19. What sacrilegious attempt was made in the time of Seleueus?

20. How was it punished?

21. What was the end of Seleueus?

22. Who succeeded him, and by what means?

23. How was the success of Antiochus Epiphanes foretold?--Dan. si. 21.

24. What was he in Daniel's vision?--Dan. viii. 9.

25. What was his character?

26. How was his preference of Roman to Greek gods foretold?--Dan. xi.

27. What terrible apostasy took place among the Jews?

28. How had Zechariah predicted the fall of the Priests? Zech. xi. 16.

29. What war was predicted in Daniel xi.?

30. What wickedness was being perpetrated at Jerusalem?

31. How had this sacrilege been foretold?--verses 30, 31.--viii. 11, 12.

32. How had the martyrdoms been foretold?--viii. 10.

33. What Psalms are applicable to this persecution?-- lxxiv.--lxxix.--lxxx.

34. What were the most remarkable martyrdoms?

35. In what apocryphal book are they recorded?

36. What was the remarkable difference between these and Christian martyrs?

LESSON XVIII.

1. What deliverers were raised up for the Jews?

2. Why was the family of Mattathias called Asmonean?

3. How was Mattathias first roused to resistance?

4. What purification did Mattathias make?

5. What were the predictions of him and his sons?--Dan. xi. 32, 33.

6. Who succeeded Mattathias?

7. How arose the name of Maccabees?

8. What was the great work of Judaa Maccabaeus?

9. What was the end of Antiochus Epiphanes?

10. How had it been predicted?--Dan. xi. 44, 45.

11. What was the death of Eleazar?

12. How was the varying success of the Maccabees foretold?--Dan. xi.

13. What was the death of the apostate Menelam?

14. How had Zechariah spoken of him?--Zech, xi. 17.

15. How had Zechariah foretold these wars?--Zech, ix. 13.

16. Who succeeded Maccabaeus?

17. With whom did Jonathan make a treaty?

18. What success did Jonathan gain?

19. What became of Jonathan?

20. Who succeeded him?

21. What work did Simon complete?

22. What was the end of Simon?

23. Who was the successor of Simon?

24. What conquest was made by John Hyrcanus?

25. What prophecies were fulfilled by the fall of Edom?--Ps. cxxxvii. 7.--Is. xxxiv. 6, to the end.--Joel, iii. 19.

26. What is the present state of Idumea?

LESSON XIX.

1. Who was the first Asmonean King?

2. What prophecy thus had a fulfilment? A. Zech. vi. 13; but this was only really accomplished in our Lord.

3. Who reigned after Aristobulus?

4. Who after Alexander Janneus?

5. What dispute broke out between the sons of Alexandra?

6. Who fostered the ill-will between the brothers?

7. To whose decision was the dispute referred?

8. What was it that made the Roman power so terrible?

9. How did the Romans extend their dominion?

10. What were the Roman triumphs?

11. How was the Roman army composed?

12. What was the Roman standard?

13. How did the Romans rule their conquered provinces?

14. Who alone could obtain law and justice?

15. Who had long ago described the Romans exactly? --Deut, xxviii. 48, 49, 50, 51.

16. What Roman general first invaded Palestine?

17. By what means did Pompey take Jerusalem?

18. What presumptuous act did Pompey commit?

19. What was the punishment of Pompey's sacrilege?

20. What became of Aristobulus?

21. How did Pompey arrange the affairs of the Jews?

22. What troubles did Pompey meet with at home?

23. Who gained the chief power at Rome?

24. What country had Julius Caesar invaded?

25. What arrangements did Caesar make in Palestine?

26. Who was Herod?

27. What became of Julius Caesar?

28. Who divided his power on his death?

29. How did Herod gain favour from Antony?

30. Who put an end to the reign of Hyrcanus?

31. What exploits were done by Herod?

32. How did Herod make himself King?

33. Who was Herod's wife?

34. Who was High Priest?

35. What crimes did Herod's jealousy of the royal line lead him to commit?

36. How were the High Priests appointed after the murder of Aristobulus?

37. How did Herod try to make up for his crimes?

38. Who had become Emperor of Rome?

39. What was the state of all the world?

40. What general expectation prevailed?

41. What had Augustus been told at a heathen temple?

42. What prophecy was fulfilled by Judea having an Edomite king? --Gen. xlix. 10.

43. How long was it since the walls of Jerusalem had been built?

LESSON XX.

1. In what year of the world did Augustus number his people?

2. What was the object of Augustus?

3. What was the real cause of this taxation?

4. What prophecies had foretold that the Messiah should be born of a woman?--Gen. in. 15.--Is. vii. 14.--Jer. xxxi. 22.--Micah, v. 3.

5. How was Bethlehem fixed for His birth-place?--Micah, v. 2.

6. How was His birth foretold?--Is. ix. 6.

7. What allusion was there to His being received into a stable and rejected by His townsmen?--Is. i. 3.

8. What were the rejoicings?

9. By what rite was He made obedient to the Law?

10. By whom had His Name been previously borne?

11. Who had prophesied of that Name?--Jer. xxiii. 6.

12. How was His presentation in the Temple foretold?--Hag. ii. 7 and 9.

13. How was Simeon's greeting of Him foretold?--Is. xxv. 9.

14. How had He been marked out to the eastern nations as a Star?--Numb. xxiv. 17.

15. What predictions were there of the coming and the gifts of the eastern sages?--Ps. lxxii. 10-15.--Cant. iii. 6.--Is. lx. 3.

16. How had the massacre of the holy Innocents been predicted?--Jer. xxxi. 15,

16, 17.

17. How had the flight and return from Egypt been foreshown?--Hos. xi. 1.

18. What was Herod's last crime?

19. What children did he leave?

20. Who first succeeded him?

21. Why was Archelaus deposed?

22. How was Palestine divided?

23. Who governed Judea?

24. What regulations for the Roman empire were made by Augustus?

25. What languages were everywhere spoken? 26. Who succeeded Augustus, and in what year?

27. What were the predictions of our Lord's childhood?--Is. vii. 15.--liii. 2.

28. How had David declared the wisdom He showed in the Temple?--Ps. cxix. 99, 100.

29. Mention the prophecies of His forerunner?--Is. xl. 3.--Mal. iv. 5, 6.

30. How had baptism with water been already employed?

31. How did our Lord sanctify baptism?

32. What had been the object of the Law which St. John brought to a point?

33. How did He show how the sins of which His disciples were sensible might be removed?

34. Who were the first disciples?

35. Whom did they acknowledge in our Lord?--Deut. xviii. 15.

36. How had the miracles been promised as marks of the Messiah?--Is. xxxii. 3, 4.--xxxv. 5, 6.

37. How had His gentleness been foretold?--Is. xi. 1 2, 3, 4.--xlii. I, 2, 3.--lxi. I, 2, 3.

38. How had the cleansing of the Temple been foretold?--Ps. lxix. 9.--Mal. iii. 1, 2, 3.

39. What was the martyrdom of St. John the Baptist?

40. What was it that prevented the Jews from recognizing the Messiah?

41. How had their rejection of Him been foretold?--Ps. lxix, 7, 8.--Is. liii. I, 2.

42. How had the triumphal entry into Jerusalem been predicted?--Ps. viii. 2.--

cxviii. 26.--Jer. xvii 25.--Zech. ix. 9.

43. How had the plots of the Pharisees been foretold?--Ps. x. 10, 11.--xxxv.--vii.--lvi. 5, 6.

44. Mention the prophecies of the treachery of Judas.--Ps. xli. 9.--lv. 12, 13, 14, 15.

45. How had the price been already made known, and likewise what became of it?--Zech. xi. 12, 13.

46. What was to be the end of the traitor?--Ps. cix. 7, 8, 9.

47. What blessed mystery was instituted on the night before the Passion? 48. How had the joining of different authorities been foreshown?--Ps. ii. 2.

49. How the testimony against Him?--Ps. xxxv. 11.

50. How the judgment?--Is. liii. 8.

51. How His silence before Pilate?--Is. liii. 7.

52. How the insults of the soldiery?--Is. 1. 6.

53. How the scourging?---Ps. cxxix, 3.--Is. liii. 5.

54. How the disfigurement?--Is. lii. 14.

55. What was the accusation on which the Jews condemned Him?

56. What that on which Pilate condemned Him?

57. Why was crucifixion the manner of His death?

58. How had it been predicted?--Ps. xxii. 17.--Is. xxv. 11.--Zech. xii. 10.--xiii. 6.

59. How had the desertion of the disciples been foretold?--Ps. lxxxviii. IS.--Zech. xiii. 7.

60. How the derision of the Jews?--Ps. xxii. 7, 8.

61. How the parting of the garments?--Ps. xxii. 18.

62. How the sponge of vinegar?--Ps. lxix. 22.

63. What had been the prediction of-the sense of desertion by God?--Ps. xxii. 1.

64. What of the dying among the wicked and the burial?--Ps. lxxxviii. 3, 4.--Is. liii. 9.

65. What of the Resurrection?--Ps. xvi. 11.--Is. xxv. 8.

66. What of the effect on us?--Is. xxvi. 19.--Hos. xiii, 14.

67. What of the Ascension?--Ps. lxviii. 18.

LESSON XXI.

1. What was fulfilled by the one great Sacrifice?

2. What were the ceremonies of the Law?--Heb. x. 1.

3. What was the difference between circumcision and baptism?

4. How had baptism been enjoined?--Mark, xvi. 16.

5. Where had its regenerating power been declared?--John, iii. 5.

6. How had the promise of being cleansed by His blood been held out in the Old Testament?--Ps. li. 2.--Is. i. 18.--lii. 15.--Joel, iii. 21.--Zech. xiii. 1. 7. How were the faithful invited to constant partaking of pardoning grace?--Ps. xxxvi. 8, 9.--Is. xii. 3.--xliv. 22.--lv. 1.--Ezek. xlvii. 9.--John, iv. 14.--vii. 37.--See Rev. xxii. 17.

8. How had the Passover come to the true fulfilment?--1 Cor. v. 7.

9. How had the deliverance of the redeemed been foretold?--Is. xxxv. 8, 9,10.

10. Which day of the week was to be kept in remembrance of their rescue?

11. How was the great Sacrifice to be partaken of?

12. How had it been instituted?--Luke, xxii. 19, 20.

13. Where had it been predicted?--Prov. ix. I, 2, 5.--Zech. ix. 17.

14. How was the bringing near in prayer made known? Is. lxv. 24.--Mai. I. 11.--Matt. vi. 9.--xxi. 22.--Mark, xi. 24.--John, xvi. 23, 24, 26, 27.

15. How had the day of Atonement come to fulfilment?--Heb. ix. 24.--Rev. v. 8.

16. How was our Lord revealed as a Shepherd?--Gen. xlix. 24.--Ps. xxiii.--Is. xl. 11.--Jer. xxxi. 10.--Ez. xxxv. 23.--xxxvii. 24.--Zech. xiii. 7.--xi. 7.--Matt, xviii. 12, &c.--John, x. I, &c.

17. How is the Old Testament shown to be only explained in our Lord?--Is. xxix. 11, 12.--Rev. v. 1-5.

18. What were the believers in the new Covenant to be called?

19. What is the meaning of Church?

20. How many believers met at first?

21. Whom did they choose into the place of Judas?

22. How was he consecrated?

23. What gift was thus bestowed on him?--John, xx. 21, 22, 23.

24. What was the meaning of the name Apostles?

25. What was the second order of the ministry?

26. What festival was taking place?

27. What did the Feast of Weeks commemorate?

28. How was the great work completed?

29. What is the inward work of the Holy Spirit? 30. With what outward signs was His coming manifested?

31. What was the promise of His coming?--Joel, ii. 28, 29,---John, xvi. 7.

32. What were the first-fruits of His coming?

33. What was the occasion of the appointment of the deacons?

34. Who was the first martyr?

35. What was the end of Pilate?

36. Who succeeded Tiberius?

37. What was the history of Herod Agrippa?

38. Who was the great Pharisee convert?

39. How was it made known that the Gospel might be preached to the Gentiles?

40. What had been the promise to Abraham's faith?

41. How had it been foretold that the Gentiles should come in?--Ps. ii. 8.--xix. 4.--xviii. 43, 44.--xxii.--lxviii. 11.--lxxii. 17.--xlix. 6.--Is. lii. 7-10-15.--liv. 1.lvi. 6, 7.--lix. 19.--Matt. xxiv. 14.--Luke, i. 79.--John, x. 16.

42. Who was the first Gentile convert?

43. Which Apostle was first martyred, and by whom?

44. What was the end of Herod Agrippa?

45. What were the different missions of the Apostles?

46. What is the tradition about the Creed?

47. What are the texts thought to be allusions to the Creed?--Luke, i. 4.--1 *Tim*. vi. 20.--2 *Tim*. i. 13.

48. Why was not the Creed commonly rehearsed?

49. Which was the first of the Gospels?

50. What was the difference between the treatment which the Apostles received from the Jews and Romans?

51. To whom did they always go first?

52. What advantages did they derive from the Roman power?

53 What was going on in Britain?

54. Who was Roman Emperor?

55. How had the persecutions been predicted?--Matt. xxiv. 9.

LESSON XXII.

1. How had St. Paul first been converted?

2. How did he spend his time after his conversion?

3. How bad education fitted him to be an apostle to the Gentiles?

4. How was he introduced to the apostles?

5. What was his first mission?

6. What name was first given at Antioch?

7. How were SS. Paul and Barnabas first set apart?

8. What was their first journey?

9. Who was their companion?

10. What was the occasion of the first Council of the Church?

11. Why must the decisions of a truly general council be right?--Matt, xviii. 20.

12. What was the decision of the first Council? Antioch?

13. What question arose between SS. Paul and Peter at

14. How did St. Paul differ with St. Barnabas?

15. What was the further history of St. Barnabas?

16. Who were the companions of St. Paul's second journey?

17. How far did his second journey extend?

18. What argument did he hold at Athens?

19. Who were the Athenian philosophers?

20. What were written at Corinth?

21. Which Gospel is said to have been here written?

22. When did St. Paul's third journey begin?

23. What was his first station?

24. What was the cause of the tumult at Ephesus?

25. Which Epistles were written in his third journey?

26. How far did his third journey extend?

27. What caused his return to Jerusalem?

28. What were his troubles at Jerusalem?

29. How was he rescued from violence both of Jews and Romans?

30. Before what tribunals was he brought? 31. Why could he not be set at liberty?

32. What were the events of his voyage to Rome?

33. How did he live at Rome?

34. What are the Epistles of his captivity?

35. To what bishops did he write instructions?

36. What apostle ruled the Church at Rome?

37. What are the writings of St. Peter?

38. Which Gospel was superintended by St. Peter?

39. What became of St. James the Less?

40. Which was the first persecution?

41. Which is St. Paul's last Epistle?

42. How did St. Paul and St. Peter die?

43. How had the manner of St. Peter's death been foretold?--John, xxi. 18, 19.

44. What Church was founded by St. Mark?

45. What was the death of St. Mark?

LESSON XXIII.

1. How had the apostles been martyred?

2. What Church was left in Ethiopia?

3. What Church was left by St. Thomas?

4. Which apostles left writings?

5. Who alone survived to hear of the destruction of Jerusalem?

6. How had this been foretold?--John, xxi. 22.

7. How did the Jews bring punishment on themselves?

8. How did they misread the prophecies?

9. How had our Lord predicted their self-deception?--Matt. xxiv. 5-11.

10. What Roman was sent against them P

11. How was he called off?

12. What warning was thus given?--Luke, xxi. 20, 21.

13. How did the Christians profit by the warning?

14. How were our Lord's predictions of fearful sights and signs from Heaven fulfilled?

15. Why was the city more than usually filled?

16. Who was the Roman general?

17. In what year did Titus besiege Jerusalem? 18. How had the Jews called down vengeance on themselves?

19. How had our Lord mourned for them?--Luke, xiii. 34.--xix, 41.

20. How had St. Paul mourned for them?--Rom. ix. 2,3.

21. How had the manner of the siege been predicted?--Deut. xxviii. 52.

22. How had the dreadful famine been foretold?--Luke, xix. 43.

23. What was the state of the city?--Deut. xxviii. 53-56.--Lam. ii. 20, 21.

24. How was the entrance effected into the Temple?

25. What had been the intention of Titus with regard to the Temple?

26. Why could not the Temple be saved?

27. What condition was the city found to be in?

28. What prophecy was fulfilled?--Matt. xxiv. 2.

29. What became of the treasures of the Temple?

30. What became of the Jews?

31. How had their dispersion been predicted?--Deut. xxviii. 64-68.--Ps. lix. 11.

32. How have they lived ever since?

33. What warning does St. Paul give the Gentiles?--Rom. xi. 18.

34. Why were the Jews so utterly rejected?

35. Who were accepted in their stead?

36. How had the acceptance of the sons of Japhet been foretold?--Gen. ix. 27.

LESSON XXIV.

1. What were the events of Domitian's persecution?

2. How was St. John a martyr in will?

3. What was revealed to St. John in a vision?

4. Where was the latter part of St. John's life spent?

5. What were the instances of St. John's love?

6. What are the writings of St. John?

7. In what year did he die?

8. What were the habits of the early Christians?

9. How did they meet for worship? 10. What was their practice on the Lord's Day?

11. How did they arrange themselves at their assemblies?

12. How did the heathen try to find out what they did?

13. Why did Trajan dislike them so much?

14. What had befallen the old Roman temper?--Dan. ii. 41.

15. Who was the great martyr of Trajan's persecution?

16. What is told us of St. Ignatius as a child?

17. What is a Father of the Church?

18. How was St. Ignatius put to death?

19. What did he say of himself?

20. Who was St. John's other pupil?

21. What had been said to St. Polycarp in the Revelation?--Rev. ii. 10.

22. In what persecution did St. Polycarp suffer?

23. What did he say of himself at the tribunal?

24. What was his last thanksgiving?

25. What was the manner of his death?

26. What was the story of the Thundering Legion?

LESSON XXV.

1. How had our Lord forewarned His followers of their sufferings?--Matt. x. 16, 17.--John, xvi. 2.

2. How had they been told to meet their afflictions?--Matt. v. 12.--1 *Peter*, iii. 14.

3. What had He said of confessing or denying Him?--Matt. x. 32, 33.

4. What had been promised through St. John to such as overcame?--Rev. ii. 17.--iii. 5 and 21.

5. How had the lot of the martyrs been shown to St. John?--Rev. vii. 14-17.

6. How many periods of persecution had been predicted?--Rev. ii. 10.

7. Name the ten chief persecutors.

8. How is Severus memorable in Britain?

9. Who were the martyrs of Carthage?

10. Who were the chief martyrs of the persecution of Valerian?

11. What were St. Lawrence's treasures? 12. Why did Sapricius fail?

13. What became of Valerian?

14. Whose was the fiercest persecution?

15. How did the Theban legion witness their confession?

16. In what manner were Christians brought to trial?

17. Mention some of the martyrs of the Diocletian persecution.

18. Who was the British martyr?

19. Who shielded the Britons?

20. How was the Empire divided?

21. What was the difference between a martyr and a confessor?

22. What was the remarkable end of Galerius?

LESSON XXVI.

1. Who was the first believing monarch?

2. How was Constantine converted?

3. Tell me a few of the promises that Gentile sovereigns should obey the Church?--Ps. lxxii. 11.--Is. xlix. 23.--lx. 4.--lxvi. 12.--Rev. xi. 15.

4. What was the date of Constantine's conversion?

5. What was Helena's expedition to Jerusalem?

6. How did she do honour to the holy places?

7. What did Jerusalem thenceforth become?

8. What prophecy thus had a partial and material fulfilment?--Is lx. 10.--lxvi. 20.

9. How did Constantine change the capital of his empire?

10. To whom was his chief church dedicated?

11. Who were the patriarchs of the Church?

12. What name was given to the patriarch of Rome?

13. What were those called who retired from the world?

14. What is a heresy?

15. How had our Lord foretold that heresies would arise?--Matt. xviii. 7.

16. What warnings had He given against them?--Matt. vii. 15.

17. What warning had the apostles given?--Acts, xx. 29, 30.--1 *Tim*. iv. 1.--Titus, iii. 10.--2 *Peter*, ii. 1, 2. 18. What had St. John given as the test of the truth?--1 *John*, iv. 15.

19. What was the heresy of Arius?

20. What council was held against it?

21. Who was the great champion of the truth?

22. What creed was drawn up at Nicea?

23. How many bishops signed the Nicene Creed?

24. How was Arius punished?

25. Into what error did Constantine fall?

26. How was the Church spared from communion with Arius?

27. In obedience to what commands were obstinate sinners cut off from the Church?--Matt. xviii. 17. 1 *Cor*. v. 4, 5.--Titus, iii. 10, 11.

28. When was Constantine baptized?

29. How was the Church tried under Constantius?

30. How was it tried under Julian?

31. What profane attempt did Julian make?

32. How was it frustrated?

33. What is the meaning of Catholic?

34. What great confession of Catholic truth was drawn up at this time?

LESSON XXVII.

1. Who were the two brothers who reigned together?

2. What evil habit prevailed in their days?

3. What was the great work of St. Jerome?

4. Into what tongue did he translate the Bible?

5. What was the bishopric of St. Ambrose?

6. How was he chosen?

7. How did St. Ambrose resist the Empress Justina?

8. Why did he hold out against her?

9. Who was the Catholic Emperor?

10. What fresh heresy had arisen?

11. What fresh confession of faith was made at the Council of Constantino-

ple?

12. What was the sedition of Antioch?

13. Who preached repentance at Antioch?

14. How were the men of Antioch relieved? 15. What offence was given at Thessalonica?

16. How did Theodosius punish the murder?

17. How was he brought to a sense of his cruelty?

18. How did he humiliate himself?

19. What prophecy was literally accomplished in his reign?--Is. lx. 14.

20. How soon did St. Ambrose reconcile Theodosius to the Church?

21. What Father of the Church was converted at this time?

22. What writings did St. Augustine leave?

23. What hymns are ascribed to St. Ambrose?

24. Who finished the conversion of the Gauls?

25. How was St. Chrysostom promoted?

26. How was he persecuted?

27. What prayer is known by his name?

LESSON XXVIII.

1. How had the Roman power decayed?

2. Of what were the feet of Nebuchadnezzar's statue made?

3. What nations had attacked the Romans?

4. What was the faith of the Teutons?

5. Under what form did they first learn Christianity?

6. Who ruled the Roman empire?

7. What portion first was lost to Rome?

8. Who conquered Britain?

9. How was Ireland converted?

10. What prophecies were there that these distant places should be won to the faith?--Is. xlix. 1.--lxvi. 19.

11. What great act of self-sacrifice marked the last Triumph?

12. Who conquered Rome?

13. How did Alaric treat Rome?

14. Who was the first Christian King of France?

15. How was Spain brought to the Catholic faith?

16. What led to the conversion of the English?

17. Who was the first missionary to the Saxons?

18. Who sent St. Augustin? 19. Who was the first Christian Saxon King?

20. What devotions were arranged by St. Gregory?

21. What did he do for Church music?

22. What was the work of St. Benedict?

23. What were the habits of the monks and nuns?

LESSON XXIX.

1. What evils prevailed in the East?

2. What heresies were there taught?

3. What threat had been made in the Revelation?--Rev. ii. 5.

4. What alarm befell the East?

5. How was the true Cross recovered?

6. What false religion sprang up?

7. Who was Mahomet?

8. What was his false prophecy called?

9. What were the requirements and promises of the Koran?

10. In what year was the flight of Mahomet?

11. How did he spread his religion?

12. Where did he die?

13. How do the Mahometans honour Mecca?

14. What was the chief Arabian tribe called?

15. How did they treat Jerusalem?

16. What did they build there?

17. What did they do with the library at Alexandria?

18. How far did they extend their conquests?

19. Where were they brought to a stop?

20. Who turned them back?

21. Are there any sayings in the New Testament that can be applied to such a falling away as the Mahometan heresy?--2 *Tim*. iii. 13.--Rev. ix. 2 to 11. (sup-

posed.)

LESSON XXX.

1. What was the danger of the Western Church?
2. Why were the people so ignorant?
3. What respect did they pay to religion?
4. What errors began to prevail?
5. What Greek emperor tried to prevent image worship?
6. What different decisions were arrived at in the east and west?
7. Who was the great western emperor?
8. What power did Charles le Magne give the Pope?
9. What miseries came upon the west?
10. Who was the great and good English King?
11. How were the Northmen converted?
12. What harm did Charles le Magne's grant do at Rome?
13. What difference of opinion was there between east and west?
14. Why did the Greeks object to the new words in the Creed of Constantinople?
15. What claim had the Popes set up?
16. Who resisted their claim?
17. How was the rent made between the Greek and Latin Churches?
18. In what year did the schism begin?
19. How is the Church still one inwardly?
20. What rule did the Roman Church make about the clergy?
21. What error did she make in the celebration of the Holy Communion?

LESSON XXXI.

1. How many horns had sprung up in Daniel's vision of the Roman power?
2. What do these horns signify?
3. How had our Lord shown how Christianity should work through the nations?--Matt. xiii. 33.
4. But how had Solomon shown that too few would really honour the Lord?--Eccles. iv, 15, 16.

5. In what were the people too prone to trust?

6. Why was it wrong to trust in the intercessions of the Blessed Virgin?--1 *Tim.* ii. 5.

7. Who had the chief power in the Western Churches? 8. What was the old way of choosing a bishop?

9. How did the Romans prove that they could not be trusted with the choice?

10. Who took the choice of the Pope for a time?

11. Who took the choice of the Pope from the German Emperor?

12. How has the Pope been ever since elected?

13. In what manner did the western Church regard the Pope?

14. What rule did the Pope bear?

15. How did he punish disobedience?

16. How was the power of the Popes misused?

17. What saints lived about that time?

18. What good works were done?

19. What were built at this time?

20. Why are churches turned to the east?

21. Why does the font stand near the entrance?

22. Why are the people allowed to come into the chancel, not kept out like the Israelites?

23. What prophecy is fulfilled by constant services?--Ps. lxxii. 15.--Is. lx. 11.

24. What is partly fulfilled by the peace impressed around the Church, even upon fierce warriors?--Is. xi. 6-9.

25. What vows were knights made to take?

26. What wars were preached in the Middle Ages?

27. What reward did the Pope hold out?

28. What was meant by purgatory?

29. What was meant by an indulgence?

30. What success did the crusaders meet with?

31. How long was Jerusalem in the hands of the Christians?

32. How was the schism increased between the Greek and Roman Churches?

33. Who were the chief crusaders?

34. Why could not the Holy Land be kept?

35. What race of Mahometans came from the east?
36. What country did the Turks conquer?
37. What prophecy was fulfilled at Tyre?--Ezek. xxvi. 14.
38. What country was won back by the Christiana?

LESSON XXXII.
1. How had the Services of the Church come to be in an unknown tongue?
2. What deceit was practised upon the people?
3. How were those who found fault punished?
4. How was it that there was less ignorance than formerly?
5. Who began to preach against indulgences?
6. What translation did Luther make?
7. How did England separate from the Pope?
8. What became of the English monasteries?
9. Why did the Italian clergy hinder inquiry?
10. What were Luther's party called, and why?
11. Who was the Swiss reformer?
12. Who tried to obtain a General Council?
13. Where was the meeting held?
14. Why was it not a true Council?
15. How was the English Church purified?
16. In what reign was the Prayer Book translated?
17. After what pattern were the Services moulded?
18. What danger did the English Church undergo?
19. Who were the martyrs of the English Reformation?
20. How did it again become prosperous?
21. How did the Council of Trent end?
22. What decision did the foreign Reformers come to as to their Bishops?
23. How did the Roman Catholics treat them?
24. What Churches have Bishops?
25. How are such Churches still one?
26. What countries are Roman Catholic?
27. Which are Lutheran?

28. Which are Calvinist?

29. Which are Greek Catholic?

LESSON XXXIII.

1. Who discovered America?

2. Who were the first inhabitants of America?

3. Why did the Pope think he had a right over them? 4. To whom did he give them?

5. How did the Spaniards use the Indians?

6. Who tried to prevent their cruelty?

7. What people were brought to the West Indies to work for the colonists?

8. What prophecy was thus fulfilled?--Gen. ix. 27.

9. What work did the Jesuits do in South America?

10. What harm did the Jesuits do at home?

11. What bad spirit rose up in Europe?

12. What prophecies were there that the Church should stretch out far?--Isaiah, liv. 2, 3.

13. Which part of America was settled by the Spaniards?

14. Which by the English and Dutch?

15. Who caused our present translation of the Bible to be made?

16. What did Charles I. try to do for Scotland?

17. How was he treated in England?

18. How was the Church persecuted?

19. How did St. Paul speak of such times?--2 *Tim*. iv. 3

20. How long did these evil times last?

21. How was the Church in England restored?

22. Why are Calvinists called Presbyterians?

23. What evils were prevailing in the colonies?

24. How were they neglected?

25. What was the great sin of France?

26. What was the consequence of French unbelief?

LESSON XXXIV.

1. What schism arose in England?

2. How has St. Paul warned us against separations?--Romans, xvi. 17.

3. Why is it dangerous to follow any unordained minister?--St. John, x. I.

4. How has our Lord taught us to cling to His Church?--St. John, xv. 4.

5. How can we be sure that ours is a true branch of the Church?-- A. Because our Bishops come straight from the Apostles, and our faith and our Sacraments are the same as theirs, and agree with Holy Scripture.

The Codes Of Hammurabi And Moses
W. W. Davies

The discovery of the Hammurabi Code is one of the greatest achievements of archaeology, and is of paramount interest, not only to the student of the Bible, but also to all those interested in ancient history...

Religion   **ISBN:** *1-59462-338-4*   QTY

Pages:132
MSRP $12.95

The Theory of Moral Sentiments
Adam Smith

This work from 1749. contains original theories of conscience amd moral judgment and it is the foundation for systemof morals.

Philosophy **ISBN:** *1-59462-777-0*   QTY

Pages:536
MSRP $19.95

Jessica's First Prayer
Hesba Stretton

In a screened and secluded corner of one of the many railway-bridges which span the streets of London there could be seen a few years ago, from five o'clock every morning until half past eight, a tidily set-out coffee-stall, consisting of a trestle and board, upon which stood two large tin cans, with a small fire of charcoal burning under each so as to keep the coffee boiling during the early hours of the morning when the work-people were thronging into the city on their way to their daily toil...

Pages:84

Childrens   **ISBN:** *1-59462-373-2*   QTY

MSRP $9.95

My Life and Work
Henry Ford

Henry Ford revolutionized the world with his implementation of mass production for the Model T automobile. Gain valuable business insight into his life and work with his own auto-biography... "We have only started on our development of our country we have not as yet, with all our talk of wonderful progress, done more than scratch the surface. The progress has been wonderful enough but..."

Pages:300

Biographies/   **ISBN:** *1-59462-198-5*   QTY

MSRP $21.95

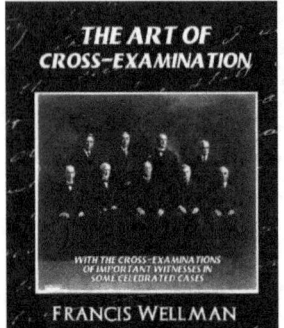

The Art of Cross-Examination
Francis Wellman

QTY

I presume it is the experience of every author, after his first book is published upon an important subject, to be almost overwhelmed with a wealth of ideas and illustrations which could readily have been included in his book, and which to his own mind, at least, seem to make a second edition inevitable. Such certainly was the case with me; and when the first edition had reached its sixth impression in five months, I rejoiced to learn that it seemed to my publishers that the book had met with a sufficiently favorable reception to justify a second and considerably enlarged edition. ..

Pages:412

Reference   ISBN: *1-59462-647-2*   *MSRP $19.95*

On the Duty of Civil Disobedience
Henry David Thoreau

QTY

Thoreau wrote his famous essay, On the Duty of Civil Disobedience, as a protest against an unjust but popular war and the immoral but popular institution of slave-owning. He did more than write—he declined to pay his taxes, and was hauled off to gaol in consequence. Who can say how much this refusal of his hastened the end of the war and of slavery ?

Law   ISBN: *1-59462-747-9*   **Pages:48**

MSRP $7.45

Dream Psychology Psychoanalysis for Beginners
Sigmund Freud

QTY

Sigmund Freud, born Sigismund Schlomo Freud (May 6, 1856 - September 23, 1939), was a Jewish-Austrian neurologist and psychiatrist who co-founded the psychoanalytic school of psychology. Freud is best known for his theories of the unconscious mind, especially involving the mechanism of repression; his redefinition of sexual desire as mobile and directed towards a wide variety of objects; and his therapeutic techniques, especially his understanding of transference in the therapeutic relationship and the presumed value of dreams as sources of insight into unconscious desires.

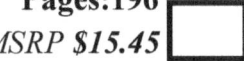

Dream Psychology
Psychoanalysis for Beginners

Sigmund Freud

Pages:196

Psychology   ISBN: *1-59462-905-6*   *MSRP $15.45*

The Miracle of Right Thought
Orison Swett Marden

QTY

Believe with all of your heart that you will do what you were made to do. When the mind has once formed the habit of holding cheerful, happy, prosperous pictures, it will not be easy to form the opposite habit. It does not matter how improbable or how far away this realization may see, or how dark the prospects may be, if we visualize them as best we can, as vividly as possible, hold tenaciously to them and vigorously struggle to attain them, they will gradually become actualized, realized in the life. But a desire, a longing without endeavor, a yearning abandoned or held indifferently will vanish without realization.

Pages:360

Self Help   ISBN: *1-59462-644-8*   *MSRP $25.45*

www.bookjungle.com *email: sales@bookjungle.com fax: 630-214-0564 mail: Book Jungle PO Box 2226 Champaign, IL 61825*

QTY

The Rosicrucian Cosmo-Conception Mystic Christianity *by Max Heindel*   ISBN: *1-59462-188-8*   **$38.95**
The Rosicrucian Cosmo-conception is not dogmatic, neither does it appeal to any other authority than the reason of the student. It is: not controversial, but is: sent forth in the, hope that it may help to clear...   New Age/Religion Pages 646

Abandonment To Divine Providence *by Jean-Pierre de Caussade*   ISBN: *1-59462-228-0*   **$25.95**
"The Rev. Jean Pierre de Caussade was one of the most remarkable spiritual writers of the Society of Jesus in France in the 18th Century. His death took place at Toulouse in 1751. His works have gone through many editions and have been republished...   Inspirational/Religion Pages 400

Mental Chemistry *by Charles Haanel*   ISBN: *1-59462-192-6*   **$23.95**
Mental Chemistry allows the change of material conditions by combining and appropriately utilizing the power of the mind. Much like applied chemistry creates something new and unique out of careful combinations of chemicals the mastery of mental chemistry...   New Age Pages 354

The Letters of Robert Browning and Elizabeth Barret Barrett 1845-1846 vol II   ISBN: *1-59462-193-4*   **$35.95**
by Robert Browning and Elizabeth Barret Barrett   Biographies Pages 596

Gleanings In Genesis (volume I) *by Arthur W. Pink*   ISBN: *1-59462-130-6*   **$27.45**
Appropriately has Genesis been termed "the seed plot of the Bible" for in it we have, in germ form, almost all of the great doctrines which are afterwards fully developed in the books of Scripture which follow...   Religion/Inspirational Pages 420

The Master Key *by L. W. de Laurence*   ISBN: *1-59462-001-6*   **$30.95**
In no branch of human knowledge has there been a more lively increase of the spirit of research during the past few years than in the study of Psychology, Concentration and Mental Discipline. The requests for authentic lessons in Thought Control, Mental Discipline and...   New Age/Business Pages 422

The Lesser Key Of Solomon Goetia *by L. W. de Laurence*   ISBN: *1-59462-092-X*   **$9.95**
This translation of the first book of the "Lernegton" which is now for the first time made accessible to students of Talismanic Magic was done, after careful collation and edition, from numerous Ancient Manuscripts in Hebrew, Latin, and French...   New Age/Occult Pages 92

Rubaiyat Of Omar Khayyam *by Edward Fitzgerald*   ISBN:*1-59462-332-5*   **$13.95**
Edward Fitzgerald, whom the world has already learned, in spite of his own efforts to remain within the shadow of anonymity, to look upon as one of the rarest poets of the century, was born at Bredfield, in Suffolk, on the 31st of March, 1809. He was the third son of John Purcell...   Music Pages 172

Ancient Law *by Henry Maine*   ISBN: *1-59462-128-4*   **$29.95**
The chief object of the following pages is to indicate some of the earliest ideas of mankind, as they are reflected in Ancient Law, and to point out the relation of those ideas to modern thought.   Religion/History Pages 452

Far-Away Stories *by William J. Locke*   ISBN: *1-59462-129-2*   **$19.45**
"Good wine needs no bush, but a collection of mixed vintages does. And this book is just such a collection. Some of the stories I do not want to remain buried for ever in the museum files of dead magazine-numbers an author's not unpardonable vanity..."   Fiction Pages 272

Life of David Crockett *by David Crockett*   ISBN: *1-59462-250-7*   **$27.45**
"Colonel David Crockett was one of the most remarkable men of the times in which he lived. Born in humble life, but gifted with a strong will, an indomitable courage, and unremitting perseverance...   Biographies/New Age Pages 424

Lip-Reading *by Edward Nitchie*   ISBN: *1-59462-206-X*   **$25.95**
Edward B. Nitchie, founder of the New York School for the Hard of Hearing, now the Nitchie School of Lip-Reading, Inc, wrote "LIP-READING Principles and Practice". The development and perfecting of this meritorious work on lip-reading was an undertaking...   How-to Pages 400

A Handbook of Suggestive Therapeutics, Applied Hypnotism, Psychic Science   ISBN: *1-59462-214-0*   **$24.95**
by Henry Munro   Health/New Age/Health/Self-help Pages 376

A Doll's House: and Two Other Plays *by Henrik Ibsen*   ISBN: *1-59462-112-8*   **$19.95**
Henrik Ibsen created this classic when in revolutionary 1848 Rome. Introducing some striking concepts in playwriting for the realist genre, this play has been studied the world over.   Fiction/Classics/Plays 308

The Light of Asia *by sir Edwin Arnold*   ISBN: *1-59462-204-3*   **$13.95**
In this poetic masterpiece, Edwin Arnold describes the life and teachings of Buddha. The man who was to become known as Buddha to the world was born as Prince Gautama of India but he rejected the worldly riches and abandoned the reigns of power when...   Religion/History/Biographies Pages 170

The Complete Works of Guy de Maupassant *by Guy de Maupassant*   ISBN: *1-59462-157-8*   **$16.95**
"For days and days, nights and nights, I had dreamed of that first kiss which was to consecrate our engagement, and I knew not on what spot I should put my lips..."   Fiction/Classics Pages 240

The Art of Cross-Examination *by Francis L. Wellman*   ISBN: *1-59462-309-0*   **$26.95**
Written by a renowned trial lawyer, Wellman imparts his experience and uses case studies to explain how to use psychology to extract desired information through questioning.   How-to/Science/Reference Pages 408

Answered or Unanswered? *by Louisa Vaughan*   ISBN: *1-59462-248-5*   **$10.95**
Miracles of Faith in China   Religion Pages 112

The Edinburgh Lectures on Mental Science (1909) *by Thomas*   ISBN: *1-59462-008-3*   **$11.95**
This book contains the substance of a course of lectures recently given by the writer in the Queen Street Hail, Edinburgh. Its purpose is to indicate the Natural Principles governing the relation between Mental Action and Material Conditions...   New Age/Psychology Pages 148

Ayesha *by H. Rider Haggard*   ISBN: *1-59462-301-5*   **$24.95**
Verily and indeed it is the unexpected that happens! Probably if there was one person upon the earth from whom the Editor of this, and of a certain previous history, did not expect to hear again...   Classics Pages 380

Ayala's Angel *by Anthony Trollope*   ISBN: *1-59462-352-X*   **$29.95**
The two girls were both pretty, but Lucy who was twenty-one who supposed to be simple and comparatively unattractive, whereas Ayala was credited, as her Bombwhat romantic name might show, with poetic charm and a taste for romance. Ayala when her father died was nineteen...   Fiction Pages 484

The American Commonwealth *by James Bryce*   ISBN: *1-59462-286-8*   **$34.45**
An interpretation of American democratic political theory. It examines political mechanics and society from the perspective of Scotsman James Bryce   Politics Pages 572

Stories of the Pilgrims *by Margaret P. Pumphrey*   ISBN: *1-59462-116-0*   **$17.95**
This book explores pilgrims religious oppression in England as well as their escape to Holland and eventual crossing to America on the Mayflower, and their early days in New England...   History Pages 268

QTY

The Fasting Cure *by Sinclair Upton*   **ISBN:** *1-59462-222-1*   **$13.95**
In the Cosmopolitan Magazine for May, 1910, and in the Contemporary Review (London) for April, 1910, I published an article dealing with my experiences in fasting. I have written a great many magazine articles, but never one which attracted so much attention... New Age/Self Help/Health Pages 164

Hebrew Astrology *by Sepharial*   **ISBN:** *1-59462-308-2*   **$13.45**
In these days of advanced thinking it is a matter of common observation that we have left many of the old landmarks behind and that we are now pressing forward to greater heights and to a wider horizon than that which represented the mind-content of our progenitors... Astrology Pages 144

Thought Vibration or The Law of Attraction in the Thought World   **ISBN:** *1-59462-127-6*   **$12.95**

by William Walker Atkinson   Psychology/Religion Pages 144

Optimism *by Helen Keller*   **ISBN:** *1-59462-108-X*   **$15.95**
Helen Keller was blind, deaf, and mute since 19 months old, yet famously learned how to overcome these handicaps, communicate with the world, and spread her lectures promoting optimism. An inspiring read for everyone... Biographies/Inspirational Pages 84

Sara Crewe *by Frances Burnett*   **ISBN:** *1-59462-360-0*   **$9.45**
In the first place, Miss Minchin lived in London. Her home was a large, dull, tall one, in a large, dull square, where all the houses were alike, and all the sparrows were alike, and where all the door-knockers made the same heavy sound... Childrens/Classic Pages 88

The Autobiography of Benjamin Franklin *by Benjamin Franklin*   **ISBN:** *1-59462-135-7*   **$24.95**
The Autobiography of Benjamin Franklin has probably been more extensively read than any other American historical work, and no other book of its kind has had such ups and downs of fortune. Franklin lived for many years in England, where he was agent... Biographies/History Pages 332

Name	
Email	
Telephone	
Address	
City, State ZIP	

☐ **Credit Card**   ☐ **Check / Money Order**

Credit Card Number	
Expiration Date	
Signature	

Please Mail to: Book Jungle
PO Box 2226
Champaign, IL 61825
or Fax to: 630-214-0564

ORDERING INFORMATION

web*: www.bookjungle.com*
email*: sales@bookjungle.com*
fax*: 630-214-0564*
mail*: Book Jungle PO Box 2226 Champaign, IL 61825*
or PayPal *to sales@bookjungle.com*

Please contact us for bulk discounts

DIRECT-ORDER TERMS

**20% Discount if You Order
Two or More Books**
Free Domestic Shipping!
Accepted: Master Card, Visa,
Discover, American Express